Olivia From Everstille

A Novel

Susan M. Szurek

Book Three: A story from the town of Everstille

Chapbook Press

Schuler Books
2660 28th Street SE
Grand Rapids, MI 49512
(616) 942-7330
www.schulerbooks.com

Olivia from Everstille

ISBN 13: 9781948237888

eBook ISBN: 9781948237895

Library of Congress Control Number: 2021914337 (Paperback edition)

Printed in the United States by Chapbook Press.

For E.W.S.

With unconditional love

Also by Susan M. Szurek:

Everstille: A Novel

Everstille's Librarian

I.
In Everstille

In our life, there is a single color, as on an artist's palette, which provides the meaning of life and art. It is the color of love.

Marc Chagall

0-1 Light Green

My first remembered memory is seeing my mother sitting in the rocking chair in my bedroom, although I did not realize then she was a ghost. She never spoke, although there was sometimes a small smile on her face. I became used to seeing her rock on the chair Uncle Terry bought for my bedroom and was never frightened. Once I could explain to him or to Dad or to Aunt Anne about what I saw, they assured me it was only the picture of my mother on the small table next to the rocker I was seeing. But I knew better. The one time I described my mother to Aunt Anne, she gave a gasp and held her hand to her mouth. I kept quiet about my mother after that. I didn't want to upset my family.

I don't remember my bedroom walls being a light green color, but I was just born then, and it changed every year, so sometimes the colors are mixed up in my mind. Painting the walls was Uncle Terry's idea although I got to choose the color they would be. I think Dad would have been happy keeping them light green because my mother picked it out, but Uncle Terry explained that color was essential in the world, and we should enjoy all shades offered to us. Since he did most of the work, Dad just let him repaint every year once my new color was selected. As I aged and was able to have a vocal choice in the colors, I enjoyed the changes. I often wondered if the fact that Uncle Terry's hair was such a showy shade of red was the reason he was so attracted to colors. Of course, mine was the same hue as his.

Mother died when I was born. She lived a day or so and was able to hold me and kiss me, and both Dad and Uncle Terry said she gave me an entire lifetime of love during the briefness we were together. My family entertained me with stories of my mother, and my infancy, and my youth, and that is how I know all these things. They explained again and again what a wonderful woman my mother was and how smart she was, and how loved she was. I believe all those things because, why wouldn't I? After all there is the room in the town library called the **Ruth Evans Pinkerton Room** after my mother, and all the books in there are called *Ruth Books*. My mother was Head Librarian of the Greenwood Library for many years, and she was influential and valuable to the town. I have often been told the story about how friends and townspeople came to her funeral bringing copies of their favorite books she had encouraged them to read. The books were piled up, stacks of them placed around Jamison's Funeral Home room; they were later to be christened the *Ruth Books*. Aunt Anne told me about the book she offered and why she placed *Oliver*

Twist on my mother's casket, and how she would guide me through the reading of it when I was older. That never happened because of what occurred when I was ten, but since then, I have read the book. Aunt Anne sent it to me one Christmas when I was thirteen along with a letter. Unfortunately, I didn't get the letter until some years later when I found it with the others.

I loved my years growing up in Everstille with my family. Dad and Uncle Terry and Aunt Anne and I were happy together. Even though Aunt Anne didn't live with us, she was not far away. Her apartment on Charming Lane was not far from our big house, and there were many times I spent the night there. Often on Friday nights if Aunt Anne didn't need to open the library on Saturday, I would stay with her. We would walk to the Emporium, and she would let me pick out a new Golden Book if there was one, and there usually was. Before I was able to read, she would read them to me while I sat on her lap. She pointed out the colors on the pages, and I listened to her soft voice purring the words. Then she would ask me questions about the story, and we would talk about the tale just read. Once I learned to read, our roles reversed, and I would examine her understanding of the story and pictures. At night in her apartment, we played card games, and she showed me how to bake cookies. Before she took me back to my own house Saturday afternoon, we would walk to town, and she would let me pick out a dessert at Peterson's Bakery to enjoy after Sunday dinner. I treasured time with her.

I adored being with Dad and Uncle Terry too. Uncle Terry was more adventurous than Dad, and he and I played in our back yard whenever we could. Dad would sit on the white-washed back porch and watch us throw a ball back and forth, or weed the brightly ornamented flower garden, or play hide and seek in the avocado-colored bushes fencing the property line. Uncle Terry was easy to find because of his hair. I suppose I was too, but he pretended he had trouble and would stand directly in front of me, yelling my name and complaining out loud that this time I had found the perfect place to hide. When he did find me, he would pick me up and throw me over his shoulder and yell at Dad, "Well, now what should we do with this bag of cabbages?" I would laugh and scream, and Dad would say, "Terry, be careful; She's the only bag of cabbages we have, and doesn't cooked cabbage with onion sound delicious?"

Uncle Terry would let me help him do the cooking. He delighted in trying new recipes, and even though Dad's penchant was more along the line of meat-and-potato dinners, he always took at least a small helping of whatever was created. One of the jobs Uncle Terry had before he came to Everstille was as a cook in some restaurant in Chicago, so he knew how to work with food. He would take me to visit Aunt Anne at the library, and he would look up new recipes and copy them into a small notebook he kept in his pocket. On Sunday afternoons, Aunt Anne would come over, and we would have a big dinner (always a meat-and-potato type just for Dad), and then we would all help clean up. If the weather allowed, we would go for a long walk around the town and then return to eat the dessert purchased from Peterson's Bakery. We spent the rest of the late afternoon playing games, and after my bath, Aunt Anne would read me a book and tuck me in. Dad said that was Aunt Anne's own time with me, and it was exclusively hers.

Dad helped me with my schoolwork when I didn't understand something. He used to be a teacher but then became the principal at Everstille High School, and was excellent at explaining when I was confused about a math problem or the sentences I was required to write. He was better at clarifying than some of my teachers were, and I think that is why school was undemanding for me. When it was Dad's turn to tuck me in, he would often tell me something about Mother…something I didn't know. Once he told me about how they first became friends when he was a teacher and wanted his students to use the library for an assignment and how Mother helped him with the planning. He told me about the times they would chaperone the school dances, and how, when she could, Mother would attend the swim meets because he used to be the swim coach. He described Mother's eyes as "unusually green like the late summer grass", and how she kept her brown hair pulled back in a knot, and how one lock always fell across her face. While I loved these stories, I always saw Dad's eyes which were azure colored, become wet. They looked like tiny oceans when this happened.

I loved my childhood. There were friends, and church activities, and summer adventures, and the first ten years of my life were magical. I was happy with Dad and Uncle Terry and Aunt Anne. My life was joyous and pleasurable. And then one day everything I thought I knew changed.

1-2 Bright Banana Yellow

It might have been for my first birthday, but someone gave me a soft stuffed toy, shaped like a banana with a silly smiling face. According to Uncle Terry, I clung to it and had to have both it and my Raggedy Ann doll, given by Aunt Anne, before I would go to bed. I had that silly yellow banana for years and thought it was packed to take with me when I was ten, but when I opened my suitcase and checked the boxes, it wasn't there. I assumed I would never see it again.

I faintly remember my bright yellow room. I think I remember Uncle Terry painting it, but that might just be another story I was told. Dad said that once the paint was dried, I ran to the walls and laughed as I touched them. Apparently, the birthday cake for my first birthday was covered in a bright yellow frosting, and I made a real mess with it, getting it all over my face. It was my first sweet treat. I have a black and white photograph that shows me being held by Dad with Uncle Terry standing next to him, his arm around Dad's shoulders, and pointing to some frosting on my nose. They were smiling, while I just stared into the camera which, I was told, was held by Aunt Anne.

That year was the first time I visited my mother's grave although I don't remember it. But we did the same thing for years up until I left, and I remember our ritual. Every year, a couple weeks after my birthday, we would go into Mother's flower garden and gather whatever flowers were just blooming. Depending on the date…late May or early June… we would bring late-blooming lilacs, or fresh peonies. Once when I was about four, I was sick, so we didn't go to the cemetery until the end of June. The day of our trip, I went out back to the garden and gathered all the snapdragons I could find. However, I pulled the buds off the stems and was upset when I realized I could not set them in the flower holder that was on the headstone. Uncle Terry told me to gather them all and showed me how to place them in a heart-shape on Mother's grave. He could always *make lemonade out of lemons,* one of the many sayings I became familiar with once I got to know my Aunt Ernestine.

Dad, Uncle Terry, and I would ready the flowers and the picnic basket. It was filled with plates, silverware, and the cinnamon cake that was Mother's favorite and which Uncle Terry baked, and Dad would fill a container with sweet iced tea. We would go to North Cemetery and place the flowers in the holder and sit down to have our small picnic by Mother's grave. We would be there for a few hours, and Dad and Uncle Terry would tell and retell stories about Mother. When we were finished, the basket and its contents were gathered, and we would travel home. There were other times we visited the cemetery, but this cinnamon cake picnic was a special yearly ceremony. Never having known my mother, I was not sad during these times although it did upset me to note the tears in the eyes of the men who knew her. And loved her.

Once I asked if Aunt Anne could come with us, and Dad explained that this was just our time, and Aunt Anne had her own tradition to honor and remember Mother. When I asked Aunt Anne if I could go with her, she was loving and kind-hearted in giving me her explanation as to why she would go alone to the cemetery. It was during one discussion that I told Anne I would periodically see Mother on the rocking chair in my bedroom. This was the time she placed her hands against her cheeks and gasped.

I had recently had my eighth birthday (newly painted lilac walls), and it was a Friday night in late June. I was spending the night at Aunt Anne's place, and we just finished baking cookies and were cleaning up. She had explained that her visit to North Cemetery was hers alone, and I accepted the explanation, and then I asked, "Does Mother ever visit the cemetery when you are there?"

"Visit? Well, you know that she is resting there, Livie, and I am the one who is visiting. Just the way your dad and uncle and you visit."

"No, I mean do you ever see her there? Like she is real. Just like I see her in my room sometimes. On the rocking chair."

Aunt Anne finished washing and rinsing the cookie pan before she gave it to me to dry. I could tell she was thinking about what to say. I had not brought up seeing Mother for a long time, and although I did not see her as often as I used to, she had visited me on the night of my eighth birthday, and I was curious.

"Livie, we have talked about this before. Your mother is not there. You are just confused because you see the photos of her around the house and on your little table next to the rocker. Sometimes when we are falling asleep, we are in a dreamy state, and our mind plays tricks on us. It's good that you think about your mother. She loved you very much."

I thought about this. We had discussed this before, but with all the courage my newly achieved eight years brought me, I decided that this time I would not simply nod and accept this explanation.

"I know Mother is there. She looks like the photo on the table, and I know it is her. But she is dressed different. She is wearing different clothes."

There were four framed photographs of my mother around the house, and I was familiar with each one. In three of them, Mother was wearing different light-colored blouses under a woman's suitcoat, and in the fourth, she wore a long coat that was tied at the waist and had on a hat. While there weren't that many pictures of my mother, I had been shown all that Dad and Uncle Terry and Aunt Anne had. All the photographs were black and white, and in none of them was Mother wearing what she wore when she appeared on the rocker.

I explained this to Anne who listened carefully. But the look on her face told me that while she was listening to me, she had some adult knowledge that I did not. She had the grown-up look that told me I was still a child and did not comprehend fully what I was saying. She would set me straight in this matter. I had seen this look on other adults, and now that I was eight, I was sure my grownup explanation should garner more respect. Because I was eight.

"What is your mother wearing when you see her?"

"She has on a dress, and I never saw a picture of her wearing this dress before. And her hair is different. In the photos, she has her hair pulled back or piled on top of her head, but in the rocking chair it is down and curled under her chin. And I am not sure of her eye color, but it is lighter than in the photographs."

Aunt Anne stopped wiping the counter. She looked down at me as I finished drying the cookie pan and placed it on the kitchen table. She reached over to the sink and put the dishcloth on top of the faucet and asked, "What does her dress look like?"

"Well, it is like a light brown color and is the kind of dress that has a little belt at the waist and a round collar. There are a few buttons that go from the collar to the belt, and there is a small pocket on top of the dress by her heart. Then there is a little lacy handkerchief coming out of it. I can't clearly see her shoes, but they look like they are sort of dressy. And I said before that her hair is curled down close under her chin. I never saw her wear it like that in the photographs. Did you ever see her wearing that dress before?"

It was at this point that Aunt Anne put her hands to her face and gasped. She didn't speak, and then turned away from me to the sink where she picked up the dishcloth and wiped the counter again. I thought I was in trouble but didn't know why. Then she just said, "Yes, I saw her in that dress one time. Livie, would you go to the pantry and get out the cookie container? I think these cookies are cool enough to put away."

I did that, and the night went on. I ate some cookies with a glass of milk, but Aunt Anne didn't have any. She said she was full from dinner, but I know she liked those chocolate chip ones, and she always had some with me. Not that night. We played a few games of *War* with the deck of cards she had, but she was not as loud as she usually gets during our games. We put the cards away, and I got ready for bed, but Aunt Anne said she was going to sit up and read for a while. That was unusual because we usually got into bed together and talked about all sorts of things. I couldn't fall asleep, and after a while I quietly got up to look and see what she was doing. Aunt Anne was in her front room, but she was not reading. She was just sitting and staring out of the front window. Once I thought I heard her sniff and cry, but I wasn't sure. I tiptoed back into bed and fell asleep thinking about the night. Wondering if I had said something wrong.

Years later, my Aunt Ernestine talked to me about my mother. She said that before I was born, Aunt Anne and my mother went shopping for a new dress that Mother was going to wear at my christening. The dress was a light brown shirt waist with a small belt and some buttons down the front. It had a little breast pocket and a small lacy white handkerchief peeked out of it. Mother never wore the dress, but Aunt Ernestine told me it was the dress in which she was buried.

That night of my eighth birthday was the next to the last time I saw Mother's ghost. She just didn't come again, and I spent the next couple of years sleeping alone in my bedroom without the phantom in the rocking chair. When I was ten, I saw her one last time.

2-3 Pink

I met my best friend, Maggie Patterson, when we were in Sunday School Little Tots class together. We were the only girls there and were both wearing pink dresses, and the shared love of that color may have been the spark that started our friendship. I remember sorting through the crayon box and removing anything which looked like any shade of pink, and we lined them up around the small table. Once I could read the names of the colors, I called them out to her: middle red, thistle, carnation pink, salmon, flesh, and later when the Sunday School bought new coloring tools, we added: violet red and lavender. The crayons were all shapes and sizes, broken and whole, and we played with them every Sunday. We went through the Sunday School classes together, and once elementary school started, we were in the same class. Because our last names were alphabetically aligned (Patterson, Pinkerton), we were often seated close to each other.

The Patterson family, Edith and Ned with their children, Mary, and Maggie, lived close enough so that once I was allowed some self-sufficiency, I could walk to their house. Or, Maggie walked to mine. It was a short journey and even shorter if we ran. I traveled south to the end of our street, turned east, crossed one street, and walked the few houses to the Patterson home. Maggie's grandparents, Nathan and Edna Mitchell, lived across her street, and we would sometimes go to their house to play in the large yard or bother her grandparents for treats.

Maggie's sister, Mary, was a few years older than us, and she was mean. I am not calling her a name but simply repeating the one she earned. "Mean Mary" was the nickname given her by her own classmates who conferred the label upon her in first grade. Mean Mary was so deviously adept at pulling hair that it was a couple of months before she was discovered. Various boys had been unfairly blamed. Mostly by Mary who swore to the teacher she had seen the act. If Mean Mary did this to her classmates, rest assured her blood sister was not exempt from these and similar actions. Nor was her sister's friend: me. Because of our perpetual attempts to avoid Mean Mary, we spent little time at the Patterson's house. We were usually at mine or in the expansive back and side yard of the treat-transmitting grandparents.

Maggie and I became closer as we grew older. We both had other friends, but we enjoyed each other's company and found plenty to discuss and examine. Maggie loved to read, and when we were at my house, in my bedroom, she was fascinated by the Golden Books library Aunt Anne had created for me. Even when we were older and had outgrown the Golden Books, Maggie would insist upon counting the books and rearranging them in various orders. One day she was involved in this task, and I was busy watching her, and the hair issue came up again.

My hair was red and there was some curl to it. When I was younger, Dad would comb through it and allow it to remain curled and fluffy against my head. One day Aunt Anne said to him, "Toby, Livie looks a bit wild. Her hair is getting longer, and you need to comb it carefully or else it will wind up knotted. Let me show you how to manage it." And that is how the pigtails started. Later, as my hair grew longer, Aunt Anne showed Dad and Uncle Terry how to braid it. I loved this style because I could tie ribbons of whatever was my favorite color at the time to the ends of the braids. This is how I was wearing my hair when Maggie mentioned it.

"I really love your hair color, Liv, and it looks just like your Uncle Terry's hair. Except his is shorter and in a man's cut. It looks like he should be your father because your dad's hair is yellowish. And your mother's hair was like a brown color, right?"

"Yep," I answered.

"How could your uncle's hair and yours be the same?"

I knew how confusing this was. I had asked this of my own father, and because he gave me what I considered a definitive answer, I was ready to explain to Maggie.

"Well, Uncle Terry is my dad's cousin from Chicago, and because the hair color is in that part of the family, it came to me when I was born, even though my own father and mother did not have this color. Sometimes in science that happens. Dad told me about it."

I was sure this explanation would suffice. After all, I used the word *science* in explaining it, and we had studied some birds, and trees, and rocks in science class in school, and knew that *science* had an explanation for everything. I knew I had explained it almost the same way Dad had. I was sure of my facts.

"Hmmm. Well, you have the same eyes as your uncle too."

I was ready. "Well, if science can explain the hair color, it must also be the same for the eyes. Don't you think?"

Maggie nodded as she placed the Golden Books in another organizational mode. "Yes, I guess you're right. I should explain this to my mom and dad. I heard them talking the other night about you and wondering about the hair thing. They must not know *science* like we do."

I thought about this for a while as we walked back to Maggie's grandparent's house hoping to receive a treat. The idea that other people would talk about my hair color was new to me. I wondered what difference this would make, and why people in Everstille were wondering and discussing my hair color. And eyes. *Maybe science class should be held for older people too*, I ruminated, *they seem to need it.*

I'm unsure whether it was that day or another that I met Michael Jasper. His parents were visiting family in the town and they had come over to see the Pattersons. I think it was Maggie's mother, Edie Patterson, who was a cousin to one of the Jaspers. Mitch and Hattie were the adults, and Michael was their son. Michael had some little sisters, but they were much younger, and we were not as interested in them. We figured out that Michael was some kind of cousin to Mary and Maggie. He was about our age. He was friendly and fun, and I enjoyed his visits. During the summer, he stayed with his grandfather who lived in a big cabin in the wooded area west of town. Michael's grandmother died when he was small, and he didn't remember her. But whenever he stayed with his grandfather, he would be at the Patterson's house, and the three of us would play together.

During his summer visits, when Mike, and Maggie, and I were a trio, we would execute all manner of adventures. We busied ourselves at the town park rocking on the swings, gliding down the slides, taking turns pushing each other and becoming dizzy on the merry-go-round. We visited the Emporium and shared whatever candy we could purchase with our combined pennies. We played hide-and-seek in the trees and bushes and the game of *Statues* in the Mitchell backyard, and occasionally, we would visit Mike's grandfather at his cabin. On summer mornings when his Grandpa Wells came to town to get groceries from Clampet's or pick up some things at the Emporium, Mike would ask if we could get permission to go back to the cabin with him. Grandpa Wells would drive us both home before supper.

Maggie and I loved these excursions. There was so much to see in the cabin and in the wooded area behind it. A roomy yard with a large garden and an old well which was closed made the back of the cabin perfect for the games we invented. There were still some farms along the county road, and we would take hikes and look for wildflowers which we would bring back to Grandpa Wells. He would identify the coneflowers, yarrow, purple milkweed, and a few times, cowslips we held out to him.

We walked west, to North Cemetery. Once there, I showed Maggie and Mike my mother's grave, and we stood there solemnly. We would travel in and out of the cemetery lanes, reading the names and dates on the tombstones and making a game of who could find the oldest one, or the strangest one, or the biggest one, or even, because death was such an abstract idea to us, the newest one. Mike showed us the stones that he knew about because they were in his family.

"Here," and he pointed to one, "this is Emma, my grandmother. She is next to Rebecca and Vernon who were her children. They died a long time ago. And here," we walked over to a lower row, "this is my dad's mom and his brother. Dad and his brother were twins, and he died in the war. I'm named after him."

We stared at the stone which spelled out the name *Michael John Jasper*. We examined this name and asked Mike if it scared him to see his name here.

"Not really. Anyway, my middle name is not *John*. It's *Mitchell* like my dad's name. I think the man who was my grandfather was named *John*, and he is around here too, but not by these two."

We searched for *John* and found him close to *Rebecca*, and wondered why he was not with his family. We made up stories about the other people who were buried there and pointed out names of those we knew because their descendants continued to walk around town. As we left to return to the cabin, we picked and ate the wild strawberries growing along Country Road 8, and we held a stone throwing contest to determine who would get the last piece of licorice Maggie found in her pocket.

Mike and Maggie would come to dinner at my house where Uncle Terry would use the new outdoor grill he bought to make hot dogs or hamburgers for us. The three of us would sit at the edge of the back porch, trying to keep our plastic dinner plates from falling while we ate. Sometimes, Mike would stay at Maggie's house overnight, and as the summer day ended and the night beetles came out, we would chase them around and grab them, and argue about their names. Mike said they were called "lightening-bugs" and Maggie and I called them "fireflies", and when we asked Dad to settle it, he quoted "The fireflies, like golden seeds, are sown about the night", and we laughed. Uncle Terry and I would walk Mike and Maggie back home, and as the two of us returned, he would lift me up to his shoulders and ask me if I could touch the sky yet.

Those youthful summers in Everstille were gloriously free. The times I spent with friends and family, those stretches filled with adventures and delight, were grounding for me during the difficult times after my tenth summer. The years I was away from Everstille, away from friends and family, away from the marvels of the small town I missed and for which I ached, were trying and gloomy.

3-4 Still Pink

On my third birthday, I was still enamored with pink and did not want my bedroom walls repainted, so they stayed pink. Aunt Anne brought a new set of lacy white window curtains, and I thought I had the most beautiful windows in the world. By this time, I was choosing my own birthday meal and cake and had definite opinions. We ate quick lunches or dinners at the restaurant in town, and I was in love with the hot dogs and French fries Mazie served. Dad, Uncle Terry, Aunt Anne, and I celebrated my birthday dinner there, eating the reddish hot dogs served in soft steamed buns with piles of sizzling fries. We drenched the fries in homemade rosy ketchup Mazie's cook made and tried to get most of the goodness in our mouths. We washed it all down with Hires Root Beer. Afterwards, we went back home and continued the celebration with the "little cakes" I had seen at Peterson's bakery. These were sweet spongy cupcakes piled high with clouds of pink frosting covered with pink sprinkles. It was the perfect birthday celebration.

My personal new year started on May 22, my birthday, followed by my yearly holidays. A few weeks after the big day was the cinnamon cake picnic held at Mother's grave. Then June traveled on warm air into the heat of July and the July Fourth festivities gave me a chance to stay up well past my bedtime and watch the fireworks while sitting on Uncle Terry's shoulders. July and August were filled with outside fun: Vacation Bible School at the church, playing at the town park with my baby-sitter, Sally, trips to South Bend with my family to visit the zoo, Friday night walks to the Emporium with Aunt Anne.

When I was school age, there were assemblies and field trips with my class. We traveled on a big bus to museums and other places of academic interest, and Maggie and I would sit together looking out the bus window, counting the cows. The excitement of choosing a Halloween costume, and the tricks Maggie and I thought up to play on Mean Mary were wonderfully time-consuming. Then the actual holiday season came with days happening quickly and running into each other: Thanksgiving, Christmas, New Year's Day, Valentine's Day, Easter.

Icy walks, and sledding, snowball fights, and hot chocolate occurred before ice and snow melted, and the snakelike shedding of winter coats and hats and freedom from boots came. This was followed by splashed color on the ground: the hyacinths, daffodils, the delicate scent of early lilacs pulled from the branches and thrust faceward to swallow the smell. Then the end of my year coincided with school's end and the town's celebration of a new cycle with the annual Spring Festival. Finally, after much patient waiting and anxious hoping and restless expectation, my personal New Year began again. May 22. Different colors for my bedroom walls. Particularly chosen meals. Specially created birthday cake. Launching another year, joyously, older.

It was the summer when I was three (going on four) that I realized I had additional family. These family members were related to me through my father, and lived in Chicago, a far-off land. I had additional aunts and uncles and cousins, and apparently Dad and I were going to meet them at a restaurant in South Bend. I was being prepared for the reunion. Although it was not really a reunion. Dad said we had made the same trip last year, but I was just two years old and did not remember. Aunt Anne had gone with us, and she was traveling with us again.

This was explained to me carefully, and I had many questions about these strangers. Who were these people? What did they look like? Were they nice? Did they know me? Why wasn't Uncle Terry going? Would the trip take days and days? What would we eat? Would we sleep there? Could we go back to the zoo there? Were there bathrooms in South Bend? What if we got lost? Could I take Raggedy Ann and Banana with me? What clothes would I wear? Who WERE these people???

Dad had some photographs of the strangers and pulled them out. I looked carefully at the black-and-white pictures of people I was positive I had never met. He pointed out the tall woman who was my Aunt Ernestine and the man who was her husband, Uncle Amos. The two boys in front of them were my cousins, Enoch and Otis, and their last name was Denison. The shorter woman was Aunt Gladys and her husband was Uncle Warren but everyone called him Dean which was his middle name. Their two daughters were Rose and Ivy, and they were the Murphy family. I was totally confused. Too many people with strange names and frankly, none of them looked happy or friendly. I looked closely at the two girls and wondered if there was any chance of them being friends. They were older than me, and I pondered a relationship with them.

"How old are those girls?" I asked, pointing them out to Dad.

"Well, I think Rose is about ten, and Ivy is a year or so younger, so about eight or nine."

"And those boys?"

"They are a bit older. Enoch is thirteen, and Otis is eleven. I think. These are your cousins. And those ladies are my sisters."

"But they have different names. Mine is *Pinkerton* like yours, so how could they be your sisters?'

A confusing explanation followed, and I remember getting tired of the explanation about family relationships and returned to another subject.

"Can't Uncle Terry come with me and you and Aunt Anne? We could sit in the back, and he could be in the front of the car with you."

Dad looked at me oddly. "Uncle Terry has to work. And when we meet our family, let's not mention him. OK? They don't really know about him, and we could keep him a secret…our own secret. Anyway, they know Aunt Anne, and won't it be fun to go with her? And, yes, you can bring Raggedy Ann and Banana."

By this time, I was tired of the entire conversation and confused, so I wandered off to play in my room. Years later, I discovered why Uncle Terry was relegated to a secret.

We traveled to the restaurant in South Bend and ate lunch there. Everyone was polite, and Dad kissed his sisters and shook my new uncles' hands. Aunt Anne said hello to everyone, and my new cousins and I were shuttled to the end of the table, although I was next to Aunt Anne on one side and relieved to be there. I didn't expect the boy cousins to be friendly, but I held out hope for the girls. After all, they had flower names. They spent the lunch giggling and pointing at my head. I think they were making fun of my red hair.

Dad and Aunt Anne and I made the luncheon trip to South Bend when I was four years old, and five, and six, and when I was seven, we took a longer trip. That is Dad and I did. Aunt Anne didn't go with us. Neither did our secret. Apparently, Uncle Terry's work schedule continually interfered with these family get-togethers.

Dad and I were going to Chicago. We would take a long trip in the car, just the two of us, and stay Monday night at Aunt Ernestine's house, Tuesday night at Aunt Gladys' house, and travel home Wednesday. I was excited. And nervous. I was pretty sure by this time that my boy cousins, Enoch, and Otis were not going to be friends. They were old now, being sixteen and seventeen. I still held out hope for the flower cousins who were twelve and thirteen. That didn't seem so much older than my seven and a half years. I had visions of us sharing toys and talking about the kinds of things Maggie and I discussed.

During one early summer Monday morning, Dad and I got up and packed the car with our suitcases, some pillows, and blankets, some of my toys, and the snack cookies from Aunt Anne. I kissed Uncle Terry good-by, and we headed off to that land called Chicago. I was eager and nervous, and after we had traveled for a time. I knew I needed to use a bathroom.

"Dad, I really need to go. Can't we stop somewhere? Isn't there a bathroom on the road?"

Dad assured me he would stop at the next filling station to get some gas and take care of my needs, and I jiggled in the car and asked forty-two times if we were close, and just in time, we pulled into a service station. Dad jumped out of the car, ran into a little store connected with the gas station, and came out holding a big key attached to an enormous piece of wood. I just made it in, and as Dad waited outside the door for me (I had begun to be shy about such things), he instructed me to "Wash your hands twice!" I had visited Mackie's service station in Everstille, but had never needed to use the bathroom there, so this was something new for me. When I was finished, we went into the little store where I was able to get a wonderful candy necklace and bracelet which I promptly began to eat, one candy bead at a time. Dad got gas in the car, and we were on our way.

Soon I knew I needed to use another bathroom. Dad pulled in to another service station, and this time, after the bathroom procedure, the little store offered me a box of Hot Tamales, but they needed something to wash them down. Dad picked up two bottles of Seven-Up, one for each of us. This trip was turning out to be heavenly.

But the Seven-Up went through my system quickly, especially because I had eaten three or four of the chocolate-chip cookies I found in the back seat which was where I wanted to sit.

"Dad…", and he said, "Almost there."

This time he said no more candy treats were needed, but I begged for "just one more, and I won't eat it." He gave in. This time, I found a package of Peeps that were probably left from a while back, but there were four soft creatures in the package and they were the prettiest, brightest pink. As we traveled towards our destination, I was very careful to open the package quietly as I ate three of them. Suddenly, I knew there was going to be a sad end to the great candy adventure, and I yelled at Dad to "Stop, I'm going to be sick!"

After clean-up and a discussion about sensible moderation, and blaming himself for having no sense either, the rest of the candy and cookies went up to the front with Dad who settled me in the back seat against some pillows and blankets. I fell asleep. When I awoke, we were in Chicago, and Aunt Ernestine was peeking in the back window at me.

"Welcome, Olivia. Come on out of there. I'll bet you're hungry, and I have Sloppy Joes for lunch. Come on in and we'll get you settled and washed up. After all, cleanliness is next to godliness."

I didn't know what she meant, and I was sure the last thing I wanted was to eat, but after a wash-up in a small bathroom, a big sandwich with some pickles and a handful of Jays Potato Chips stared me in the face. I picked at it, even the chips, took a bite or two, and listened as Dad and Aunt Ernestine talked about people I didn't know and things that were not interesting. Dad didn't push me to eat, and I was grateful for that. I am sure he didn't want another clean-up. Aunt Ernestine asked me typical adult-type questions about school, and friends, and playing, and after receiving mono-syllabic answers, she stopped. I know I was not being a *good guest*, something I had been cautioned to be, but just didn't care.

"The boys are out, and Amos is at work, but they'll be home in a couple of hours. Tobias, is there something you would like to do with Olivia? You could take a walk and show her some of the neighborhood where you grew up. After all, don't put off till tomorrow what you can do today."

"I think that's exactly what we will do Ernie. Let me help with the dishes and clean-up."

"No, you two go on your adventure. I'm going to make dinner. I guess you remember your way around. Go on now, get going. The early bird gets the worm!"

This aunt sure talks funny, I thought, but said nothing, as I was trying to be the *good guest*. Dad and I got up, I went again to the small bathroom and washed up, and we walked down the many stairs of the front porch and walked some streets away from the house he had lived in for many years. We crossed a busy street, and I clung to Dad's hands because I had never seen so much traffic. There was a big statue of some man named McKinley who was a president, and I ran up and down the stairs where his statue was located. We walked around the park and saw many geese and some ducks in the water that Dad said was a *lagoon*. We played there, and Dad told me some stories about what he did as a boy and where he went to high school, and I was beginning to feel much better. We crossed the street again, and it was busier than ever, so Dad picked me up and carried me to the other side.

There were some people sitting on the front porch steps when we got back to Aunt Ernestine's house, and they were my boy cousins. They were nice enough and said "Hi" to me, but they were old. When Uncle Amos came home, he and Dad shook hands and talked, and the boy cousins listened, and I kicked the steps and then sat down because I was just bored. Aunt Ernestine called us to come in, clean-up, and eat. There were sure lots of clean-ups this trip.

Dinner was meatloaf and mashed potatoes, but it did not taste like the meal that Uncle Terry makes, so I just ate some of it and pushed it around on my plate. Dad watched me but didn't say much. He ate all his and took some more, and told Aunt Ernestine how good it was, and it reminded him of his youth.

"Well, you know, there's no place like home," and Aunt Ernestine smiled.

After dinner and more cleaning-up, the boy cousins offered to walk me to the corner drugstore where I could get some ice-cream. That sounded great, and Dad gave them some money to pay for it, and told them to keep the change. That made them happy, and I was happy too when I picked out an ice-cream that I had never had before. It was called *orange sherbet*, and it was the best thing I had eaten all day. Even the Peeps weren't as good.

Dad got me ready for bed in a small bedroom upstairs. He covered me with a light blanket and put Raggedy Ann and Banana close to me, and said a prayer with me. When he left, I got up and began to look around the room. I heard some voices and in a corner of the room found a grate. If I looked down the grate, I could see Dad and my uncle and aunt sitting. I could hear most of what they were saying although I didn't understand it all.

"Well, where did that red hair come from? It sure wasn't in our family."

"Ernie, I believe Ruth had that color in her family a few generations back. She told me that her one aunt and, I think, her great-grandmother had that color. What difference does it make?"

"It's just strange. That little girl is cute, but she needs a mother. Why aren't you asking Anne to marry? It has been long enough, Tobias, and you should settle down again. I just don't know how you can be a principal and a father and keep it all straight. And you know, two heads are better than one."

"Leave the man alone, Ernie, he's doing just fine. I believe some relative back in my line had some red hair. It's just not that uncommon. Hey, Toby, come on out to the back porch with me. I have a couple of bottles of beer to help us cool off."

Uncle Amos and Dad got up to leave, and Aunt Ernestine just shook her head. Then she took out a magazine to look at, and I hurried back into bed to think. My mother's family had this red hair too? I thought Uncle Terry and his family gave it to me. I wasn't sure why Dad was saying that, and I fell asleep with these thoughts swirling in my mind.

The next day, after breakfast when the boy cousins and Uncle Amos left, and long good-byes were said, Dad packed everything up and we got in the car again for a ride to Aunt Gladys' place. Aunt Ernestine stood on the corner, waved at us, and yelled, "Watch this traffic. Better safe than sorry!"

It was not much more fun at Aunt Gladys'. The flower cousins were with some friends, and when they came home for lunch (Fried baloney sandwiches with milk. Yuck! How could Dad eat two?), they weren't any friendlier than my boy cousins even though they were closer to my age. Aunt Gladys told them to take me to the back yard and play with me while she talked to Dad, but when we got there, they sat in a corner and talked and threw a ball back and forth to each other. I sat down in the grass and found some clover growing, so I began to make chains with the flowers. I thought that maybe because they had flower names, they would help. They didn't.

After dinner (A strange tasting chicken and potatoes. I was missing Uncle Terry's good cooking.), we went to watch the television, something I did not have in my house. We all watched some tiresome news, and then there was *The Bugs Bunny Show* which I liked. Then there was another clean-up and bed again. Because the flower cousins were older, they stayed up later, but I didn't care. That night I was tired, and after Dad tucked me in to another small bed, I went to sleep. Boring stuff makes me tired, I thought.

We left after breakfast and made the long trip home. I slept most of the way back, and we only stopped two times for gasoline and bathroom needs. Dad wouldn't let me get any candy. That was fine. I didn't want any. When we were almost home, I sat up in the back seat and leaned forward to talk to Dad.

"Will we go there again next year?"

"Well, maybe not, Livie. Your aunts wanted us to visit for years, and I thought this was a good time to do that. Now that it is done, I think we can just go back to meeting for lunches in South Bend. What do you think?"

I thought for a minute, and since I didn't want to hurt Dad's feelings because he did let me get all that candy, I said, "That would be a good idea. Chicago is really far away, and there wasn't anything for me to do there. But I really liked the orange ice-cream at that drugstore. Do you think there is any like at at Clampet's grocery store?"

Dad reached back and squeezed my shoulder and laughed. "I'll bet we could find some there. We'll go and look for it tomorrow. How's that?"

"That would be great. And Dad, Chicago wasn't so bad."

"Glad you feel that way, Livie."

But it was that bad, and in a few short years, I would find out just how awful it could be.

4-5 Orange Monkey

Sometimes Dad left for short weekend trips. Uncle Terry explained that he was talking to other principals and teachers about school and teaching stuff, and during these times, Uncle Terry and I would have adventures. For example, we played something called Putt-Putt Golf at a Putt-Putt Golf Course in Elkhart where I wanted to keep the little club and the ball, but it wasn't allowed. Another time, we drove the car into a big outdoor movie lot and stayed in it while we watched a movie called *Old Yeller.* It was a sad movie, but I didn't find that out until later because I fell asleep. The next day, when I asked Uncle Terry about what happened, I was glad that I fell asleep. One time, Uncle Terry took me out to the road west of town and let me sit on his lap while I drove the car. That was great, but he said to never tell Dad or he would get in trouble. I never did. But the most unforgettable time was when we went to a carnival.

I was just four years old. Dad was gone on a talking/teaching trip, and Uncle Terry asked me if I wanted to go on an adventure. Whenever he said *adventure*. I knew it would be fun. Aunt Anne was supposed to go too, but something happened, and she couldn't, so one late Saturday afternoon, Uncle Terry and I got into his car and took off. We traveled to a carnival that was set up in some farmland past Elkhart.

I had no idea what a *carnival* was, so Uncle Terry tried to explain.

"There are games to play and rides to go on, and strange things to see. Food wagons have things to eat that are delicious. Not sure they are so good for you, but they taste great. We'll eat dinner there. How does that sound?"

"Great! Will we eat in a restaurant like Mazie's? And then the waiter girl will bring our food?"

"Nope. We will stand in line and order what we want and then sit at some picnic tables to eat."

"So, we are eating outside? What kind of food is there?"

"You can get about anything you want, Cabbage. How about corn on the cob, or a corn dog, or elephant ears?"

Now I knew Uncle Terry had to be joking. But when he explained what the elephant ears really were, I couldn't wait to try them. And they were as wonderful as he claimed.

I could see the carnival as we got closer. There was a big wheel ride that went around, and lots of colorful flags on top of long poles, and tents, and booths which promised the *adventure* Uncle Terry talked about. I had trouble containing my excitement, and squirmed in the front seat pointing out the red, yellow, blue flags, and the music and laughter and noise which floated through the air. A man with a cigar in his mouth pointed to the area to park the car. There was a long line in front of us and an even longer line in back, but finally, after what seemed like one hundred hours, we parked and got out, and Uncle Terry leaned down to me to give me instructions.

"Now there are lots and lots of people here, so you need to hold my hand the entire time. Do not let go, and don't run away to see something. It will be noisy in there, so if you say something and I don't hear you, tug on my hand. Got it?"

I nodded my head and held out my hand, and he took it. We walked towards the beckoning sights and sounds, and I felt overwhelmed. Too bad Dad and Aunt Anne weren't here. Then we could all hold hands and walk and swing our arms just like the family in front of us. I couldn't wait to tell Maggie about being here on this adventure with Uncle Terry. I was sure she had never been to a carnival.

The smells were intoxicating. Some I could identify, like the popcorn smell and something deliciously fried. But there were other aromas; aromas I could not recognize; aromas whose source I wanted to discover; promised pleasures hanging in the air. I was immediately hungry, but Uncle Terry explained our plan.

"Never eat anything before you get on a ride. That's a surefire way to get sick; and rides should be done first. Then games, and if your stomach is fine, we'll eat, and finally, get cotton candy. After, we'll walk around to see if we missed anything exciting. How does that sound?"

"Can we get the cotton candy right after the rides?" I wasn't sure what cotton candy was, but it sounded too spectacular to put off for long.

"Sure, as long as you feel fine."

We walked for a time, then stopped to watch the Ferris Wheel and the Tilt-a-Whirl, but Uncle Terry said those were not meant for someone who was not at least five feet tall. I was not sure where he got the height information, but I agreed I was not yet ready for those amusements. We walked over to a booth, and Uncle Terry exchanged some money for a long row of burnt-orange-colored tickets, and we sauntered over to the Carousel to watch it turn and turn in slow motion, a leisurely twisting spectacle which gave us time to notice the fabulous creatures residing on it.

Horses of all shapes and colors were easy to recognize, as was the elephant, lion, giraffe, and swan which seemed to be the most popular rides. There were other creatures I was not able to identify. Uncle Terry pointing out the seahorse, and a dragon, and a wild looking horse with wings. Then there was a snake-like creature which frightened me, and I told him I would not go on that one. The beast which fascinated me the most looked like a bird on fire. Red and orange and purple lines flew from its wings, and the face contained bright blue eyes and long lashes. It was called a *phoenix*, and that was the one I wanted to ride. But not right away, and could Uncle Terry go on with me?

He laughed and said, "Look at the seats. There are some flat seats that you and I can sit on at first until you get used to the ride. How about that? There is a peacock seat. If we go on that first, you can ride on one of the other animals after. I'll stay right next to you and hold on so you won't fall. OK?"

We got in a long line which moved quickly, and he helped me up onto the platform where we sat together in the peacock seats. I held onto Uncle Terry's hand tightly because I felt some of those butterfly things in my stomach, but once the ride started, it was slower than riding in a car, and we waved at the people who were watching us travel around and around. Once the ride stopped, we had to get off and get in the line again, but this time I wasn't scared.

The second ride was disappointing because I was not able to get on the phoenix. Some boy had scooted up there, and I had to choose another animal. The swan was empty and Uncle Terry lifted me up and put a loose braided belt around my waist, but he stood beside me and held his hand on my back. The swan moved up and down, and this time, I didn't wave at anyone because I had to hold onto the pole that was stuck through the swan's head. When the ride was slowing down, indicating it was over, Uncle Terry said, "Wait here for a second, and hold on." He jumped off the platform and sprinted over to the man who was making the Carousel go, handed him something, and came back.

"Don't we have to get off now?" I asked.

Uncle Terry shook his head and lifted me off the swan and carried me to the phoenix where he placed me on the seat, buckled me in, and we waited while the rest of the riders clambered aboard to find their animals. I was thrilled. The third time was the best ride of all, and I pushed Uncle Terry's hand away so that I could feel as though I was flying in the air all by myself on this strange firebird. He kept his hand on the back of the bird just in case, and I laughed and yelled as I pretend-flew. Once the ride stopped, we got off, and as we passed the man who ran the ride, Uncle Terry put his hand to his head and saluted him as the man said, "Thanks, Sir. Glad your daughter liked the ride."

I glanced at Uncle Terry, but he didn't correct the man about me being his daughter. I filed this away. There were important decisions to make. We walked out of the area and Uncle Terry looked at me smiling and asked. "How about the Teacup ride over there? Then there is a Caterpillar ride you might like. Let's go and see those."

We watched others get on the rides, and once I was sure I would be safe, we waited in line. Uncle Terry put me into the seat. Then he squeezed into the small one behind me because I didn't think I could manage to go by myself. We rode the Teacup and then the Caterpillar, and they were exciting, but the Carousel was the best of all. Once we finished, I thought again about the cotton candy and asked if it was time to taste it.

"Are you feeling OK? Is your tummy sick, or do you want to go on more rides?"

I assured him I was fine, and the rides were great, but I thought it was time for something to eat. We walked over to a man who was standing in front of a large spherical moving object, swirling the most amazing confection in the world round and round on paper cones and selling the cloud-like substance to waiting customers. There was a choice of pink or blue, and Uncle Terry bought one of each, and I choose the pink one. I wasn't sure how I was going to chew this cloud, but I did what Uncle Terry showed me, pulled off a piece and stuck it in my mouth. What a surprise! It melted down around my tongue and disappeared, and I savored the taste of sugared wonder and quickly took another, bigger serving of the curiosity which did the exact same thing. I finished quickly and was left with both regret and satisfaction at the vanishment.

"That was great!" I held out the empty paper cone to Uncle Terry who put his and mine into a trash bin nearby. I touched my fingers and felt the stickiness. We walked by a water fountain and cleaned out mouths with sips, and a handkerchief dampened from the water helped to clean off fingers.

"Now what?" I looked up expectantly.

"Let's play some games," said my uncle. We walked towards the sign that was placed between two tall poles and proclaimed: *Midway: Games, Games, Games,* and gravitated to the *Duck Pond: Everyone Wins!* location. We stood and watched as several children who were in front of a moving pond with plastic ducks floating by, reached out, picked a duck out of the water, and won the prize that was printed on the bottom. Seemed straight forward. More of Uncle Terry's tickets were exchanged, and I was encouraged to pick up a duck. The first time I won a plastic ring which immediately fell off my finger. The second duck got me a whistle which didn't work when I tried to blow it in the car on the way home. Twice was enough, and Uncle Terry stored the trophies in his pocket as we traveled on.

We noticed some men who were standing and watching as one of them lifted a hammer high in the air and brought it down on a disc which rose on a pole. The object was to ring the bell on the top, but so far, not much ringing was heard. As the group moved away, the man holding the hammer looked at Uncle Terry and said, "Sir, you look like a strong man. Come on and take a chance. Let your little daughter brag about how big and strong her daddy is. Come on and try it."

This was the second time I had been called Uncle Terry's *daughter,* and I was about to correct this man when Uncle Terry said, "What do you think, Livie? Think I can ring the bell?"

I looked up and smiled and said, "Sure. I bet you can!"

Another exchange of tickets, and the large hammer was given to Uncle Terry. And he did ring the bell. Three times. The third time some people had gathered to watch and they clapped when the hammer pounded down, the disc rose, and the bell rang out loudly across the Midway. I clapped too and was proud. But Uncle Terry wouldn't try it again, and we walked away to watch some of the other games.

We stood and watched as people tried to get some small light white balls into some fish bowls. Getting one in would garner a prize, and there were lots of great prizes there, although we saw only one man win a small stuffed bear which he gave to the woman standing next to him. Then we watched something called Ring Toss which I thought was the same sort of game only plastic rings had to land and stay on bottles which were positioned on a table. The prizes were even better here. They hung down from giant hooks anchored to the top of the tent, and they were so crowded that counting them would be impossible. As I gazed up at the stuffed animals and dolls and jump ropes and bags with big question marks all over them, I saw it. Almost directly overhead hung an orange monkey. It was about the size of my Raggedy Ann doll at home, and it smiled down at me with a large loopy grin and black button eyes. There was a fluffy red bow tied around its neck, and I felt lust for the first time.

"Look, Uncle Terry, look at that monkey. I wish I could have it. It looks so soft, and it wants to come home with me. Could you get it for me? Please?"

He looked up at the orange critter, then down at me, and then over to the Ring Toss game. There were about five other people lined up trying to get the plastic rings on the elusive slippery bottles. None of them were having any luck, and soon they gave up. One or two other people paid their twenty-five cents for three rings and attempted to outwit fate.

"I'll try, but there's no guarantee I'll win, so no crying if I don't. OK?"

I nodded and squeezed his hand, and he stepped forward, handing the man behind the table a dollar. Twelve rings were handed back. Twelve chances to become a champion. A dozen tries to lower the orange monkey, place him in my arms, and bring him home to cuddle next to me and Raggedy Ann and Banana as we drifted off to sleep. My heart raced. The butterflies were back. I could not breathe.

Uncle Terry stepped back and examined the bottles. He turned his head one way and then another. He eyed the table and the bottles and squinted over the tops of them. He held the twelve rings, weighed them, and choose one. He looked at me and smiled and said, "Well, here goes nothing." Then he tossed the ring.

During my life, there were many surprises. Some good, many not. As I consider all the things about which I was shocked or amazed or astonished or flabbergasted, none of them compared with what happened. The first ring Uncle Terry tossed landed on a bottle, spun around a few times, almost slipping off, then settled down, leaving a lovely collar of dirty plastic around the dullness of the glass bottle, and the monkey, the orange smiling monkey with the fluffy red bow, was mine. Uncle Terry shrieked; I jumped up and down and yelled; the people around the table clapped, and as the Ring Toss man reached up with a large hook, removing the monkey from its spot next to a doll and a stuffed Mickey Mouse, he screamed out to the crowd that had gathered, "Come on and try your luck. See how easy it is to win a great prize! Look at the wonderful gift this little girl just got. Come one! Come all! Three rings for a quarter!"

Uncle Terry stepped back. He turned to two boys who stood there, gave them his eleven unneeded rings, and took my hand. We moved out of the way, and I looked at the monkey and up at my uncle and said, "I knew you could do it. You're the best uncle ever! Wait until Maggie sees this. Thanks, Uncle Terry!"

I held his hand and squeezed the monkey to my side, and I walked, no, floated next to my uncle where my joy was barely contained. We found an empty picnic table next to some delicious smelling food trucks and sat down. I examined the monkey closely, admiring the soft orange fur and the lovely red bow, and hugged him repeatedly. After watching me for a while, Uncle Terry leaned back against the table and asked. "Are you hungry? Do you think you could eat dinner now? I can walk right over here and get some things for us. Don't move from here, and I will watch you as I order."

He looked at the signs on the side and back of the trucks, took some money from his pocket, and went to get our dinner. I sat at the table holding tightly to my monkey, and I could see Uncle Terry watching me as he stood in the food line. It took two trips for him to return with dinner. There was sweet lemonade and some corn-on-the-cob laying in a paper plate swimming in butter, two corn dogs, and some flat, flaky cinnamon-covered fried dough which did look a bit like elephant ears. He spread out the feast, told me to put monkey to the side by him so it wouldn't get greasy, and we began our meal.

I was hungry, and the food was great although I wasn't crazy about the corn-dog and took only two bites. They were not like Mazie's hot dogs in town. But the flakiness and sweetness and crunchy-softness of the elephant ears was the best. We ate. Then, he cleaned the table and me, and we sat there sated and content, sipping on the lemonade. I played with my monkey as Uncle Terry watched, and we chatted about the rides and games and food, and then I spoke.

"Uncle Terry, I think I know what color I want my room painted this year."

"So, you want to change from the pink?"

"Yes. I want to have the walls the color of my monkey. I want an orange room. Can we do that?"

Uncle Terry looked at me and slowly nodded. "I think that is doable. In fact, on Monday, I can go to Jensen's Hardware after work and ask Mr. Jenson for the paint we need. How does that sound?"

"Thanks, Uncle Terry. I know my monkey will like to be in the room that is painted the same color as him."

We sat for a while longer. The late afternoon was becoming early evening, and the sun was creating uneven stripes of pink and orange in the west. The day was ending, and we needed to get home.

As we walked back to the car, I pointed to the sky. "Look. The sky is turning orange like monkey. It's really pretty. I'm going to like that color on the walls."

I held tightly to Uncle Terry's hand and clutched the orange monkey with the fluffy red bow to my side. I suddenly thought about the two men who called me Uncle Terry's daughter, and I glanced up at him. I loved Dad. He was kind and loved me a lot, and I knew it. He and my mother who was no longer here, were the best parents ever. But I wouldn't mind if Uncle Terry was my father. I wouldn't mind at all.

5-6 Light Blue

In first grade, my teacher, Mrs. Griffith told me I was a *little know-it-all*, and I told her she was a *big meanie*. And that was in the first month. Kindergarten was different. Indiana did not have a mandatory kindergarten program, but left the decision about offering it to individual school districts. The Everstille School Board decided to do so in 1958, and so, in 1959, the year I was five, I went to kindergarten.

Miss Jennifer Kendal was the kindergarten teacher. There was one class during the morning and one in the afternoon, and she taught both. Not all families, especially the farming families who lived further out from town and had difficulty with a half-day program, made the decision to send their young children to kindergarten, but the townspeople did. The morning class had ten students in it while the afternoon class had nine. I was in the morning class with my best friend, Maggie. Sally, my baby-sitter, picked me up after school. About once a week, Maggie would come home with me, and the two of us would eat lunch then play together in my room.

I loved Kindergarten. Except for the absence of Jesus stories, it was Sunday School with better organized activities and superior toys. Miss Kendal was a pretty, young woman with curly blond hair and blue eyes which almost matched the color of the walls I had decided on that year. She played the piano while we sang, dispensed our daily snack of milk and cookies, and wiped all our tears when Tiny, our class turtle, disappeared and was found under a shelf all dried out. Despite that early introduction to death, and the burial of Tiny in the schoolyard under a boxwood near the rear school door (I wondered if he got dug up for reburial in the afternoon class), we all learned to love our new class pet, Timmy, the turtle.

We looked forward to the scheduled playtimes. There were blocks, and clay, and coloring, and occasionally, finger painting. Once each week, weather permitting, we would take a *nature walk* all around the school building, examining the scraggly plants and flower beds that were there, listening for the annoying woodpecker sound, watching a trail of ants haul a dead bee. We learned songs and simple dances and played *Simon Says* and did the *Hokey-Pokey*. We were taught to recognize and name colors, to wash our hands which would keep us healthy, and to play nicely and take turns. Birthdays were celebrated with a plastic cake that had real candles on it, and treats were shared. Sharing, explained Miss Kendal, was an important human trait.

Then there was the letter per week program which took us through the alphabet, and prepared us for reading in first grade. Each week, a new letter appeared on the bulletin board; throughout the week, everyone had to name a word that began with the letter. During our writing class, we used enormously large pencils to trace the uppercase and lowercase letter in our workbook and were encouraged to bring in something for Show-and-Tell that started with the latest letter. The girls, brought in their favorite doll when *D*'s turn arrived, and all of us, including Miss Kendal, laughed when Martin Merz brought in a *diaper.* However, his three grasshoppers for *G* had to be turned loose outside after they eventually were caught, having escaped from Martin's paper bag.

And we counted. There were counting games and number games, and we were expected to count by ourselves up to fifty by the end of the schoolyear. This achievement placed your name on the *Counting Ladder* which was a paper ladder that went from the bottom of the wall to the very top and was located behind Miss Kendal's desk. There were two ladders, one for the morning class and one for the afternoon class. From the looks of it, the afternoon class was going to have difficulty in first grade arithmetic, which was what counting to fifty was training us to do.

I went along with it all. I counted (I was the first name on the morning class Counting Ladder), and traced my letters, and brought in my Show-and-Tell items, and danced, and sang, and shared. I did it all because I really liked Miss Kendal. She was kind, and friendly, and smiled, and the first time we met, she told me that her best friend had lovely red hair like mine, and she was sure we would be good friends. She charmed me. And because she did, and because she smelled like roses, I did not let on that I was able to count to over a hundred by both ones and twos, read most of my Golden Books to myself, and could write my first, middle, and last name as well as that of my father and Uncle Terry and Aunt Anne using a regular sized pencil. I allowed her to teach me.

First grade was a challenge. Probably more of a challenge for Mrs. Griffith than for me, although we tested each other. I know I did not like her as I liked Miss Kendal, and after the first week, I discussed the idea with Dad that perhaps I could opt out of first grade. After all, I was pretty sure I knew it all anyway. Besides, Mrs. Griffith had separated Maggie and me due to our *chatting,* even though our last names were alphabetically compatible in the girls' line.

"But Dad," I argued, "I know the numbers and the alphabet, and can read the easy stories in the book Mrs. Griffith gave us. Do you want me to prove it? I can read them to you," and I ran to my room to get the primer I had brought home. I read quickly through the first few pages, then stopped to look at my father, expecting the same look of disdain I had for the mindless stories.

My father listened to me and then nodded. I was sure he would agree with me that staying at home with Sally would be a much better use of my time. First grade required me to be in school all day, and Sally met and walked me home in the afternoon and stayed with me until Dad or Uncle Terry arrived home. I could simply stay with Sally all day. I was willing to hide in the house. That way no one would know that I was not in school, and no one would get in trouble. Dad did not see it that way.

"Livie, school is mandatory. That means children must attend, and you are going to go. Even if you think you know everything, there are always new concepts for you to learn. Being in school teaches us how to get along with each other; how to appreciate the differences in people and accept them. That includes learning to get along with adults like Mrs. Griffith. Both Uncle Terry and I expect you to behave and listen and not talk back. I know you can read, but not all your classmates are as advanced as you are. Perhaps you can help some of them. Let Mrs. Griffith see that you are willing to take her instructions, and don't be a show-off. There is something to be said for humbleness. Do you understand?"

No, I did not. I was sure Mrs. Griffith did not like me. I disputed the notion that there were any new concepts I would learn in first grade. I presented my best arguments, but after a few more minutes I could see that my father was unbending. I knew defeat when it showed its distasteful face to me. I sighed, and shrugged, and went to put the stupid easy book back in my room. The following morning, I was glum as I got up and prepared for school. For the next few days, I was so quiet that Maggie asked if I were angry with her. I assured her I was not, but I missed not being able to stand next to her in line. I had been placed at the back, after Cathy Wesselmann, and she and I were not friends.

I attempted to make the best of the bad situation, and I tried to behave. I honestly did. I read my line in the reader when called on, counted my numbers with the class, and walked quietly with my arms folded as required, when we marched down the halls. Whenever we passed the kindergarten room and I saw rose-scented, blonde-haired Miss Kendal playing the piano while a new group of fortunate students sang, a wave of melancholy washed over me. I was certain that as I walked by her classroom, a small piece of my heart, red as my hair, fell upon the kindergarten floor. Soon the entire heart would be left in fragments there. But I said nothing and became quieter, and attempted to accept my fate. And then, one day, towards the end of the first lengthy month in first grade, my good behavior streak ended.

Mrs. Griffith was engaging us in what she called the *Word Game*. She would hold up a card with a word on it and everyone would say the word. Once we got through one set of the cards, she would begin again, but this time, she would call on one student to say the word. Then the next student would get the next word. It was boringly repetitious, and I was constantly amazed at the stupidity of some of my classmates when they could not recognize the easiest words; as they stumbled over *stop, go, play, ball;* as they attempted and failed to sound out *who, them, thank, eat.* One day, as I stared out the window and saw the fall colors beckoning to me, teasing me with their hues, demanding that I come outside and play, I decided to invent my own game to liven things up. As the word card was held up, I muttered the word *sotto voice* just before the chosen student gave the answer. At first, no one paid much attention, but soon, as I continued to raise my voice slightly, one decibel with each answer, I began to be noticed.

At first, only one or two classmates paid attention, but after about a half dozen rounds of the game, more began to turn their heads towards me, towards the sound, towards the word spoken louder and louder. I was unsure whether Mrs. Griffith was ignoring me or just couldn't hear me, but soon someone giggled, and she looked around.

"Is there a problem? Does someone need something? We all know that being polite means to be quiet and listen. If something is needed, please raise your hand."

No one moved. There was complete stillness in the room. Then she held up another card and called on the next student, Robert Stevens, who sat right behind me. This time, I didn't bother to whisper, but as soon as the card was held up, said clearly and well before Robert could figure it out, "Fish!"

Mrs. Griffith stopped and looked at me. "Olivia, it's not your turn yet. Please allow Robert his turn. Robert, try this card."

She held up another one. "House!" I spoke up clearly.

Mrs. Griffith stared at me. "Olivia, wait your turn. Robert, try this one."

The next card was an unfortunate choice. The entire class broke into laughter as the card came up and I, without any thought to safe-guarding my future, yelled in as piercing a voice as I could manage, "PIG!"

The card was slammed down, and Mrs. Griffith stood up. The entire class immediately stopped breathing. They had never seen a murder before, and obviously one was going to take place.

"Olivia Pinkerton, come here!"

I hesitated, but there was nowhere to hide, so I walked to her desk to meet my fate.

"Young lady, step into the hall and wait there. I will deal with you in a minute. Everyone else, get out your pencils and copy down this sentence on your paper," and Mrs. Griffith turned and wrote on the chalkboard: **We must be polite**. I stepped into the hallway and waited while she read the sentence and made sure everyone started their task.

When she came into the hallway where I was standing and, I admit, shivering with fear, Mrs. Griffith glared down at me, told me that I was impolite, and worse of all, had proved myself a *little know-it-all*. I believe she was waiting for me to cry, but I was determined not to, and I countered by telling Mrs. Griffith she was a *big meanie*. We both stood there for a long minute, not sure where to go next in this war, but I knew I had lost.

"Young lady, your father is going to receive a telephone call from me. He can deal with your impertinence. Now, get into the classroom and begin to complete the assignment."

The remainder of the afternoon dragged on, and when Sally met me after school, I threw myself into her arms and sobbed. She got me home and settled. I wanted no after-school snack and went to my bedroom where I cried until I fell asleep. When I awoke, it was to the sound of my father and Uncle Terry talking in the kitchen. I couldn't hear the words, but knew the tone, and I was afraid to get up.

Dad came into my room and sat on the end of the bed. I looked at his face, at his bright blue eyes, and began to cry again. He waited for me to finish and then spoke.

"Well, I guess you know Mrs. Griffith called me today. I heard her story and now want to hear from you. Sit up and tell me what happened."

I did. I explained it all to him. There was no sense in telling a lie. The entire class witnessed the act. The only part I kept from my father was what I had called Mrs. Griffith. I waited for him to pronounce sentence.

He talked about *respect* and *politeness*. He remarked about *manners* and *patience*. The word *humbleness* came up again, and *acceptance of others*. There was something about *waiting my turn* and *honoring our elders*, but I was waiting for the bombshell to explode. It never did. The phrase *big meanie* was never mentioned. And I did not repeat what Mrs. Griffith had called me. I supposed I was a *know-it-all*. I had never misbehaved like this before, but I would need to learn a lesson. Punishment would be given. I would have to apologize to Mrs. Griffith the next day, and I would not be allowed to go to Maggie's house on Saturday. Did I understand what was expected of me? Did I know how to behave from now on? Would a telephone call from Mrs. Griffith or any other teacher I would ever have in any grade ever, be received again? Then that was the end, and now, I should wash my face and hands because Uncle Terry had dinner ready.

I had never gotten in trouble or been punished before, but now, I knew what it was about. There was a weight upon my shoulders I had not felt before, but it wasn't totally oppressive. I felt some remorse and was mildly repentant, but there was another feeling I could not yet name. Strangely enough, I felt more grown up. I had been punished for my actions in class but not for my words in the hallway. I had gotten away with something. I had avoided dire consequences. There was a reprieve of sorts. I didn't know exactly what to feel, so I washed my face and hands and sat down to eat dinner with Dad and Uncle Terry.

Bedtime came. Dad came in and sat with me for a few minutes even though it was Uncle Terry's turn to tuck me in. He took my hand and held it, and then he leaned over to kiss my head.

"Good-night, Livie. Sometimes days are difficult, and today was one of those days. For both of us. Now tomorrow, do you know what to say to Mrs. Griffith?"

"Yes, Dad."

"Good. I love you, Livie. Uncle Terry will be in soon," and Dad planted another kiss on my head and left my room. I waited for Uncle Terry.

When Uncle Terry came in, he sat on the floor next to my bed, placing our heads level with each other. He looked at me for a few seconds and then said, "So, my Cabbage got into some trouble today. I guess I should ask if you learned your lesson, but I'm sure you did. You're a smart one. Right?"

I nodded. He could always make me feel better about anything. I could confide in him, and I felt I wanted to unburden myself about the rest of the incident from today.

"Uncle Ter, if I tell you something, will you keep a secret?"

"Yes, I will."

I took a deep breath. "Dad doesn't know about everything that happened today. There was another part."

"I'm listening. Tell me."

I took another breath and did. I didn't hide the truth. I told him about how when Mrs. Griffith called me a *know-it-all*, I called her a *big meanie*. I did not change any words, or cover up my part in the shamefulness, or excuse myself in any way. I just told him. Then I waited for his response.

He looked down at the floor for a few seconds, and then I saw his shoulder shake. He was laughing. And the laugh got louder, and when he looked at me, I began to laugh too. We giggled, and I was not sure what was so funny, but it felt good to laugh with him after spending so much of the day crying. Then we stopped, and I looked at my uncle with the red hair who was sprawled on the floor in front of my bed. He smiled and reached over to stroke my head.

"Listen, Livie, I am going to tell you how to get along with the Mrs. Griffiths in this world. You will need to pretend. You and Dad and I know you can read and count and do many of the things some of the other kids in your class haven't leaned yet. Don't shove their noses in it. And people in charge, like teachers, want to feel they are needed; that their knowledge is just a bit more than yours. Sometimes, it is. So, just go along with it. Tomorrow, apologize to your teacher and be sincere about it. You know that you did show off, and frankly, no one likes a show-off. Sometimes in life, you will need to pretend to be someone else. I know this sounds like you're not being true to yourself, but as long as you know in here…" and he pointed to his heart, "who you are, that's what matters."

I took in his words not completely understanding them, but knew they were important. I nodded and looked in his eyes.

"Uncle Ter, did you ever have to pretend to be someone else?"

He became serious. He looked down at his hands and then back at me. "Yes, Livie, I have had to pretend."

Then he reached over to pat my cheek. I put my hand up to his, and we were still for some moments.

"Now, go to sleep. Tomorrow will be better. And this conversation is just between us."

I smiled and was suddenly ready for sleep. He reached over to the side of my bed and pulled out my orange monkey which had slipped down between the bed and wall and settled him into the crook of my arm. I hugged the softness to me as a comfort. Uncle Terry reached over, kissed my head, leaned down close, and whispered to me.

"Sweet dreams Cabbage. And one more thing just between you and me…Mrs. Griffith *is* a big meanie!"

***

The following day, I marched up to Mrs. Griffith and apologized. Slowly the situation in first grade improved, and there were some new things I did eventually learned. Second grade was better with Mrs. Jenkins, and third grade with Mrs. Smith was downright fun. Fourth grade was difficult but not because of the work or the teacher. Miss Harris, my fourth-grade teacher was kind and understanding, and not just because she had to be. She helped me through a trying time, and I was grateful. The fifth-grade teacher, Miss Miller, was rumored to be the best teacher at Everstille Elementary. She was funny, made school enjoyable, and encouraged learning through inventive projects, but I never got a chance to complete any of them. I spent my fifth-grade school year elsewhere, employing Uncle Terry's advice, and pretending to be someone I was not.

6-7 Strawberry Blue

On a Thursday in May, the last full day of school, the kindergarten class went on a field trip to the Tillerman Farm where we would pick the early strawberries and eat our picnic lunches. Aunt Anne was going to go with me, and I was so eager for this day to come I could barely get to sleep the night before.

Uncle Terry had packed us a lunch, and when Aunt Anne came to pick me up, I insisted upon dragging the picnic basket out to her car and placing it in the back seat. I usually walked to school with Maggie, but today was special. Many of the mothers and a few grandmothers and aunts would accompany the class on this trip, and I was thrilled Aunt Anne would be part of the adult population.

Maggie's mother, Edith Patterson, and Aunt Anne took the bus seat behind Maggie and me, balancing the lunch baskets on their laps, while Maggie and I sat and wondered to each other what the coming first grade year would be like.

"My sister said that Mrs. Griffith is sometimes mean and sometimes nice, and on Fridays if the class has been good, she gives everybody a piece of candy."

"What kind of candy?" I asked. "I hope it's something good like licorice or those candy bracelets," thinking of my favorites.

"I don't know, but a couple times Mary said she gave out some butterscotch circles, and those are icky," and Maggie wrinkled her nose and stuck out her tongue. "I don't think Mary's class got too many candy treats. They were a bad class. At least, that's what I heard Mary say."

We began to name our favorite candy, and as the bus traveled down the country roads, we were jostled in our seats. Once, everyone laughed as Martin Merz fell on the floor and proclaimed "Noooo!" loudly. In a short time, we were at the Tillerman Farm, and Mrs. Tillerman was explaining to everyone what to look for and how to pick the berries. We lined up for our strawberry collection baskets, and then after the adults placed the picnic baskets, boxes, and bags on the waiting wooden tables, we were cautioned to remain close to the adults and sent out to gather the newly ripe and waiting berries.

Maggie and I ran ahead, down into the middle of the long row filled with the bright red fruits and began to alternate picking and placing them in our baskets and into our mouths. The sun was warm but not too hot, and I thought this had to be the best day of the entire year so far, even though I had just celebrated my sixth birthday last weekend.

"Are you thinking of what color you want your room this year?" asked Maggie through a mouth filled with berries.

"I don't know yet. I like my blue walls, but don't want to keep them another year. I think I might like this red, like the strawberries. That would be fun. I could think about this day all year then," and stood for a few seconds to consider what those walls would look like.

"You are lucky. My mom said the yellow walls I have are just fine for a few more years. She said that maybe when I'm ten they can get repainted, but that's such a long way off."

We worked our way down the row and bent over to get the ripe big ones that were hanging low on the bushes. I glanced up to see where Mrs. Patterson and Aunt Anne were and to make sure they were not lost. I stood up, placed my half-full basket down on the ground, stretched out my arms and was promptly stung by a bee.

"OUCH!" I screamed loudly enough that most of the surrounding strawberry pickers stopped what they were doing and looked towards me. "I GOT STUNG," I yelled and immediately began to cry and run towards Aunt Anne who was making her way towards me. I had never been stung before, and the pain was overwhelming. I was sure my life was in peril, and as Aunt Anne and I continued our journey to each other, tears began to roll down my face. Thoughts of strawberries and painted walls were gone replaced by visions of me lying in bed with family and friends all around, sobbing over my eminent demise.

I stopped and held out my arm to Aunt Anne who looked closely at it and scrapped her nail against the bite.

"Ouch," I yelled again.

"There. The stinger is out. Let's go back to the barn and I'll take care of this. You're going to be fine, Livie. Bee stings are part of life," and she held one hand as I stuck my bee arm out, and we walked past Mrs. Patterson who was moving to get closer to Maggie. "Bee sting. Will you bring our baskets up when you are finished?" Mrs. Patterson nodded and patted my head as we made our way to the barn and the picnic tables.

Mrs. Tillerman was coming out of her barn, and when Aunt Anne told her about my predicament, she walked us to her house and into the bathroom where the sting was washed and an iced towel was applied. I had stopped crying although the bee sting still hurt, and I thought I was being extremely brave. Perhaps a medal for bravery would be issued. We thanked Mrs. Tillerman and walked out to sit in the shade under a tree. Aunt Anne reached into the picnic basket and pulled out a sandwich for me although I could only take a couple of bites given my weakened state.

"You'll be OK, Livie. If that was a honey-bee, do you know that after they sting, they die?"

"What? Then that was a stupid bee. Didn't it know it would die? Why was it even around me?" I took another small bite of my sandwich. I was beginning to revive.

"It was probably searching for nectar to make honey, and that's just the way bees work. Creatures are programmed certain ways. I am sure that bee didn't mean to hurt you. That was its nature. Look, here comes everyone now. I'll ask Mrs. Patterson if she has a band-aid. Feeling better?"

I was. And I was also the center of attention, at least for a while. Miss Kendal came over and pulled her picnic basket to our table and ate lunch with us. And while Mrs. Patterson didn't have a band-aid, one of the other mothers did. Maggie and her mother had continued to pick the strawberries and shared their bounty with us, so Aunt Anne and I went home with full baskets of the berries. I was glad, because Uncle Terry said he would make strawberry shortcake for dessert.

On the bus ride back to the school, I sat next to Aunt Anne and she put her arm around me, and we talked about the day, the bee sting, the end of the school-year, the bee sting, the upcoming weekend festivities in town, the new color of my walls, and the bee sting. I was feeling better and spoke to her about Uncle Terry painting my room again,

"I would like the walls to be red like the strawberries. A strawberry wall would be fun, but I like my blue walls still."

"Well, what if there would be a pattern of strawberries on one of the blue walls? That way you could have both colors. I think I know how to do that. I could get some plastic sheets and make a stencil of the berry, and Uncle Terry could paint the stencils all over the wall. We could paint a green stem on them, and that way you could keep the blue and add the red. What do you think?"

"I think that's a great idea. Make sure you tell Uncle Terry. But Dad won't be home tonight because of the parade stuff. Do you think he'll agree?"

Aunt Anne was sure he would. And in a couple of weeks, I was thrilled to help Uncle Terry and Dad stencil the strawberries on my wall. I was responsible for the green stems, and there were hardly any mistakes. The wall painting did have to wait until after the Spring Festival because Dad was so busy planning and organizing that. He did it every year.

Everstille enjoyed its parades and celebrations. There was the Spring Festival which celebrated the end of the schoolyear and often coincided with the Memorial Day holiday. July Fourth was a spectacular celebration ending proudly with the city council's fireworks display. The Fall Festival was held yearly just as school and football season were in full swing; and the Winter Lights Parade with Santa Claus as the honored guest, was a favorite of the town's children. The Spring Festival was my favorite, and for several years when I was younger, I thought it was the town celebrating my May 22 birthday with a parade.

Dad chaired the committee to plan the spring and the fall parade and activities because they involved the school band, teams, and clubs, and offered the senior class a last celebration. The marching band from the high school and the junior high practiced together for the month before. They marched first in the parade, after the color guard and the Grand Marshall, who was the mayor, followed by the members of the city council. I loved seeing the band in their red and white uniforms and their high red hats, being led by the Drum Major. Listening to them was another matter. They knew two marches: *Stars and Stripes Forever* and *Washington Post March*, and some hymns. *Nearer My God to Thee* was the only one I recognized, but the hymns were played at the same loud, specific march tempo, so they were like marches.

There were two wagons used as floats which, when not in use, were housed behind Jamison's Funeral Home. They were both decorated with about a million red and white crepe paper flowers made every year by the girls in the various clubs. On the first float, which was pulled by whichever senior boy had the best-looking truck, were as many members of the senior class as could fit, with the rest walking along side. That float was followed by various school clubs and civic organizations, waving flags and banners, and banging small drums. They were followed by the second and last float which was pulled by the two old, kind, black horses that Mr. Jamison kept in the barn at his brother's farm. Mr. Jamison himself drove the float. Unless there was a death in the town. Then his brother drove it. Seated on the float was either the Rachel Circle from the Methodist Episcopal Church or the women from the First Baptist Church. They had agreed, after heated discussion, to take turns. No one wanted to walk behind the horse-drawn float (the younger children in the town laughed and held their noses as the horses passed) which is why it was always last in the short but enthusiastic parade.

The July Fourth parade followed the same pattern with the first float holding any of the town's veterans who could be talked into sitting on the wagon to wave at the crowd. For July, blue crepe paper flowers were added to the red and white ones on the floats. Depending on weather and vacation plans, the crowd at the July Fourth parade was sometimes smaller than in the spring. But it was still fun for the young of the town, especially the summer I was seven. Mike Jasper was in town to visit his grandfather, and Maggie and I included him in our plans to have a real sleep-out in my back yard. We planned to sleep in a tent the same night after the parade and picnic which was to be held in Maggie's grand-parents' large yard.

Once Maggie told me that her cousin would be spending all of July at his grandfather's cabin, we began to organize our outdoor sleepover. The tent would be created with two or three very large blan-kets placed across the clothesline in my backyard. We drew dozens of pictures showing how we wanted it to look and then took the crayon-col-ored papers to Uncle Terry. He was our *ace in the hole*, a phrase I had heard my Aunt Ernestine say when Dad and I stayed in Chicago in early June. I wasn't sure what it meant, but it sounded correct, and I repeated it to Maggie as we planned.

"I know Uncle Terry will help us. He is our *ace in the hole* and will know what to do with the blankets. I know he is good with making things. Look at the strawberries on my wall. He did that because he is the *ace in the hole*," and I swung my arm around, pointing out the lovely large berries splattered all over my blue wall, conveniently ignoring Aunt Anne's part in the decorating

When we took our plan to Uncle Terry, we were disappointed at first. "We need to check with Dad, and Maggie's mother, and Mike's Grandpa Wells. And the night of July Fourth might not work. July Fourth is on a Tuesday, and I go to work on Wednesday and so does Dad. Sally will be here, but I'm not sure she will want to deal with three kids sleep-ing outside. Why don't we check with everyone first and then plan this for the Friday after the parade and cookout at the Mitchell's? Both Dad and I will be here then, and I can make everyone my buttermilk pancakes for breakfast on Saturday. How does that sound?"

It sounded like Plan B, but an acceptable Plan B, so Maggie and I waited impatiently until Uncle Terry made the phone calls. Once all assented to the sleepout plan, Maggie and I began to count the days and prepare the games the three of us would play. We gathered flashlights and drew and colored pictures to decorate the tent's inside. We practiced making what Uncle Terry explained was a *bedroll*. We would have liked real sleeping bags, but made do with the multiple blankets and pillows we repeatedly rolled incorrectly until we decided they were perfect. We rolled one for Mike because he was not there to do it himself. Finally, on Sunday, July 2, Mike's parents, and younger sisters drove him from Chicago to Everstille where he would stay with his Grandpa Wells until the end of the month.

The July Fourth parade and the following cook-out at the Mitchell's back yard were amusing diversions, but the three of us spent most of the afternoon planning our sleepout activities. There would be hamburger eating followed by marshmallow roasting over the coals on Uncle Terry's outside grill which he promised to keep hot and blazing for us. Once it was sufficiently dark, we would engage in hide-and-seek with the flashlights, star-gazing with three cardboard "telescopes" Maggie created by unrolling her mother's wrapping paper from a longer tube, nocturnal animal watching with the one pair of binoculars we could find, and scary-story telling. We were each responsible for coming up with our own story, and then we would, being totally fair, vote on whose story was best. We stopped the planning to enjoy the town's fireworks, and then, because it was late, and the adults needed to rise early for their jobs, we parted to go home and rest in ordinary beds for the night.

On Friday after lunch, I ran to Maggie's house and waited impatiently as she gathered her things for the sleepout. With Sally supervising and Uncle Terry's directions in our heads, the tent, using three blankets and a fourth for the floor, was maneuvered over the backyard clothesline and secured in place using all the clothespins we could find. Straight pins held the pictures on the blanket/walls, and the bedrolls were rerolled again until perfect. Uncle Terry came home from work just as Mike was dropped off by his grandpa, and we ran around and around and then sat in the tent and talked until time for the cook-out. Everything worked out as planned. Hamburger eating and marshmallow roasting completed, we played the games. When it was completely dark and time to tell the stories, the three of us settled down and told our story in the scariest possible fashion. However, voting for the best was an issue because we each voted for our own story no matter how many votes were taken. Finally, I ran to get Dad and Uncle Terry who were convinced to be judges at a retelling. They crawled into the tent, and the five of us sat squished together as the stories were retold. When the vote was decided, Mike's story was judged the winner, and we all clapped and then rolled out our bedrolls.

"Alright, each one of you take a turn and go into the bathroom to brush your teeth and wash your hands and face," Dad instructed as Uncle Terry checked once more around the yard to chase out the tiger Maggie was positive she had seen during the animal watching portion of the evening.

We settled down for the night. Well, not quite settled. We whispered to each other in the dark, and giggled at nothing, and listened for the possible growl of a loosened tiger. When answers to softly spoken questions were not forthcoming, and the crickets faded away, sleep arrived.

I awoke when it was just becoming light. The marginal grayness of the sky made it clear that night had come and gone, and we were safe. No tiger arrived. I whispered to Maggie but she did not answer. I then called quietly to Mike but was ignored. They slumbered still, and I was awake. I needed to use the bathroom and wondered if either Dad or Uncle Terry was awake and if the buttermilk pancakes were being assembled, so I left the tent and walked to the back porch.

Mrs. Wilson's large striped yellow cat, Henry, was seated on the porch, and when I bent to pet it, it hissed and ran away. *Bet that was the tiger Maggie saw*, I thought to myself, and gently pulled open the back door. There did not seem to be anyone awake, and no delicious aromas were noticed, so I assumed Uncle Terry was still upstairs asleep in his bedroom, and Dad was in his. I tip-toed into the hall bathroom, carefully closed the door, and remembered to wash my hands when I finished. I wiped my hands dry on the towel, opened the door, and stepped out to the hall. I saw Uncle Terry coming out of Dad's bedroom. I watched as he softly shut the door and tied the belt on his bathrobe. Then he saw me.

"Livie," he whispered, "What are you doing here? Is anything wrong?"

"No. I was awake and had to go to the bathroom. The others are still sleeping," I looked back at the closed door to Dad's bedroom and then at my uncle. "Why were you in Dad's room? Is he OK?"

My Uncle Terry never lied. At least, I had never known him to lie, and I knew he valued the truth. He always said so. But as he answered me, I knew he was lying. I did not know why or what was being kept from me, but I knew he was not being truthful just as I knew Henry was the tiger Maggie saw last night. There was a tone to his voice, a catch in the words, a quality, a pitch, a timbre I had not heard before. He was hiding something.

"Dad is fine. He is still asleep, so let's not wake him. I just thought I heard a noise and went to check on it. Since you are up, do you want to help me make the pancakes? You can break the eggs and whisk them. Sound good?"

It did, and I was glad to help. Within fifteen minutes, Maggie and Mike wandered into the kitchen, and Uncle Terry gave us all jobs to complete. Soon after that, Dad woke up, joined us, and started the morning coffee. We were talkative and happy and looking forward to a day of playing together, and the brightness of the early Saturday mirrored the happiness in the kitchen.

We sat in the dining room, and ate the buttermilk pancakes, bacon, and fruit, and drank our juice, and discussed the events of the sleepout. Uncle Terry looked at me and winked as he passed me additional pancakes, and I smiled back at him. But the conversation between us and the uneasiness I felt remained. I tucked it back into a small fitted recess of my brain and tried to ignore the uncomfortable tightness it created.

7-8 Violet Lilacs

In 1962, when I was in second grade with Mrs. Jenkins, who was a million times better than Mrs. Griffith, I did something totally new; something I had never given any thought to before; something that consumed me for weeks and helped me decide on the new color my walls would be. I went to Miss Kendal's wedding. My favorite teacher in the whole world was getting married at our church, and Maggie and I were allowed to sit in the back and watch *Miss Kendal* magically become someone called *Mrs. Milton* when some special words were pronounced by the minister. She would be getting married on Saturday, April 14, the first Saturday of our week-long spring break, and for weeks, Maggie and I talked about little else.

Maggie's mother had been asked to sing at the wedding. When she was younger, Mrs. Patterson had taken voice lessons from Mrs. Wilson, and since Mrs. Wilson was music director at the church, she would play for the wedding and accompany Mrs. Patterson. We got special permission to sit quietly in the back pew and watch the proceedings. The only bad thing about it was that we had to sit with Maggie's sister, Mean Mary, who was supposed to make sure we didn't cause any commotion.

"What does your mother think we are going to do? Jump up and yell 'PIG'?"

Maggie giggled. "That was so funny, Livie! I have no idea what Mom thinks. I told her we would be perfect, and she said we'd better, and Mary thinks she is so smart just because she is older and gets to eat cake after. Anyway, the wedding is at three o'clock, and Mom needs to be there early. Could you be at my house at two o'clock? We are going to have to sit still for a long time, but it'll be worth it."

We discussed the mysterious ceremony. Neither of us had ever been to a wedding, and we weren't sure what would happen, but we were excited to find out. Afterwards, we would have to leave since we weren't invited to the cake-and-coffee reception in the church basement, but Uncle Terry said he would take us out for ice cream to celebrate. The wedding day couldn't come quickly enough.

Because Dad had to go to some meeting on that Saturday, Uncle Terry combed through my hair which had grown quite long. He found a blue ribbon almost matching my dress and placed it in my hair using about twenty hairpins. Finally, I was ready, and he walked me over to Maggie's house. It was a few minutes before two o'clock, and he bent down to kiss my cheek and told me to *behave and have fun, and those things are not mutually exclusive!* I laughed because he was always saying things like that to me, and although I didn't understand most of them, I knew they were meant to be funny.

There were a few people standing outside the church, but Mrs. Patterson moved the three of us in and showed us where to sit. She said that the last pew would give us a perfect view of the wedding party before they walked down the aisle. Mary tried to act all grown up, telling us to behave and sit still, but Maggie and I ignored her and watched as the church began to fill up. We saw lots of the teachers and their husbands move into the pews, and when Mrs. Griffith and her husband passed by, I whispered *pig* to Maggie, and we laughed until Mary muttered she would tell on us.

The wedding music started, and Mrs. Patterson sang, and then we heard a rustling behind us. Two bridesmaids were there wearing the most beautiful lilac/violet-colored dresses I had ever seen. They were tea-length (I found this out later), and full-skirted, and they had on white lacy short gloves and little round hats with lilac-colored veils covering their hair. Miss Kendal was beautiful, and her dress was long and lace-covered, and when she saw us, she smiled. That was wonderful, but I was struck by the bridesmaids' dresses and right then, knew what color my room would be. We couldn't see or hear very well from where we were seated, but when the bride and groom kissed, Maggie and I clapped the loudest.

Wedding over, we walked out of the church to Uncle Terry who was in the car, waiting to take us to Banter's Drugstore for ice-cream. Mary was going to be with her mother, so it was just the three of us. Maggie and I couldn't stop talking about the wedding all the time we drove to town. We walked into Banter's, took over one of the three booths, and ordered ice-cream sundaes. While Maggie and I sat together, Uncle Terry was on the other side listening as we continued our review of the wedding.

"Uncle Terry, I know the color I want my bedroom walls to be for my eighth birthday. Do you know the lilacs in our backyard? That is the color. The bridesmaids' dresses were just like that, and they were perfect. I know my birthday isn't for weeks yet, but could we at least get the paint this week? I can help you to paint too. So can Maggie because we don't have school this week. Maybe the two of us can paint the walls as far up as we can reach, and you can paint the top after work. Sally will be there and she can watch us," and I stopped talking to take large bites of my ice cream that was slowly becoming soup.

My uncle pushed his emptied dish to the side and took large swallows of his water. Then he smiled at us. "We can go to Jensen's Hardware and look for the color you want and then order it. We can do that when you finish your ice-cream, but I think painting the walls will need to wait until Dad and I are able to do it. But thanks for the offer. Now, when you two finish, how about a walk to pick out the paint?"

We completed the ice-cream and walked the few streets to the hardware. Mr. Jensen hauled a large book to the top of a counter, and Maggie and I discussed which of the many shades of violet would be the perfect one. We found it; Uncle Terry ordered it. Lilacs, spring, and bridesmaids' dresses appeared in the paint cans he brought home from Jensen's one day after work the following week.

One Saturday in early May, with my bedroom furniture moved out or covered with cloths, Dad taped around the window, door, and baseboards while Uncle Terry began what he called *cutting in* around the edges and ceiling. I stood excited and ready to help with the wall painting, a job which I would help to complete. Last year, I practiced by painting the green stems on the strawberries, and this year, Uncle Terry was going to show me how to paint the walls. I had on an old shirt of Dad's that was rolled up and safety-pinned so the sleeves would not dip into the paint.

"I think this wall with all the strawberries is going to take two coats, but the blue walls should be able to be covered with just one," Uncle Terry got down from the ladder and stood back to examine the job. "What do you think, Cabbage? Will this match those bridesmaids' dresses?"

I cocked my head and looked up at the cut-in paint. "I think that is EXACTLY the color. It's beautiful, don't you think?"

Dad finished the taping around the door and looked at the wall. "Well, it looks like the early lilacs in the back. I'll bet that wedding was a lovely one, wasn't it, Livie?"

"The best wedding I ever went to! Dad, when you and my mother got married, what color did the bridesmaids wear? Was Mother's dress big and fluffy like Miss Ken—I mean, Mrs. Milton's? Do you have any pictures? Could I see them?"

"We had a very small wedding, Livie. There were no bridesmaids, but Aunt Anne did stand up with your mother. She didn't wear a dress, but wore a suit of some kind. It might have been navy. No big wedding dress for your mother. She wore a suit too, and I remember she called the color *teal*. I'll look for more pictures. I know some were taken because someone sent them in the mail to us. I'll see if they are in the bottom drawer of my bureau. In fact, I am sure they are there. Terry, do you need more help?"

Uncle Terry was stirring more paint around and he looked up and spoke, "Thanks, Toby. I'm almost done cutting in, and then my helper here and I can get the walls done. Shouldn't take more than a couple hours. I know you have some school thing this afternoon, so Livie and I will be fine. By tonight, we can move her furniture back in and she can sleep in lilacs!"

"Great. Then I'm going to clean up and get to that meeting. Liv, I'll look for the photos and leave them on the dining table for you. See you later." And he bent down to kiss my head.

"Sure, Dad," I was anxious to begin the painting. Uncle Terry leaned over with a brush and placed a dab of paint on my nose. "Hey!" and I started to wipe it off.

"Leave it, Liv. That's for good luck. Now you won't get any more on you," and to our surprise, I didn't. At least not much.

He showed me how to load my brush with paint so it wouldn't drip, how to move it carefully back and forth to cover the blue wall, and, and how to wipe up any splotches with the cloth he gave me. We worked together and were silent for quite a while, and then I glanced at him.

"Uncle Terry. You never got married, right?"

"No, I did not."

"Do you think you will?"

He stood back and moved his shoulders around, and let out a sigh. "I believe there are some people who are not meant to be married, and I think I am one of them. I got close to getting married once, but am glad I didn't. I think that might not have been a good thing."

"Who did you almost marry? Someone I know?"

"Nope. This happened a long time ago, when I was still living in Chicago. Her name was Betsy, and she was a nice woman, but I think it wasn't meant to be."

"Well, if you didn't marry her, did you find someone else you might have? What did you do after Betsy?"

Uncle Terry turned to look at me. There was a weird look on his face, and he did not answer right away. Then he smiled and said, "Well, after that, your dad talked me into coming here, to Everstille, and I came and stayed with him and your mother. I just never left, and then you came along, and here we are. How about getting back to work now? We don't have that much more to do. I am going to open this window and let some fresh air in and the paint smell out. Back to work, Cabbage!"

We worked and finished the room. It looked great. I was tired and said, "I'm glad we're done. This painting is hard work. My arm hurts and so do my fingers. Now what do we do?"

"If you can go and clean yourself up, I'll finish the cleaning up here. Make sure you wash your nose, and leave that shirt on top on the washing machine in the laundry room. I'll get cleaned up too, and then make us sandwiches for lunch. How about if we go to Mazie's for dinner tonight? We can call Aunt Anne, and she can meet the three of us there for those great hot dogs and French fries. Maybe one of those chocolate shakes you like so much."

"Yay! Great! Going to clean up now." I stood in the doorway and looked around at the room. "Thanks, Uncle Terry. This looks great! I picked the right color for my birthday, and Maggie will be jealous. She said her room has to stay the same color until she is ten!"

I cleaned up, washed my hands and face, and tried to pull my hair back into a neater ponytail. When I walked the painting shirt to the laundry room, I paused at the dining table where the photos Dad left for me lay. I threw the shirt on the washing machine and rushed back to look at them. There were only a few. Two of them showed Dad and my mother standing next to each other. In one of them Dad was looking at Mother and smiling and in the other, they were both smiling at the camera. There was another one of Aunt Anne and my mother, two more with some people I didn't know, and some with folks I did recognize. There was my Aunt Gladys with an unfamiliar older woman. The photos were all in black and white, so I couldn't tell what my mother's teal suit looked like. She had on a hat and was holding some flowers.

When Uncle Terry came into the kitchen to make lunch, I held the photos out to him and asked about them. "Who is this lady?" and I pointed to the woman standing next to Aunt Gladys. "I don't know her."

"That is Dad's mother who died before you were born. She and Aunt Gladys came to the wedding, but Aunt Ernestine couldn't for some reason. No, I don't know who those other people are, but I know some of the teachers from the school came to the wedding. I don't see any photos of your mother's family, but I know some of them came. Maybe Dad has more. Anyway, he can tell you who everyone is when he comes home."

"What color is teal?" I wondered.

"Sort of a blue-green color. Sometimes it's green-blue. Depends on how much of each color is in it. I think there are several shades, both light and dark, a bit like all the purples and lilacs you were looking at in Mr. Jensen's paint book. I'll look around and see if I can find that color. Wait, go look at your crayons. Maybe one of them is a teal color."

I went to my room, but forgot that things were hidden under cloths and in drawers because of the painting. I came out disappointed.

"I can't get to them because of the painting."

"Oh, I forgot. Well, I'll look around and try to find the color. Come on. Let's eat lunch, and then we can go for a walk while the room dries."

We ate. Then we walked. Then Dad came home, and we talked more and looked at the photos, and he told me who all the people were. Later, we met Aunt Anne at Mazie's for hot dogs, and when we returned home, my bedroom was put back in order and, as Uncle Terry said, I slept in lilacs that night. He was always saying things that sounded like poetry. Dad once said that he was a poet in his heart and his soul, and I think that perfectly described Uncle Terry.

The last day of the school year was Thursday, May 24, and my birthday was the Tuesday before. It was a busy time because the annual Spring Festival was the weekend of the 25th, and Dad had lots of meetings. But the night of my birthday, Aunt Anne came over with the Peterson's Bakery chocolate cake with chocolate frosting I wanted, and we shared it after we ate the fried chicken and mashed potatoes Uncle Terry made especially for me. It was a warm, breezy, comfortable night, and we sat and ate cake and talked about the upcoming summer. Dad and I were going to South Bend for our annual luncheon with the Chicago relatives. No visit to Chicago this year, and I was relieved. Then the July Fourth parade and picnics, Vacation Bible School, visits with Maggie's cousin Mike, and weeks and weeks which stretched ahead before September came and third grade started. Mrs. Smith would be my new teacher, and I was looking forward to what I was told by other students would be an enjoyable year. I went to bed happy. And a year older.

Both Dad and Uncle Terry tucked me into bed that night. I was smiling as I cuddled in my bed, not able to see my lilac walls, but still faintly able to smell the paint, and I knew the smell was violet. I glanced at the small table next to the rocking chair where I could barely make out the photo which I asked Dad to put there. It was the wedding photo of Dad and Mother; the one where Dad is smiling at her, and although I did not yet know what teal looked like, I knew that next year it would be the color of my walls.

I sighed and thought I would fall asleep and when I woke up, it would be the last day of school, and the start of summer fun. I was dozing off when suddenly, I felt a presence, and through the slits I created with my eyes, I looked at the rocking chair. My mother's ghost was there. She wore the same dress she had worn before, the one with a lacy white hanky in the breast pocket and the rounded collar which met where the buttons came down to the belt around her waist. Her hair was not in a knot like in the photos I had seen, but was curled under and fell lightly to just below her chin.

She had not visited for a while, and I was surprised but unafraid to see her. I had never spoken to her, but something about my eighth year of life gave me additional daring. Quietly, so softly that I was sure no one would hear me except for Mother, I spoke to her.

"I know you are my mother. I miss you even though I never knew you." I glanced at her and thought her mouth moved in a miniature smile.

"When you come here, do you visit Dad too?" Perhaps there was a slight shake of her head. I wasn't sure.

"Do you remember when I was born? Dad and Uncle Terry said you held me for as long as you could." I was pretty sure there was a nod of her head.

"I am eight years old today. Is that why you are here?" This time I was sure there was a smile.

"Well, I want you to know I love you even though we aren't together. Do you still love me? Do you still think of me?" I noted that there was a movement of her hand as if she were trying to hold mine. But I felt no touch.

"I'm tired, Mother, but glad you came tonight." I closed my eyes and was sure I heard a voice softly say my name: *Olivia*. I tried to keep my eyes open but couldn't, and when I forced them open just to see her once more, there was no one there. I went to sleep.

The next morning, I wasn't sure I dreamt last night's vision, but I felt comforted. I would not mention her visit to either Dad or Uncle Terry. I knew it would upset them. I got ready for school and went to the kitchen where my family was eating breakfast, waiting for me. Keeping my secret vision to myself, I sat down and Uncle Terry put the bowl of oatmeal before me. As I ate it, I thought about my mother. I didn't know it then, but I would only see her once more.

8-9 Teal

During the fall of my eighth year, I was enjoying third grade with Mrs. Smith, and learning more *science*. We learned about clouds. For two weeks, we had to keep a "Cloud Diary" and look at the sky before school and after to notice and name the clouds and draw them in our folded paper diaries. It was fun and gave me an idea for next year's bedroom walls. I wanted to keep the teal walls for a while because Dad and Aunt Anne and I had spent so much time looking at Mr. Jensen's big paint book to find the right shade. Dad remembered it one way, but Aunt Anne thought it was another, and I had to choose. I went with Dad's color. After all, he married my mother in her teal suit. Besides, Dad hadn't been feeling well. He had visited Doctor Grenville who gave him some small white pills that would help his heart. I was worried about him.

After the science about the clouds, we began to learn about wind and rain and all kinds of weather. That wasn't as interesting, but we kept a weather diary for a month in our folded paper books. We also kept a reading diary listing everything we read that was not a school book, and a vocabulary diary listing words we did not know with their definitions. Mrs. Smith was big on diaries. Nevertheless, third grade was fun.

In early October, the Fall Festival took place. For the first time, Dad was not at the parade. He was home in bed. Uncle Terry was caring for him while Aunt Anne took me to the parade and other activities. I tried to have a good time, but I was concerned about Dad because I couldn't remember him being sick before. Aunt Anne took me to Mazie's Saturday afternoon, and we sat down on one of the outside picnic benches because there were so many people inside. We ordered my favorite hot dog and French fries, and as we waited, I questioned Anne about Dad.

"Livie, don't worry so much. He'll be fine. Doctor Grenville is looking after him and has given him some helpful medicine. Uncle Terry is at home and keeping him company. Dad is just tired. He works hard, you know. In fact, Uncle Terry and I have almost convinced him to stop his traveling and lecturing for a time. Then he can be at home with you more often."

Aunt Anne always spoke to me as if I were an adult, and I appreciated it. I ate part of my hot dog with a few fries and pushed the rest away. I heard Aunt Anne sigh, and she stopped eating too. We sat for a few minutes watching the crowds around us eating, laughing, and pointing to the various sale booths which had been set up along Main Street. Everyone appeared to be in good spirits, and I thought back to last year when Aunt Anne and I were with Dad and Uncle Terry. We were part of the laughing crowd then.

"Livie, do you want to look at the booths? I saw some pretty hair ribbons at the Emporium. And if you are still hungry, Peterson's Bakery is selling those donut holes you like. We could get some for later. Do you want to walk along the street?"

"I guess so," I answered, but I really didn't feel like joining the crowd or even finding Maggie even though we said we'd look for each other. Aunt Anne asked if I wanted more to eat, but I didn't. She cleaned up our lunch and didn't say anything about me not finishing. We walked down the street towards the Emporium and bakery and glanced at the items that were offered for sale. At the Emporium, Aunt Anne found some hair ribbons that were almost the same shade as the teal bedroom walls I had. She bought them for me, and we purchased donut holes to take home later for Dad and Uncle Terry. We stood with our purchases, and looked at the crowds which were getting larger. There was going to be a football game with Everstille's team playing another local high school, and everyone seemed excited about attending.

"I thought we could go to the field for the game. Maybe Maggie will be there, and we can sit with her. How does that sound to you?"

I looked at Aunt Anne and shook my head. "Can we just go home now? I don't want to see the game and am worried about Dad."

Aunt Anne looked at her watch and said, "I think he might be taking a nap. I know Doctor Grenville was going to stop over before the game and check on him. If you don't want to go to the field, what if we go to the library? There are some things I want to get done, and you can help me. After that, we can go home and check on Dad. I'm sure he's fine, Livie. Let's give him a chance to rest. I think Uncle Terry is making dinner, and if you want, we can call from my office, and you can check on him."

I agreed. We walked through Main Street which was teeming with townspeople, and I reached over to hold Aunt Anne's hand, something I was sure I was too old to do. It made me feel better, and Aunt Anne squeezed it and smiled as we went to the Harrison Greenwood Public Library, the institution Aunt Anne oversaw, and the place my mother had spent so many of her living hours.

I visited the library often. Dad and Uncle Terry took me there, and sometimes, after school, I would stop to see Aunt Anne and pick out another book from the growing *Young Readers' Section*. I visited the **Ruth Evans Pinkerton Room** where the books townspeople donated after her death lined the walls, each one containing a special dedication sticker announcing the fact that it was one of the *Ruth Books*. Once Aunt Anne opened the locked door and turned on the lights, I headed there.

"Turn the lights on, Livie, and I'll bring the papers from my office and work in there with you."

I reached up and hit the switch and stood looking around. This room comforted me. Maybe it was my mother's name on a plaque beside the door, or her framed picture just inside it, or the thought that so many people brought copies of the books she had suggested they read as an offering to her memory. Whatever it was, I was often here, and today, I felt need of the familiar security. I walked around the room, looking at the book titles, running my hand along the shelves' edges. Aunt Anne came in and sat down at one of the tables to complete her work, and I continued to walk around the entire room. When I finished, I went over to sit next to her and sighed.

"How many books are in this room?"

Anne added her signature to the bottom of the sheet she held and then looked up and around. "I'm not sure. I counted them once, and there were about one thousand, give or take, but now I don't know. Periodically, someone brings in another book and asks that it be placed here. Sometimes people are somewhere and see a book or think of something your mother told them about it, and they just get the book and bring it to me. Sometimes the books are old, in bad shape, and need to be replaced, and I try to do that. I tried to keep track of the number, but just didn't. I had to order more dedication slips about a year ago, and I should check to see how many are left. Maybe you can make that your job one time and count the books for me."

I nodded my head thinking I might do that. Then Aunt Anne continued to do her paperwork, and I watched her for a time. I pushed back my chair and got up and said, "I think I am going to look for a new book to take out. Is that OK?"

"Sure," she answered, never looking up. I left the room. I walked out to the main area and stood there. I knew the library had undergone a renovation and enlargement, and I wondered what it was like when my mother had been in charge. Walking up and down the stacks, filtered light coming in from the front windows, I tried to imagine my mother doing the same thing years ago, before I was born. There were full magazine racks I ran my hand over and a couple stray books I picked up and placed on the rolling book cart. I came around to the Circulation Desk and pushed open the swinging half-door which separated it from the rest of the library and looked at the tall stool I was sure my mother had once occupied. I climbed up onto it, leaned forward, putting my fists on my chin, observing the dimness where books my mother had touched regarded me, silent and aware.

Anne came out of the room and saw me. "Did you get a book?"

"No, I'm just sitting here. Are you done? Can we call home to check on Dad now?"

"Sure. Go on. Use the telephone there, and I'll put these papers away and grab my purse."

I reached over and dialed, and when Uncle Terry answered and told me Dad was feeling better and currently taking a nap, I was relieved. "Aunt Anne and I are coming home in a few minutes. Do you want to talk to her?"

"No," he said, "I'll see you both soon. Tell her I am making meatloaf for dinner, Dad's favorite, and I am expecting her to stay. Tell her to pack her overnight bag and tomorrow I'll make buttermilk pan-cakes for all of us. How does that sound?"

"Sounds great, Uncle Terry. Bye."

I felt better as we walked over to Aunt Anne's apartment, picked up a few things she needed, and got into her car. I would have my family around me. Dad seemed to be better, and all would be well, I thought.

School was out, summer started, and I was sure things would be fine. Usually, the first weeks in June, two events would occur: our cinna-mon cake picnic at North Cemetery and the annual lunch in South Bend with the Chicago relatives. We visited the cemetery as usual, but did not go to lunch. Dad called his sisters and told them he needed time to rest and would like to put off the visit until later in the summer. When later in the summer came, he put it off until early fall, and then later fall. We did not meet with them that year, and I was relieved. I thought Dad was too although he never said so.

Dad stayed home with me much of that summer which was unusual. Usually, he would be at school overseeing the summer session, and sometimes he would even teach an English class. "Like to keep my skills sharp," he would say. The summer I was nine, he rested at home. "Let Richard take over some things. He is capable and will do well," Dad explained. Richard Winslow was the assistant principal at the high school, and when fall came and the Fall Festival parade and activities were planned, he organized them. I thought Dad would be upset at this and asked him about it, but he said it was his idea. I looked at him and noticed that my tall father looked just a bit shorter, and there were some wrinkles around his blue eyes, and his bright blonde hair had started to turn white just above his ears. "Reaching that half century mark in a few years," he joked, "time to slow down," and he reached down and tried to lift me up. He couldn't and blamed it on my growth and not his frailty.

It was during the end of a school day, right after Thanksgiving, when my third-grade class was finishing up writing in our Essay Diaries that Mrs. Smith received a note from the office. As we got ready to leave, she called me to her desk and told me that I was to go to the library and see Aunt Anne right after school. I should not walk home with Maggie. No, she did not know more than that, and she was sure everything was fine. It was not.

When I pulled open the door of the library, Aunt Anne was waiting for me. Just inside. "What's the matter?" I asked. She took my books from me, and we walked into her office and shut the door.

"Dad and Uncle Terry wanted me to talk to you. First, don't worry. Things will be alright. Dad had a spell at school this afternoon, and he and Uncle Terry went to Doctor Grenville's office, and he sent them to the hospital at Elkhart for some tests, and that's where they are. You and I will be together until we hear from them. Don't cry, Livie; I am here and as soon as he can, Dad said he would call you. We can stay here until then. Do you have any homework to complete? Best to keep busy."

I wiped my eyes. I wasn't sure what a *spell* was, and wondered if there was a *spelling test* that Dad needed to take, but immediately knew that was incorrect. I questioned Aunt Anne, but she said she didn't have any other news, but was sure things would be fine. This was a medical test just to find out what caused Dad to feel sick. As she was talking, her phone rang, and I was relieved when Dad was on the other end.

"Now, Livie, I will be fine. Doctor Grenville is just trying to find out what caused me to faint. I feel much better now and don't want you to worry. However, I think I'll be staying here overnight. Uncle Terry won't be home until late, and we think it's a good idea if you stay at Aunt Anne's tonight. Does that sound acceptable? Great. Listen, I love you and will see you after school tomorrow. Now be good, and let me talk to Aunt Anne."

I handed the phone to her and listened carefully to her answers. Aunt Anne smiled at me as she spoke to Dad. Then Uncle Terry came on the phone because she said "Hi Terry", and spoke for another minute or so. She hung up and smiled the counterfeit smile that sometimes grown-ups use when they want you to think things are fine.

"We'll stay here about another hour, and then go home and pick up your pajamas and some clean clothes since you will stay with me tonight. How about Mazie's for some dinner?"

I shrugged and nodded my head at the same time. Aunt Anne let me sit in her big chair to do my arithmetic homework while she checked on some things at the Circulation Desk. I think this was her night to work late, and she needed to get someone to take her place. She never said that, but I could figure things out.

We left and went to my house to gather some things. It seemed strange because the house was dark, and no dinner smells were evident, and when we left, Anne turned on the outside porch light. "So Uncle Terry doesn't trip," she explained. She let me order what I wanted from Mazie's menu, but when my hamburger and fries came, I just wasn't that hungry. She asked for two servings of Mazie's special baked apple pudding to take home with us for later, and we left. I heard her tell Mazie that she was sure Dad would be fine, but nothing was known yet. News travels quickly in a small town.

I was thrilled when the next day, after school, Dad was home. He was seated in the big chair across from the small television set Uncle Terry had bought for us, and was watching some news program. Uncle Terry was in the kitchen making soup, and things almost seemed normal. I dropped my books and ran over to Dad and crawled up on his lap even though I knew I was too old to do that. I didn't care. It seemed like I hadn't seen him for a week, and I was happy to see that he looked the same.

Things were normal for the rest of the year. Dad was taking something called a *sabbatical* and did not plan on going back to his job as high school principal until after the new year. Uncle Terry moved his bedroom downstairs. He explained he needed to be close in case Dad needed him during the night. At first, he slept on the sofa in the parlor, but then he complained that it hurt his back, and decided that since Dad had a large bed, he would just sleep in there. It sounded to me like Uncle Terry was taking really good care of Dad, and I was glad.

Our Christmas was quiet. We took our usual Christmas shopping trip to South Bend to see the lights and have a special dinner and pick out a new ornament for the Christmas tree. Aunt Anne came over to help decorate the tree, and we took photographs with Uncle Terry's new camera, and ate Aunt Anne's chocolate chip cookies, and watched and listened as a large choir sang Christmas carols on a special television program. We opened gifts and went to church, and when the snow came, Dad watched out the front window as Uncle Terry and I made three snowmen on the front lawn and fashioned them with extra hats and scarves so that they looked like the three of us. I stayed up until midnight on New Year's Eve, and was glad when the new year started. Dad seemed well, and he started back to his job. It all seemed routine and ordinary and conventional, but it was the last Christmas season that would be that way.

9-10 White Clouds

In 1963, at the beginning of May, just before my ninth birthday, I told Uncle Terry and Dad that I wanted to keep my teal walls, but would like to paint clouds on them. The white paint was easy to obtain, and I drew the clouds I wanted on a sheet of paper. Uncle Terry did an excellent job of outlining them, and then he steadied me on the ladder as I painted the cirrus and cumulus clouds all along the upper third of the teal walls. I didn't want stratus, stratocumulus, or the cumulonimbus because they were grayish, and one was a thundercloud. I wanted only fluffy, friendly clouds on my teal skywalls. In hindsight, thunderclouds would have been more appropriate.

In 1963, I enjoyed the summer with my best friend Maggie and spent time with Dad who was, once again, leaving the summer school operation to Richard Winston, the assistant principal. Once a week, on Wednesdays, Dad would go to his office and meet with him to discuss school-related issues. Then he would come home and spend the afternoon in bed resting. I stayed at Maggie's house during this time, and in July, when her cousin Mike visited, the three of us continued our adventures together. Vacation Bible School was in early August, and Dad and I went to South Bend to meet with the Chicago relatives in late August. None of my cousins came, and I was stuck listening to the adults talk about people and situations which were totally uninteresting. I was glad when the day was over but sad that Dad was too tired to visit Robertson's where I was hoping to find a *SuperBall.* Maggie and I were hoping to bounce one to the top of our school.

In 1963, when school began in September, I was in Miss Harris' fourth grade class where science lessons were about light and colors and the rainbow. During art class, we learned about primary and secondary colors, and our entire class painted an enormous rainbow on lots of sheets of paper taped together. When it was completed, and the paint dried, and parts of the rainbow which had fallen off were retaped and stapled, the rainbow was curved on the wall over the door to our school room and stayed there until January. When we came back from our winter break, we found the rainbow in separated sheets all over our room, but by then we were studying light and reflection and refraction, and we just picked up the shattered rainbow and placed the papers on the art table in the back of the room.

One day after school, as Maggie and I were filling up additional papers with rainbows, it struck me that I had been living in rainbow rooms. "The red was the strawberries, orange was my orange monkey color, and yellow was the banana color. The green was when I was a baby and my mother had the room painted light green. I had a light blue and a lilac for the violet. But I didn't have indigo. I'm not sure what that is, but I know that when I am ten, I'm going to have indigo-colored walls. Then, I will have had all the rainbow colors. And some not in the rainbow. What do you think?" and I turned to Maggie.

Maggie looked at the clouds on the wall and sighed. "I think you are lucky to have all those colors. At least when I am ten, Mom said my walls can get repainted to the color I want. I am not sure what color that will be. Indigo sounds great, but I think I will go with my favorite color: pink." She wrote her name in pink under the rainbow she had just created. *Yes*, I thought, *I am lucky.*

In 1963, during early October, the Fall Festival was held, and this time, Mr. Winston was totally in charge. Dad did not have to go to the many meetings, but during the parade, he got to sit on the reviewing stand with the mayor and city council after they finished marching. I sat there too and waved to everyone who passed. Afterwards, he went home to rest, and I stayed with Aunt Anne and Uncle Terry. The three of us walked up and down Main Street and ate donut holes and drank cider and then went to the football field to watch the game. Everstille High School lost, but I sat with Maggie and we had a great time anyway. When we got home, Dad was sitting on the front porch waiting for us, and Uncle Terry made hamburgers on the grill. We could see the fireworks from our corner, and I went to bed thinking that this fall festival had been much better than the sad one last year.

In 1963, in November, a terrible thing happened. President John Kennedy was shot and killed. I didn't understand it all, but I watched Aunt Anne cry and Dad and Uncle Terry wipe their eyes. School was cancelled, and the four of us watched the sad funeral on our television. It was a strange time. I wasn't sure exactly how I should feel, but seeing all the adults around me being sad and talking about little else made me realize that life could be difficult. I would find out just how difficult shortly.

In 1963, on Tuesday, December 10, when I was nine and in the fourth grade, and looking forward to the Christmas season, and wondering exactly which shade of indigo I would have my walls painted next year, and if I would get the *EZ Bake Oven* I wanted for Christmas, and whether Robert Stevens who sat in back of me in class would ever stop kicking my rear end, and deciding about cutting my long curly red hair the same way Maggie had hers cut, Tobias Pinkerton, the man I called "Dad", the center of my life, had a heart attack and died.

It was a continuation of the sadness begun in November. When I think back, I'm unsure of the order of events. I was picked up from school early on that Tuesday afternoon by Aunt Anne, and we went to my empty house. Aunt Anne had the same look on her face I had seen only a couple weeks earlier as we watched the President's funeral. I remember Uncle Terry coming home and taking me into the front room and trying to explain how sick Dad had been, and how the doctors really tried to help him, and how his last words were to "take care of my baby" and that meant me. At some point I wondered if there would be more snow because just two weeks ago, about five inches fell. I thought that maybe there would be no Christmas this year, and that I might not get that oven. I remember Aunt Anne crying and holding me, and I know that I did not go back to school until about a week later, after the funeral.

The funeral for Dad was not like the one for President Kennedy. There were no horses or lots of people walking behind Dad's casket. Anne did not wear a long black veil, and neither did Dad's sisters or the flower cousins who were there. There was something called a *wake* on the Friday of that week at Mr. Jamison's Funeral Home, and lots of people were there, and they came up to me and hugged me and shook everyone's hand, and when I saw Dad looking like he was sleeping, I whispered to Aunt Anne that we should just wake him up. He was fine. And when I went to him and touched his hand, it was cold. All my teachers were there. In fact, all the teachers from the elementary and high school came, and lots of students did too. It was confusing, and when Maggie came with her parents and grandparents, I started to cry, and so did Maggie, and Mrs. Patterson took us to a small room at the back where there was coffee and cookies and she said we could eat some.

My Chicago aunts and uncles and cousins all stayed at our house for about four days, and it was noisy, and they talked for a long time to Uncle Terry, and I think there was some yelling, but I was in bed when it happened, so I wasn't sure. They were surprised that Uncle Terry was living there, and they didn't seem to know him, and I was confused by their questions. I was glad when the funeral was over on Saturday and the Chicago relatives went home. On Sunday, Aunt Anne came over and stayed until Wednesday which is when I went back to school.

My teacher, Miss Harris was really kind to me, and all the kids were too. The girls would hug me, and some of the boys walked by and patted my shoulder. Robert Stevens stopped kicking my rear when he was sitting behind me. When we went to gym class, and I started to cry, although I'm not sure why, Miss Harris left the class with Mr. Ambers, the gym teacher, and took me to the Teachers' Lunchroom, and talked to me, and made me feel better. I was so shocked to be in the special room for the teachers that I stopped crying to look around to see if all the rumors about there being lots special foods and scary objects was true, but it just looked like a regular room with lots of chairs and tables and an old refrigerator. Life was strange for a long time.

There were some changes. I no longer walked home with Maggie after school, but went across the street to the Greenwood Library and stayed with Aunt Anne. Then she took me home. On the nights she worked late at the library, I waited until Uncle Terry came to pick me up. There were plenty of phone calls from the Chicago relatives, and when I answered the telephone, whichever aunt was on the other end always asked me how I was, if I was eating and sleeping, if I was sad or happy, and then they asked for Uncle Terry, but never called him *uncle*. They said, "Good talking to you Olivia. Now would you get Mr. Douglas and tell him your Aunt Gladys (or Aunt Ernestine) wishes to speak with him?" He always told me to go to my room while he talked, and I did, but I stood just inside my open door trying to figure out the conversation. I knew it was mostly about me. Something was happening. Things were not right, and it wasn't just that Dad was not there. I picked up bits and pieces of conversations, and vocabulary I didn't know, and decided that after Christmas, I would ask Aunt Anne about things.

I know both Aunt Anne and Uncle Terry tried to keep things happy for me during Christmas. The three of us went to South Bend for our usual luncheon. We picked out a new ornament for the tree which we all decorated together. Aunt Anne stayed over most nights because the library had shortened hours during the winter break. She even stayed with us Christmas Eve instead of going to her parents where she would normally have a party with her brothers and sisters and their families. I received the *EZ Bake Oven,* but it wasn't as much fun as I thought it would be. Aunt Anne and I made real cookies in a real oven while Uncle Terry went to work, and while we baked, I started to ask questions and tried to find out what was happening.

"Aunt Anne, I know I call you *aunt*, but are you really related to me? Are you Mother's sister?"

"No, Livie, I am not related to you or your mother, but we all decided before you were born that you would call me that. I met your mother when I was eleven. I've told you those stories…how she taught me to understand books and ask questions about the ideas in them, and how I started working at the library then. Remember?"

"Yes, I know all that. But why don't I know any of Mother's family? My real aunts. No one ever mentions them."

Aunt Anne looked at me for a few seconds. "Why all these questions, Livie? Is something wrong?"

"I just want to know."

"Your mother's parents died before you were born. There was a brother, but he was killed in the war, and Ruth was never close to her sisters who all live in different parts of the country. She had one sister she would periodically write to, but after your mother died, and the sisters moved, none of them kept in touch with Dad."

I thought this through while we continued to move cookies around, put more in the oven, and wash and dry the baking dishes. I wanted to ask about some of the things I had overheard, but wasn't sure how to approach it, so I just began to talk.

"Is Uncle Terry my real uncle?"

"That's what you call him. Right?'

"But an uncle is a brother to your father or mother. He's not Dad's brother, is he?"

"No, he is not Dad's brother."

"Is he Dad's cousin?"

Anne hesitated. She looked at me. "Livie, I think you should talk to Uncle Terry about that. These are some questions he should answer for you."

I changed the subject. "What is a *lawyer* used for? What is a *life insurance policy*?"

Anne stopped wiping the cookie pan and looked at me. "Why are you asking me that? Where did you hear those terms?"

"I heard Uncle Terry and Aunt Gladys talking about it. I think it has to do with me, and I want to know what it is. What are they?"

"A *lawyer* can help figure out problems or write up papers which are legal and make sure certain things are done in a certain way. A *life insurance policy* means that you pay a company some money each month, and if something happens to you, then a person you want the money to go to gets it."

"Is twenty-five thousand dollars a lot of money?"

Anne sighed and turned to me. "Livie, I don't know what all these questions are about or where you heard all these things, but I think there are some things you should discuss with Uncle Terry. If you want me to, I can talk to him first and let him know you have questions and would like some answers. I am not trying to skirt the issue, but there are things I don't have any right to discuss with you. Do you understand?"

I thought about it, and decided she was right. "OK. I'll ask him about stuff. And, Aunt Anne, I just want to call you *Anne* from now on. Is that alright with you?"

She rolled her eyes and then she smiled. "Sure, Livie, that's fine. And, yes, twenty-five thousand dollars is a great amount of money. Let's finish up these dishes and put the cookies away. Except for a few. I think we earned some."

"Sounds good to me, ANNE," I said, and she laughed.

***

A couple days later, as snow fell outside, and snow on our television set ensured no programs were going to be seen that night, Uncle Terry piled logs in the fireplace and started a blaze, and after dinner, the two of us sat down and prepared to play my new Junior Scrabble game. It felt cozy and right, and I was feeling better than I had for some weeks. Uncle Terry took his tiles and set them up, and I was getting mine in just the right order when he looked at me and spoke.

"So, Anne tells me there are some questions you have about things you have overheard. What do you need to know, Livie?"

I sat back, holding some of my tiles and thinking about how I should start. There were many things I wanted to know, and other things I didn't know how to put into question form. I sighed and then put the tiles down. "I know that Dad is not here, and there are things you and my Chicago aunts are talking about, and I know it has to do with me. I am afraid I did something wrong and don't know what to do about it." Tears filled my eyes, and I wiped them away. I did not want to cry.

Uncle Terry sat back and looked at me. He patted the seat next to him, and I crawled there as he put his arm around me. We sat quietly for a few minutes and listened to the crackling of the fire logs and the wind blowing outside. He hugged me and then shifted sideways to face me.

"Livie, there are things I need to talk to you about and tell you. But I was hoping to hold off for a while. It seems to me that you are ready to hear some of them. I'll tell you what is happening, and then you can ask questions about it. Your aunts want you to go and live in Chicago with them, and…"

"NO!" I yelled, "I won't go!"

"Well just listen because things are confusing. Do you know what a *birth certificate* is?"

I wiped my eyes. "No."

"When a baby is born, a legal piece of paper is written and issued. It tells who the baby's mother and father are. Your birth certificate lists Ruth Evans Pinkerton as your mother and Tobias Pinkerton as your father. Because the paper is legal, I don't really have any claim to you, even though I helped to raise you. We are not related, legally. Your aunts don't think I would be a good person for you to live with and want you to go with them. Dad was their brother, and legally, they are your closest blood relatives."

"But aren't you and Dad cousins? Why doesn't that count?"

Uncle Terry sat still for a few seconds, staring into the fire before he answered. "Dad and I were never cousins. We were very close friends in Chicago when we met in college, and when I came to Everstille to live, the easiest way to explain my living with Dad and your mother was to tell people I was his cousin. That is why I never went to the South Bend lunches with you and the Chicago relatives. They never knew I was living here and just found out when they came here for Dad's funeral. Legally, I have no right to raise you."

I let this sink in for a while. I wasn't sure exactly what to ask. "Then why did you come here? Why didn't you marry that Betsy woman and stay there? I don't understand."

"That's a complicated answer. I loved your father and came to love your mother. The three of us were happy here together, and if your mother had lived, we decided that the three of us would raise you. Before you were born, we thought that you calling me *uncle* would be the easiest thing to do, and when your mother died, Dad and I stuck to our original plan. The two of us, with the help of Anne, raised you. If I could, I would continue to do that. There is something else."

Questions were crowding my mind and I wasn't sure I could hear any more, but I knew I needed to. "What?"

"You obviously have overheard some of the conversations your aunts and I have been having. I know this because of the questions you asked Anne. I have hired a lawyer to try and keep you here with me and continue to raise you. But my chances are not very good. I want you to know this. The other thing is that Dad had a life insurance policy that left a lot of money to you in case he died."

"Twenty-five thousand dollars?" I asked.

"Yes, Cabbage, and that's lots of money. You will not get it. It will go to your guardians and is to be used to help care for you…to buy you clothes and things you need, and maybe some will be available for college in the future. The lawyer I hired said that will be part of what the judge in the case will decide. Do you know what a *judge* is?"

"Someone who makes decisions about other people and things?" It had been one of our spelling words.

"Right. Now, I know that is a lot for you to understand. I will need to go to court and answer some questions, and maybe a lawyer will ask you questions too. Don't worry about it now. There is nothing you or I can do about this. For now, we will continue to live here, and have Anne over, and you will finish fourth grade, and I will work, and we will be fine. Now if there are other questions you have, ask me any time. Just know that I love you like you are my own daughter, and I will do my best to keep us together. Should we continue to play Scrabble?"

But I had lost interest in the game and said I just wanted to sit and talk, and we did. As the fire burned and I asked a few more questions, many of them having no answers, Uncle Terry and I sat comfortably next to each other, watching the fire inside and the snow outside. Our red hair, his and mine, mingled, and I thought that anyone who saw us would be correct to assume we were a family; to believe we were a father and daughter, talking, and laughing, and delighting in being together.

***

Everyone around me tried to keep life as normal as possible. As spring appeared, I was, once again, allowed to walk home from school with Maggie and stay at her house until Uncle Terry came home from work. We continued to go to church with Anne, and she spent most of the weekends at our house. Kids in my class stopped patting my shoulders and hugging me for no reason, and Robert Stevens began to periodically kick my rear in the classroom. Outwardly, everything was routine and conventional. Inside my heart and head, I was anxious and panicky. And as it turned out, for good reason.

The judge decided that I should live with my blood relatives. The *birth certificate* made it clear, so he said, that my Chicago aunts and their husbands were the ones who could give me a family and a home. He ignored the fact that Uncle Terry had helped give me a rainbow filled life for ten years. The house I grew up in was legally Uncle Terry's since his name had been placed on something called a *deed* a few years ago. The *life insurance policy* would go to my aunts so they could use it to buy me the clothes and things I would need. I didn't understand it all. I was the saddest I had ever been, and I could tell Uncle Terry and Anne were too. The judge was, without a doubt, a big meanie.

I was supposed to finish the school year and leave for Chicago on June 1, but Uncle Terry's lawyer talked the judge into allowing me to stay in Everstille and with my family, my real family, part of the summer, so the date was moved to Monday, August 3. On that day I would leave to live in Chicago at Aunt Gladys' house with her and Uncle Dean and the flower cousins, Ivy and Rose.

I tried not to think about the horrible things that were happening to me, but my eyes filled with tears most nights, and Uncle Terry was at my bedside those nights comforting me, and telling me stories, and holding my hand until I finally fell into a sorrowful sleep. Uncle Terry, who was not my real uncle, but had hair that matched mine, and eyes that matched mine, and a heart that was as shattered and crushed and devastated as mine.

10 Indigo

I refused to repaint my room for my tenth birthday. Uncle Terry thought I should pick out the shade of indigo I wanted and complete the rainbow colors I had been so excited to do, but I would not. I had given up the idea. For the first time ever, when he brought it up again, I went to my bedroom and slammed the door. There was complete quiet from both sides for an hour or so, and when I came out and went into the front room where Uncle Terry was sitting on a chair, looking out the window, I broke into tears, and he held me until I stopped crying.

"It's fine, Livie. We won't repaint this year. Don't cry now. You've cried enough," and we both sat on the chair, me on his lap, and looked out the window until I felt calm again.

My tenth birthday was sad even though Anne and Uncle Terry tried to make it a happy day. They wanted to invite Maggie and Mary and some of the other kids from my class, but I told them I didn't want to have a bunch of people here when I would never see them again.

"Livie, I am sure you will see them again. Don't worry so much. Things will work out," and Anna tried to encourage joy, but I would not change my mind.

"So, my newly decade-old girl, what would you like for your birthday dinner? Or, would you rather go to Mazie's this year? She has some great French fries, and we can get a hamburger or hot dog to go with them. Then a milkshake would be great! I could go for one of her chocolate ones. And name your cake. I need to get started on that," and Uncle Terry tried to make things better, but I saw the sadness in his eyes, and knew that this tenth birthday would be nothing like the other ones. Dad wasn't here. And soon, I would be gone.

"Honestly, I don't care what we eat. And I don't care about the cake either. I don't understand why I can't stay here. You two can raise me. Maybe you can get married. I can live with you as your daughter, and we can still be together. We have been doing that for all my life, and that dumb judge should know that," and I burst into tears. Again.

The birthday dinner was at home with just the three of us. Uncle Terry made three of my favorites: fried chicken, meatloaf, and hamburgers on the grill, and there was so much food we had leftovers all week. I tried to take a bite of everything, but with each bite, I thought, *Is this the last time I will have this?* and it just spoiled the taste for me. Even my favorite strawberry shortcake dessert with two candles, one the number **1,** and another the number **0,** was tasteless and I left half of it on my plate. I attempted to be happy and smile, but my stomach hurt all night. It continued to hurt all summer.

The Spring Festival came right after my tenth birthday, and I went with Uncle Terry and Anne, but all I could think about were sad things. I would never see the red and white striped uniforms of the Everstille High School band as they played *Nearer My God to Thee* at the fast march tempo. This was the last time I would watch the city organizations and the various clubs and groups march together waving their banners and banging the small drums. Gone would be the sight of the Jamison horses pulling the float carrying either the Rachel Circle from the Methodist Episcopal Church or the ladies from the First Baptist Church, with everyone laughing as the horses drop their loads, and the little kids point and yell as they hold their noses. I would view no more fireworks or watch the July Fourth Parade. Picnics, and hot summer days, and ice-cream cones, the donut holes at Peterson's Bakery, and August's Vacation Bible School were to end for me. Maggie would find another best friend, maybe that awful Cathy Wesselmann, and I would miss being in fifth grade with Miss Miller, the best teacher at school. These things were overwhelming, and when I thought of them, I could not help that my eyes filled with tears and my nose ran.

At the cinnamon-cake picnic at North Cemetery that summer, Anne came with Uncle Terry and me. It was particularly sad that year because there were two stones, side by side: one for my mother, Ruth Evans Pinkerton, and one for my father, Tobias Pinkerton. I started to cry, and Uncle Terry held me as Anne wiped first my eyes and then her own. None of us felt much like eating the cake or drinking the sweet iced tea, and after a time, we just sat together, all of us, holding each other's hands and looking at the two graves.

"Will I ever be here again?" I asked.

"Of course, you will," answered Anne, and Uncle Terry nodded. "Livie, Chicago is not that far away, and I will send you letters and the books I know your mother would want you to read, and we will figure it all out."

Uncle Terry hugged me tightly and kissed the side of my head. My ponytail had come loose, and he did his best to pull my hair back from my sweaty face. I glanced at him and saw there were tears on his cheeks, and I reached up to wipe them away.

"It's really warm today, and since it's Sunday, I think it would be a great day to rest at home. Maybe tonight the three of us can go to Mazie's for a root-beer float. What do you think, Anne?"

"That's a great idea, Terry. Let's clean up here."

We moved the cake and plates and tea and napkins into the basket and walked to the car. I did not let go of Uncle Terry's hand, and instead of sitting in the back seat, I scooted into the front, sitting between him and Anne, feeling close to them, sensing the security of their nearness, and not minding the warmth from the summer day. We drove home slowly and unpacked everything and rested. By that evening I was feeling better, and when Anne suggested we get Maggie and take her with us to Mazie's, I quickly agreed. We slurped our floats, and for just a while, I felt that everything was normal; it was correct and ordered and proper.

I squeezed in as much of that summer as I could. I spent as many days in the library inside the Ruth Evans Pinkerton room as possible. There were not enough hours in the day for packing and stuffing and cramming the sights and sounds and smells of Everstille, and my house, and Maggie's friendship, and the fun of Mike Jasper's visit, and Anne's cookies and stories, and Uncle Terry's fried chicken and love into my memory. And August 3 came too soon. Much, much too soon.

I had packed up my clothes and most important items. My favorite books, given to me by Anne, were placed in a box along with the games and toys and stuffed animals I wanted to keep. When I said my good-by to Maggie, I gave her my *EZ Bake Oven,* and we both cried so hard that her nose started to bleed, and we ended up laughing. We pledged eternal friendship, and her sister, Mean Mary, even hugged me. And this time, did not pull my hair.

The Sunday before the Chicago aunts were coming to steal me (this is how I thought of the move), we didn't go to church. I didn't think I could take everyone saying farewell again, and Uncle Terry agreed. Anne came over after the Sunday service, and the three of us went for a walk along Main Street, and then Uncle Terry made hamburgers for a late afternoon lunch. We finished eating and cleaned up the kitchen, and then went outside on the back porch to sit. I had said my good-byes; my suitcase and boxes were packed. I had no interest in doing anything except spending my remaining time with the two people I thought of as my parents.

As we sat quietly, looking out over the yard and the flower garden and into the avocado-colored bushes lining the edge of the property, Uncle Terry reached into his pants packet and pulled out a small jewelry box. He looked at me and spoke.

"Livie, I know you didn't want to paint your room the indigo color which would finish your rainbow plan, but I have something for you that will. This is really an adult gift, and you might put it away until you grow into it, but I want you to have it, and remember that life is filled with colors, and we are meant to enjoy them all."

I took the box he held out to me and opened it. Inside, nestled in the velvety softness was a necklace. I pulled it out and held it up before me. At the end of the real silver chain hung a jeweled teardrop pendant whose indigo color danced in the sunlight. I watched as shades of blue, gray, purple, and even a bit of green flashed and sparkled, and my throat became tight, and I had trouble talking.

"It's beautiful. Thank you. Can you put it on me?"

Anne said, "Come over here," and I handed her the necklace which she didn't need to unhook because it fit over my head.

I looked down at the jewel and smiled. Then I smiled at Anne and Uncle Terry, and it felt strange because my mouth had not practiced making that movement in months. I hugged Uncle Terry and then Anne, and said, "This is great. I'll be careful with it because it's special. I love the indigo jewel."

I had Anne help me take it off, and before I placed it back into the box, held it up once more. I squinted and looked closer at it and then held it next to Uncle Terry's eyes.

"Look, Anne, this is the color of his eyes, don't you think?"

She looked closer and then smiled. She took the necklace from me and held it close to my face. "It's the color of your eyes too," she said, and she was right.

***

I didn't think I would be able to sleep that night. I kept thinking that this would be the last night I would sleep in my own bed. But, I did, and when I awoke, it was Monday, August 3.

Anne had stayed overnight. She and Uncle Terry had taken the day off work to make sure things went smoothly. I wasn't hungry for breakfast, even though Uncle Terry made the buttermilk pancakes I loved. As I looked around at the three of us, sitting at the table, moving the bits of pancakes with syrup around our plates, I saw there were plenty of pancakes left over. No one seemed to have an appetite. We did dishes and waited on the porch. Aunt Ernestine and Aunt Gladys said they would be driving together and should be at the house by ten o'clock or so. It was ten-fifteen when the car turned the corner and drove slowly into the driveway. My stomach hurt so much I was sure I needed to go to the hospital.

The Chicago aunts came out of the car and greeted everyone. They didn't shake hands with Uncle Terry or Anne, but just nodded and said "Good Morning."

"Are you all packed?" asked Aunt Ernestine. "We want to get started back right away. Mr. Douglas, I'll open the trunk so you can bring Olivia's things out. Olivia, why don't you go to the bathroom, then say your good-byes? We will stop for lunch and gas, but don't want to make any unnecessary stops other than that."

I turned and did what she said, and passed Anne and Uncle Terry as they were carrying my belongings to the car. Once everything was packed, and the Chicago aunts said good-bye, Aunt Gladys said, "We're ready. Olivia. Say good-bye and get into the back." I turned and threw myself into Uncle Terry's arms.

I held on tightly and cried and said into his ear, "I don't want to go. Please, please!"

He held back a sob and tightened his arms around me. I reached over and pulled Anne into our hug and the three of us stayed like that, and I thought maybe we could just float up to the sky like this and never let go. But I knew that would not happen.

Anne let go first. She reached into her pocket and pulled out two handkerchiefs, giving me one, and holding the other to her eyes. Uncle Terry carried me to the car and before he put me down, whispered. "You are mine, Cabbage. You always have been and always will be." Then he let me go.

I crawled into the back seat of Aunt Gladys' car. She started the car, and Aunt Ernestine turned around and said, "Remember, we'll stop for lunch, but that will be a while, so do you need to use the bathroom once again before we leave? Better safe than sorry." I shook my head and she turned around. Aunt Gladys slowly backed out, and we began the trip to my new home. Chicago.

I turned around and looked out the back window to see my house and yard and Uncle Terry and Anne. They were standing on the front steps. Anne was holding a handkerchief to her eyes, and as they saw me looking out the window, they waved, and Anne blew kisses.

I placed my hand flat against the back window and left it there as I watched them. As I looked back, inside the house, standing at the front window, I saw a familiar figure. The ghost of my mother was there. I could see the lacy handkerchief peeking out of the breast pocket and noted her hair curled just under her chin. She leaned forward and placed her hand on the front window, echoing mine. I stayed there, kneeling on the backseat, ignoring my Aunt Ernestine's demands to turn around and sit down, and I watched until the car turned the corner, and they were no longer in sight. I would not see Anne for many years, and it would be even longer until I saw Uncle Terry. And that was the last time, the very last time, I ever saw the ghost of my mother.

II.
In Chicago

Our most basic instinct is not for survival but for family.

Paul Pearsall

Christmas Gift Books and Inscriptions

1964, Age 10
The Borrowers
(Mary Norton)

Dear Livie,
You have a new special home, just like these small creatures. Make the best of it. Live joyously. A.O.R.

1965, Age 11
Harriet the Spy
(Louise Fitzhugh)

Darling Livie,
Do you enjoy watching others? Harriet does. She has lessons to teach you about friends, and family, and being yourself. Always, A.O.R.

1966, Age 12
*The Lion, the Witch,
and the Wardrobe*
(C.S. Lewis)

Dearest L,
A wonderful adventure that contains good and evil. This will prepare you for the next book. Be good!
A.O.R.

1967, Age 13
Oliver Twist
(Charles Dickens)

The first book, Livie, your mother instructed me to read and to figure out who is good, who is evil, and why. You should do the same.
 A.O.R.

1968, Age 14
To Kill a Mockingbird
(Harper Lee)

Oh, Livie, what a joy to read this for the first time. Walk in their shoes. Understand others. Not always easy. Yours, A.O.R.

1969, Age 15
Jane Eyre
(Charlotte Bronte)

Livie dearest: Life has rules, and at times they are not fair. You do belong. You are loved. You are missed.
A.O.R.

1970, Age 16
Of Mice and Men
(John Steinbeck)

Dear Livie,
How much responsibility do we actually have for others? Think about that as you read.
Always, missing you, A.O.R.

1971, Age 17
Ethan Frome
(Edith Wharton)

Sweet Livie,
It is true that you should be careful
for what you wish; it may come true.
Wishing only the best for you.
A.O.R.

1972, Age 18

?

No book was sent.

Grade 5

Olivia pulled out the piece of yarn hanging around her neck which had the key attached to it, positioned it into the keyhole, jiggled it, and turned. She pushed the door open and walked into the kitchen, placing her books, notebook, and folded brown paper lunch bag on the table before she went back to the door, closed, and locked it. She sighed with relief. Sometimes the key got stuck, and she remembered the first day when she could not open the door, and her cousins found her sitting on the back steps crying. Ivy, older and kind, showed her how to shake the key around a bit to guarantee opening. "These old doors are sometimes tricky," Ivy told her. Rose, younger and mean, looked at her, and whispered, "Stop whining, Clown-Girl. Such a baby!"

The day was Thursday, October 8; she had been living with Aunt Gladys, Uncle Dean, and her girl cousins since August 3. On Tuesdays and Thursdays after school, she had tasks to complete in preparation for that night's supper. Aunt Gladys always left a note telling Olivia what to do, and today she was to wash and dry the dishes in the sink, set the table, peel, and cut the potatoes sitting on the counter, then place them in a pot of cold water. She was to turn the oven on to 350 degrees, take out the prepared meatloaf and deposit it in the oven at 4:15. Some days she had only the dish-washing and table-setting to complete. Tuesdays and Thursdays were the days Aunt Gladys worked at a grocery store. She also worked on Saturday, but was home by early afternoon. Ivy and Rose didn't get home from high school until four-thirty, and Olivia's earlier arrival put her in charge of the tasks. "It's good for you to take responsibility. You have been too coddled," explained Aunt Gladys while Aunt Ernestine added, "Idle hands are the devil's workshop."

The aunts weren't being cruel. It was just their way. They had spent many hours discussing the raising of Olivia, their brother's only child: deciding with whom she should live, what she would be allowed to do, how often she would be allowed contact with Anne Rivens and that man, Terrence Douglas. The answers, after debating and discussing were: Aunt Gladys, very little, and never. It was all for the little girl's good. She was sweet enough, and pretty enough (oh, but for that red hair), but had been spoiled by the adults who had raised her. Habits needed to be broken. Behaviors must be corrected. Routines required establishing. And Gladys had experience with girls, having two of her own. Olivia could learn from the older girls. Besides, Ivy would be graduating high school in a couple years and there was that extra small bedroom upstairs. Ernestine had two male lodgers in her upstairs rooms and wasn't sure how a ten-year old girl would fit in. Olivia would be fine with Gladys and Dean. Things would work out. Ernestine and Gladys would, together, make decisions about Olivia and raise her. They owed it to their brother. Their poor, dead brother. The brother they had never really known. And Olivia could not be left with that man, Terrence Douglas, who clearly had taken advantage of Toby. In many ways.

Then there was the money. Olivia came with money from the Life Insurance Policy. The money would help with the expenses connected with raising a child: clothing and food, school supplies and incidentals, doctor visits and dental check-ups. And transportation to those places. Dean's new car wasn't driven by Olivia of course, but then she did ride in it. And it was only fair to share the money because both Gladys and Ernestine would help to raise her.

Olivia had been taken shopping for new school clothes. Uncle Dean drove them, in the new family car, to Goldblatt's Department Store where she got three skirts: navy blue, dark gray, and black; three new simple white cotton blouses; a half dozen ankle socks (white, no lace), and a sturdy pair of brown oxfords. Olivia would have preferred the patent leather Mary Janes she saw, but why buy two pairs of shoes? She would outgrow them before she could outwear them. Besides, there were all the clothes Gladys had saved from her girls which were perfectly good. She could use her new sewing machine to take the clothes up or in, and they would be perfectly acceptable for Olivia to wear. Gladys examined the clothing Olivia brought with her. The dresses were frilly and colorful, the shoes totally unacceptable for walking to school, and everything was fashionable. Unsuitable for a ten-year old. Olivia needed toning down. No red-head should be wearing pink or scarlet.

So, Olivia was taken care of. She seemed to have adjusted after a week or two of crying. Gladys hadn't heard anything lately, although it was difficult to hear anything from that small bedroom in the corner upstairs. Olivia followed the simple orders left for her, got along tolerably well with her cousins, and was quiet and polite to the family. At least Tobias had installed courtesy in her. Gladys was certain it was her brother and not that Terrence Douglas who trained her. She just did not understand that friendship. Too bad Ruth hadn't lived. If she had, it was very possible Terrence Douglas wouldn't be around. And that he had been deeded that house…well!

On Tuesdays and Thursdays, Olivia got through her chores as quickly as she could. She had about an hour until her cousins were home, and once it was completed, she could disappear upstairs and stay in her bedroom until dinner. That way she didn't have to be around for Rose's teasing. Ivy was kinder, but she mostly ignored Olivia which was one of her kindnesses. Rose had taken to calling Olivia "Clown-girl" because of her hair. "Really, clown wigs are just like your hair. Maybe we should rename you *Bozo*," was one of the first things Rose said to Olivia on the first day she moved into the small bedroom. Of course, Rose was careful not to let her mother or father hear her comments. Olivia thought about Maggie's sister, Mean Mary, and decided that compared to Rose, Mary was only unfriendly. Rose was downright malicious.

On this Thursday in October, the weather was warm, and Olivia was anxious to get to her bedroom and change her school clothes. She was still able to fit into most of the clothes she brought with her, and wearing them made her feel better. A reminder of her previous rainbow life. She completed her chores, moved the brown-paper lunch sack to the side counter for later use, grabbed her books and notebook and hurried upstairs just as she heard Ivy's key turning in the lock. She closed her door, opened her window, and turned on the small fan she had been given to ward off the sweaty nights. At times, there was a cool breeze from outside, but the wind was as still as a statue today.

Olivia hung up her blouse and the navy skirt she had worn, smoothing out wrinkles and shaking out the lone potato peel that clung to the skirt. Clothes should be worn three times before they were washed, and be careful while wearing them. Aunt Gladys make this clear. There were other rules in the house. Olivia and the flower cousins received one brown paper-bag per week in which to pack school lunches ("Waste not, want not," explained Aunt Ernestine). Don't throw it away, but bring it home nightly for the next day's use. She forgot to do that the first week of school and had to withstand a scolding by Gladys while Rose stood behind her mother, laughing silently, and pointing her wagging finger at Olivia. Saturday mornings she was to remove her bedsheets and bring them down to be washed by Ivy and then remake her bed with the clean sheets she was given. Olivia had to be taught how to put sheets on because Uncle Terry had always changed her linen. And when he did, he left a surprise on the pillow for her. Often, it was a funny note with a drawing, but periodically there was a small toy or new colorful hair ribbons. There were no toys or ribbons or notes anymore.

Olivia reached into her closet and removed pink shorts and a ruffled striped top and put them on. She immediately felt better. The outfit was cool and reminded her of home. And then, instantly, she felt wistful and unsettled. She had only spoken once on the telephone to Anne, and had not heard from Uncle Terry although she was sure he had called. There were times the telephone rang, and she overheard Aunt Gladys whisper into the receiver "No, she is (outside, sleeping, unavailable), and you shouldn't expect to talk to her. Please stop calling." Olivia felt tears pricking her eyes and wiped them away. She couldn't be caught crying again. Aunt Gladys had told her she needed to stop, and Aunt Ernestine said. "It's no use crying over spilt milk." She took deep breaths and decided to complete her math homework before supper. Thursday night was meatloaf and mashed potatoes, and it was one of the least odious meals Aunt Gladys made.

Meals followed a regular pattern too. Monday's supper was either left-overs from Sunday or baked mac-and-cheese. Tuesday was some sort of "chop suey" with rice. Wednesday supper was over-cooked spaghetti and a red tomato sauce Aunt Gladys called "marinara" and every so often she would shop at the Italian grocery store and get some Italian sausage to serve with it. Thursday was meatloaf, and Friday was left-over night. Saturday, when the weather was nice, Uncle Dean made hamburgers or hot dogs on the grill outside in the backyard, and during cold weather, he made chili. That project took all afternoon, and he was proud of his concoction which he had perfected over the years. Every other Sunday, the family went to Aunt Ernestine's and Uncle Amos' for roast beef, and on the alternate Sundays when they came to the Murphy's, it was roast or fried chicken. The food was plentiful if not particularly tasty, and Olivia never missed Uncle Terry more than on Thursday nights meatloaf supper and those Sundays when fried chicken was served. Nothing compared with Uncle Terry's cooking.

Olivia took out her math book and notebook and sat at the small desk under the window. She placed the fan on the floor so it would blow upwards at her and worked at the assignment. After completing it, she took out the copy of *Pippi Longstocking* she had taken out of the school library and began to read. There was comfort in discovering another red-haired girl in the world; even if she were fictious. Downstairs, Aunt Gladys was home, completing dinner preparations and talking to Ivy and Rose. Soon, Olivia was summoned to supper by Ivy. She washed her hands and walked down the stairs.

"Come on everyone. Let's sit down. Dean, would you like to start the potatoes? Ivy, pass the meatloaf, and Rose, sit down. Olivia, take some of those green beans. They are good for you," and Gladys moved the supper along and kept an eye on everyone's plate. The family tended to not eat enough vegetables.

"Mom, did you see the new shoes at Montgomery Wards? They were advertised in today's paper and are darling. They have a bow and small kitten heels. Could I get them? I could wear them to the Homecoming Dance and for other special occasions," and Ivy looked at her mother who was the one in charge of the family's finances.

"If she gets new shoes, then I should get something too," complained Rose.

"No one is getting anything right now. No, Ivy, I did not see the ad, but I will look at them. Are you and Jeffrey going to the dance together?"

"He hasn't asked me yet, but he will. He just hasn't thought about, and I'll remind him."

Olivia watched her older cousin. This boyfriend stuff was new to her, and while Jeffery seemed nice enough, she couldn't understand Ivy's attraction to him. He was quiet, and when he did speak, it was difficult to hear him. But Ivy seemed happy. Olivia took another bite of her green beans, but these, like the entire meal, were not as good as the ones Uncle Terry made. He left them long, not short and stubby like these, and there was a delicious sprinkle of some toasted, slivered almonds on the top. These were both bland and too salty. Aunt Gladys believed in salt. It was her favorite seasoning, and she used it generously. Olivia took another bite and chewed quickly, then washed it down with her milk.

"Let me know if you and Jeffrey are going to the dance, and then we can discuss the shoes. And yes, Rose, we can consider something new for you too. Dean, would you like more potatoes? Olivia, pass your uncle the dish, please."

Olivia handed the potatoes to Ivy who handed it to her father who took the smallest spoonful of potatoes he could manage and put the dish down in front of him. The family continued to eat and discuss various unimportant neighborhood happenings, and Olivia sat and listened. She wasn't sure who the neighbors being mentioned were, and didn't really care about their happenings. She had completed her supper and was waiting for a chance to disappear upstairs again. Her silence was noticed by Aunt Gladys when she remembered Olivia was there.

"Olivia, how was school today? Did you bring your lunch bag home? Do you have homework to complete?"

"It was fine, Aunt Gladys. Yes, my bag is on the counter, and I have some reading to complete."

"*Chatty Cathy* speaks," teased Rose, "Such interesting things to say!"

"Stop teasing, Rose," cautioned her mother, "Olivia is still adjusting to a new life. There is fruit cocktail for dessert. Who wants some? Olivia?"

"No thank you, Aunt Gladys. May I be excused now?"

Gladys looked at her, and said, "Are you sure? Fruit is good for you."

"And there are red cherries that match your hair," hissed Rose.

"Stop the teasing, Rose, or you will have to go to your room and not watch television tonight. Have you done your homework?"

Rose gave Olivia a side glace and said to her mother, "Yes, I did it in study hall. I'll take some dessert, Mom."

"And does everyone else want a dish?"

Dean and Ivy nodded, and Gladys turned to Olivia and said, "Well, if you don't want anything else, take your plate to the sink and make your lunch for tomorrow before you go upstairs. Rose, it's your turn for dishes tonight," and she went into the kitchen to dole out the brightly colored canned fruit.

Olivia placed her dish and glass in the sink and made a peanut-butter and jelly sandwich for the following day. She found an apple, and wrapped two fig newton cookies up, and placed everything in the used brown paper bag. Making her own lunch was also a new task for her. She didn't mind this one. At least she knew what she liked. For the first week, Aunt Gladys made her lunch and gave her those disgusting baloney sandwiches. When she offered to make her own lunch, Gladys was pleased with her. "What a good idea, Olivia. See. You really are growing up!"

Lunch made, good-nights said, Olivia went to her bedroom and gathered her pajamas. She took then to the bathroom and cleaned up, brushed her teeth, and readied herself for bed. No one would be tucking her in. She completed the night-time rituals and went back to her room, closing the door behind her. She turned the light switch on, feeling a cooler breeze come in from the window and was glad. She stood for a minute and looked around her bedroom wondering again how it was possible to create such a colorless room.

The walls were some sort of gray or beige or perhaps a dirty white color, and the two small area rugs in the room were just as non-descript. There was a white coverlet on the bed and the sheets were also white. Olivia missed her pink and blue flowered sheets as well as the ones with green and yellow daisies. The furniture was wood or a material meant to look like wood, and it was dull. Clean, but dull. Olivia walked over to the small desk under the window and took the library book from it. She paused to look at the photograph of her mother and father, the one where Dad was smiling at her mother. She leaned forward and kissed it and whispered, "Love you Mother and Dad. I miss you both."

Olivia crawled into bed, grateful that the warm October day had settled into a breezy October night. She opened her book, but the words swam before her eyes. She sat with her back to the wall and thought about her life. Her head dropped to the side, and as she leaned into the bed, she reached over and switched off the reading light on the small table next to her. It was early evening, but she felt herself slipping into sleep and allowed herself to go. The book closed and fell off the bed onto the small non-descript rug, and she would step on it the next morning as she got out of bed to ready herself for school. Olivia's eyes closed, and she felt around until she found her Raggedy Ann doll and pulled to her. She fell asleep dreaming of pink, and strawberry, and blue, and orange walls.

Christmas, 1964

Friday, December 18, was the last day of school before the two-week winter break. Olivia was glad to be done with school for a while, but sad that she had to spend the time at the house with her new family. It was cold. No snow, but it was suggested in the outside air. On Fridays, Aunt Gladys didn't work, and she was home baking Christmas cookies, something she had been doing all week. Her cooking was mediocre, but her baking was excellent, and she enjoyed creating the dozens of cookies gifted to friends and neighbors during the holiday season. Olivia had watched her bake the sugar cookies, thumbprints filled with apricot and strawberry jam, and molasses chewies. Today she was baking a cookie called *melt-in-the-mouth*, and Olivia changed her clothes, washed her hands, and came to the kitchen to see if she could help.

"Olivia, if you want to help, you can do those dishes. Then remove the baked cookies from the cookie sheet and place them on the racks over there. Careful not to burn yourself. Use the potholders. Is it snowing out yet?"

"No, Aunt Gladys," and Olivia washed the large bowl and put it in the drying rack, "but it's really cold outside. I can't find my winter scarf, and I think I might need one. Is there an extra one here?"

"We'll look later. Glad this is leftover night. These took longer than I thought they would, and everyone will be home shortly and be hungry." She looked over at Olivia and pursed her lips. *The girl is coming along,* she thought. *Toby would be proud of her. Poor man.*

The dried dishes were put away, and Olivia carefully scooped up the hot cookies and put them on the racks to completely cool. She took a deep breath and said, "Umm, these smell great. I've never eaten this kind of cookie before."

Aunt Gladys glanced over and smiled. "Then go on and try one. Just don't let it spoil your dinner, and don't tell the girls you had one."

Olivia searched through the cookies, took what she thought was the largest one, and took a bite. "Wow," she said, "these ARE melt-in-the-mouth good!" As she chewed, she smiled and felt almost happy.

***

Dinner and dishes completed; cookies put away; baking equipment left on the counter for the next day's work, and Olivia went upstairs to get ready for bed. It was getting colder, and she was tired. There was a Bob Hope Special on television that the family was going to watch, but she wasn't interested. She thought she would spend the evening looking through the Golden Books from Anne. She was too old to reread them, and besides, she knew most of them by heart, but going through them brought back happy memories.

She settled herself on her bed with the books all around her and picked up *Raggedy Ann's Tea Party*, one of her favorite books, and decided that perhaps she was not too old, so she opened it up and began to read. She heard the doorbell, but she didn't pay attention to it until there was a sound that drifted up to her, to her hearing, to her memory; a voice whose tone, pitch, resonance was familiar even though she had not heard it in months. Almost five months. Olivia listened closely. She decided she wasn't just dreaming, then pushed the Raggedy Ann book out of the way and hurried to her door where she heard a few sentences.

"No, she is in bed. It's a bad idea. I've asked you not to contact us. She is better off here, and you need to go," and this was followed by a hard closing and clicking of the lock on the front door.

"Uncle Terry, Uncle Terry," yelled Olivia as she rushed down the stairs to the front door where Gladys, with Dean behind her, were returning to the front room. To Bob Hope and the television. To join their daughters who were laughing at the humor exuding from the set. The new television set. Money was not such a problem lately.

"Where is he? Where is my Uncle Terry?" and Olivia ran to the door and attempted to pull it open. The lock had been turned, and she struggled to open it, started to cry, and yelled for Uncle Terry to stop. To wait. To see her. To hold her. To take her home.

Gladys turned back and took Olivia's arm and began to move her away from the door, but with the strength of an angry and lonely ten-year old, Olivia simultaneously pulled her arm away and got the door open. She ran out to the front where the darkness was interrupted by some flashing multi-colored Christmas lights decorating a few houses on the block. She looked through the flashing glare to see if a tall man whose red-hair matched hers was around, but all she could see were some moving cars. One might be his, but she didn't know which way he might have driven, and she rushed down one way and then the other, calling out his name, ignoring the freeze on her feet which her slippers were not protecting, and the chill on her arms and neck and head. As she turned to run back the opposite way again, strong male arms caught her, lifted her up, and Uncle Dean carried the sobbing girl back into the warmth where the blanket placed around her shoulders and the sweet warm tea offered to her did nothing to melt the lump of frost that used to be her heart.

***

Christmas morning came, and Olivia was feeling better. She had spent a few days in bed feeling ill after the previous Friday night when her present almost met her past. Her temperature was normal, and there was no sickness although she didn't eat much. Not even the Christmas cookies offered to her. Not even those melt-in-the-mouth ones or the new ones which had red and green sprinkles on them. The cold outside remained, and the snow was lightly falling that morning. The family was up and awake and eating pancakes when Olivia ventured downstairs.

"Merry Christmas, Olivia. Glad to see you. Come on and sit down and have some pancakes," and Uncle Dean reached over to give her a quick hug and moved her into the chair next to him. He got up and poured her a glass of milk while Aunt Gladys filled a plate for her with freshly made pancakes and a couple strips of bacon. Everyone was being nice to her. Even Rose hadn't called her *Clown-girl* all week.

"Thanks," answered Olivia, and she poured syrup on the breakfast and began to take small bites.

"After we eat, everyone should get dressed, and then we'll meet in the front room for gifts. Aunt Ernestine and Uncle Amos will be here about eleven, and I think Enoch and his wife will be here later. Olivia, you haven't seen your older cousins in a while, and they are all grown up. Of course, Otis is in the army, so he won't be here. More pancakes anyone?"

The group ate and talked; then they dressed for the day and went to the front room for the gifts. There were happy exclamations and hugs and thanks, and Olivia thought that the Christmas tree, although not as big or fully decorated as the ones she remembered at her real home, in Everstille, was moderately attractive. There were three gifts for Olivia. One from Aunt Ernestine and Uncles Amos, another from Aunt Gladys and Uncle Dean. Olivia received a light gray skirt and a white blouse, and a new winter scarf set with matching mittens and a warm hat. The scarf set was beige. The third gift was a book. It was unwrapped, and no note or letter accompanied it, but inside the new copy of *The Borrowers* was an inscription and the initials: A.O.R. Anne Olivia Rivens. It was Olivia's favorite gift.

May 22, 1965

The Saturday Olivia turned eleven was a lovely spring day. She was given a break from her regular chores which were done by Ivy and, grudgingly, by Rose. Dinner that night was prepared by Uncle Dean and they had hamburgers on the grill. She didn't get a choice of cake, but Aunt Ernestine brought over the sponge cake she made for all the family birthdays and holidays. It had powdered sugar on top, not frosting, and was served with vanilla ice cream. Somehow, Aunt Ernestine's sponge cake was dry. The vanilla ice cream helped.

There was a combined birthday gift from the aunts. Olivia opened the box hoping it was the cute pedal pusher set she had seen and mentioned to Aunt Gladys. Her colorful clothes which were hanging in her closet were mostly too small for her now. The set she saw had a striped red, white, and blue top which perfectly matched the red bottom which had ties at the end. She opened the box and pulled out the package of undershirts and another of underpants. There were also new socks. No lace. Everything was white.

"Thank you," said Olivia.

Grade 6

The Chicago Public School Olivia was attending was different from the Everstille Elementary School Olivia had attended. Very different. For one thing, it was much larger. The school building had three floors. Everstille Elementary had one. In Chicago, grades kindergarten through eighth grade were all in the same building, while Everstille had three separate buildings for elementary, junior high, and senior high students. But the biggest different was in the class size. The entire fifth grade in Everstille had twenty-one students while last year's class in the Chicago school, and it was one of three, had thirty-six. Olivia was in a sixth-grade class this year, and class size was increasing. The first day there were twenty-five students, but by the second week of school, she counted twenty-nine. And now, after almost four weeks of school, for some reason Olivia never understood, the sixth-grade classes were being reorganized. There were now thirty-three students seated alphabetically in her classroom, room 304. And directly behind her was a new girl named Karolina Pinkus.

As the students took their reassigned seats and Mr. Taylor (a male teacher was a revelation to Olivia) called out their names, Karolina went past Olivia's desk and smiled at her. Olivia was surprised. She had made no friends last year but was hoping for one this year. This girl seemed friendly and approachable, and Olivia thought about what to do to get to know her. Perhaps at lunchtime they could sit together. That would be a start.

Lunchtime came. In the crowded lunchroom which was in the basement of the school building, Olivia decided not to get into the long line just to get a carton of milk. She would spend time looking for Karolina. Somehow, as the classes merged into the lunch area, she lost sight of her possible friend. After being pushed for what seemed like the tenth time by some older students, and told to "Move, Red!", Olivia gave up her search and took her usual seat towards the back of the large room where she knew no one. She scrunched herself into a corner of the table, hurriedly ate her lunch and cleaned up her space. Olivia threw out her paper bag because this was Friday, and she would not need to fold it carefully and bring it home, took a long swallow of the lukewarm water from the water fountain, and walked up the stairs and out to the surrounding playground. She walked around watching for the blonde-haired girl, but did not see her. The first bell, the "line-up" bell, sounded, and she wandered over to the place where *Room 304,* painted in red on the sidewalk, indicated where that class should line up. As she moved into her alphabetically assigned spot, she saw Karolina looking for the number. Olivia caught her eye and waved and smiled. Karolina smiled as she got into line behind her. "Hi," she said, and Olivia answered, "Hi." This began their friendship.

Karolina and her family had just moved into the neighborhood because *Tata,* her father, got a better paying job at one of the nearby factories. *Mama,* her mother worked for a company that cleaned houses, and *Babcia,* her grandmother, lived with them. Alex and Steve were her older brothers, and both were in high school although Alex was fighting with their father about ending his education and getting a job. They lived on the street right behind Olivia's family in an apartment building on the third floor, and no, she didn't really know anyone in the neighborhood. Olivia discovered all these things as the two of them walked home together from school on Friday afternoon. The excitement of finding each other, and of living so close was overwhelming. They made plans to meet at the corner of the street on Saturday afternoon at one o'clock. Karolina's family did not have a telephone in their apartment yet, but Olivia gave Karolina her telephone number anyway. They parted at the street, and Olivia practically floated home.

She was in a great mood all night and didn't even mind when, because it was her turn to do the dishes, Rose purposely dirtied more dishes than necessary. The next morning, Saturday, she got up to do her chores, removing her white sheets from the bed, taking them downstairs to Ivy, then receiving the clean white sheets with which she was to re-make her bed. She was surprised to find Aunt Gladys at the washer doing the job Ivy would usually do.

"Where is Ivy? Aren't you at work today? It's Saturday."

"And good morning to you, too," replied Aunt Gladys taking the sheets from Olivia and placing them into the washing machine. "Ivy started a job at Kresge's Dime Store, and she will be working on Saturdays. And I am not working anymore. Olivia, please hand me that box on the desk behind you."

Olivia picked up the box of laundry detergent and handed it to her aunt. "Why aren't you working? I thought you said the money was needed."

"Now, Miss Nosy, things sometimes change. Don't worry about the money. We are fine. Better, actually. Now, go and do your chores, and then make sure you wash up. Comb that hair back. Right after lunch we're going to Aunt Ernestine's. Your cousin Otis is coming home from the army, and we are going over to have a family party at their house. Ivy will join us there after work. Go on now. Get your chores done."

Olivia stood still and stared at her aunt. Not today! This was the day she and her new friend Karolina were going to meet at the corner.

She shook her head and said, "I can't go. I have something to do. You can leave me here, and I'll be fine."

Gladys finished placing the sheets into the washing machine. started it, then opened the dryer, taking out the dried towels. "Nonsense. We are not leaving you here alone. Whatever you think you have to do can wait."

"NO!" yelled Olivia, panic in her soul, "I have to be here. You don't understand. I can't go!"

Gladys turned, holding the towels she had just removed and looked at Olivia. This child had not acted like this in over the year she had been here. What was going on? "Olivia, there is no discussion about this. We are leaving right after a quick lunch. I want to be there to help Ernestine by one o'clock. Now, go do what you need to, and lower your voice."

"Please, Aunt Gladys. I made a friend, and we are meeting today at one o'clock. I have to be there." She was close to tears.

"A friend? Well, good for you. I'm happy to know you have one. But you won't be able to meet her today. Go ahead and use the telephone. You can call her and meet another day," and Gladys shook out the towel and folded it. Then she took another.

"I can't call her. She doesn't have a telephone yet. Her family just moved here. I have to meet her," and Olivia was desperate in her explanation.

"Olivia, this is an important day for this family. Otis is coming home, and we are going to be there. I'm sure your friend will understand. Go on now. And get yourself some breakfast. There's cereal on the counter," and she turned around to complete the folding.

Olivia took her white sheets, ran up the stairs, and threw them on her bed, ignoring them. She ran back down the stairs, disregarding Rose who was coming out of the bathroom and called to her, "Hey, Clown-girl, what's your hurry?"

Olivia ran down the stairs, out the back door, and went to the front of the house. She looked at the corner where she was supposed to meet Karolina and ran there. She turned the corner, running down the street Karolina lived on. She lived on the third floor of an apartment building, so Olivia would just find her apartment, knock on the door, and explain to her about the change of plans. She stopped when she came to the apartment and looked up. Then she looked to her left. And then again to the left. There were three apartment buildings. They all looked the same. They all had three floors. Olivia felt her stomach churn and she was sure her brain was on fire. The was nothing else to do. She would start with this building and check all of them.

She went to the door of the first apartment building and pulled it open. She checked the mailboxes, but not all of them had names on them. If Karolina and her family just moved here, maybe they couldn't get their name on one yet. She walked up one flight of stairs and went into the hallway to look around. Three doors. Three apartments. The second floor was the same. When Olivia went to the third floor, she stood for a few seconds deciding what to do. There were numbers on the doors but no names. She took a deep breath and walked to the closest door. She knocked. There was no answer, so she knocked again, harder. Still no answer. Then she balled up her fist, hit the door again, and stood back. No one seemed to be home. She went to the next door and knocked loudly. Then again. She stood back when she heard someone walking to the door. The door cracked open and a face appeared. A woman looked out and scowled, "What do you want?"

"Does a girl named Karolina live here?"

"No," and the door closed with a slam.

One door left, and it had to be hers. Olivia walked over to it and raised her hand to knock. Just as she did, the woman from the second apartment opened her door to say, "That apartment is empty. They moved out a week ago. Whoever you are looking for isn't there." Then her door shut again.

Olivia stood for a few seconds wondering whether to believe her or not, and then decided not to waste time. She hurried down the stairs, went out to the sidewalk, and ran over to the second apartment. After she glanced at the mailboxes which gave her no clue, she rushed up to the third floor and proceeded to knock and ask at all three doors. No, no little girl named Karolina had recently moved in. Then, Olivia decided, she had to be in the third apartment building.

Down the stairs. Out to the sidewalk. Over to the third building. Into the main floor. Glance at the mailboxes. Up to the third floor. Knock. No answer. Knock. Ask. *No* was the answer. One door left. This had to be the one. Olivia knocked loudly because by now, she had the right one. She was sure of it. There were no more apartments. No more apartment buildings. The door opened, and a teenaged boy looked out.

"What do you want?"

"Are you Karolina's brother? Is this where she lives? I am her friend from school. Can I see her?"

The boy scrunched up his face and shook his head. "No Karolina lives here. Sorry," and he started to close the door. Then, as Olivia stood there in disbelieving shock, he reopened it and said, "Oh wait, you're looking for that new family. Yesterday they moved down to the second floor to the larger apartment there. That's where they were," and he pointed to the first door, "but when the second floor one was cleaned, the father and boys moved their stuff. Pretty sure they have a sister," and he closed the door.

Olivia turned and ran down to the second floor. She walked into the hallway and lifted her hand to knock on the first door when she heard her name.

"Olivia? Why are you here?"

She turned and saw Karolina coming out of the second door holding a garbage bag. She was happy and relieved and pleased and her smile grew as she walked over to her friend. "I didn't know which building you were in and I had to find you. You don't have a telephone yet, and I can't meet you because we have to go to my other aunt's house. You said you were on the third floor."

"Come on. Walk with me to the garbage outside. I have to dump this. When I got home yesterday afternoon, my family was moving to this apartment. It's bigger, and the second floor isn't so far for Babcia to walk. It became available, but I didn't know it. Glad you found me. No telephone until next week."

The girls walked down the stairs discussing the move, and school, and generally got to know each other. Karolina showed Olivia where the garbage cans were in the alley behind the building, and they stood there for a while talking. Suddenly Olivia looked around the alley and when she realized where she was, she laughed.

"What?" asked Karolina.

"Look over there," and she pointed across the alley and to her left. "That's where I live. That's the house my Aunt Gladys and Uncle Dean own. Look how close we are. All I have to do is to go out the back gate and across the alley. That's great!"

The two of them looked and smiled and made plans to walk to school together Monday morning. Then Olivia waved good-bye to Karolina, or Kari, as she wanted to be called, and ran across the alley to the backyard. She felt proud of herself. She solved her problem; she figured it out. And things were settled.

As she walked through the back door, Rose was in the laundry room and when she saw Olivia, called out, "Here she is, Mom; Olivia is here." And then she turned to Olivia and crowed, "Too bad, Clown-girl, you're in trouble now!"

And she was. Aunt Gladys yelled and shook her finger and told Olivia she had left the house without permission. They had looked all over for her, and she was disobedient and careless and defiant and on and on, and Olivia just stood there and took the yelling and didn't even try to explain where she had gone or why. And when, later, she had to listen to Aunt Gladys tell Aunt Ernestine about her disobedience and carelessness and defiance, and when Aunt Ernestine looked at her and shook her head and said, "Well, spare the rod, spoil the child, I suppose," Olivia did not care. She had a friend.

She had to wash the dishes and could not have dessert for a week. She was also given Ivy's job of throwing out the garbage permanently. Olivia didn't mind. In fact, when she took the garbage out to the alley, she could look down the way and see Kari's apartment, and who knows…perhaps she and Kari would be emptying their garbage at the same time. That hadn't happened, but it could. And who wanted fruit cocktail or canned pears anyway?

Sixth grade became better. Once Aunt Gladys calmed down and when Kari came over and was introduced to her, and after Aunt Gladys was sufficiently appeased by Kari's general politeness and sweetness, Olivia was absolved of her sin. Kari and Olivia walked together to and from school, spent as much time in each other's company as possible, and because they lived so close, Aunt Gladys didn't care. Olivia was occupied many afternoons and Saturdays at Kari's apartment and often ate dinner there. She was welcomed by Kari's Babcia, Mama, and even on the rare occasions she saw him, Tata. Kari's brothers, Alex, and Steve, were kind to their young sister and did not tease her the way Rose teased Olivia.

And the food! Olivia had not tasted such delicious things since Uncle Terry's cooking. There was *pierogi*, dumplings stuffed with various fillings: meat and cheese and fruit. And lusciously soft yet crunchy potato pancakes eaten with sour cream. Creamy, earthy, salty mushroom soup which taught Olivia that she liked mushrooms. She also liked the garlicy sausage called *kielbasa*, fried doughnuts known as *paczki* filled with gooey sweetness, and the soft envelopes of cookies called *kolaczki* with letters of apricot or prune or cheese folded inside and stamped with powdered sugar which became her favorite. Olivia was introduced to an entirely new category of fare she didn't know existed. Not in Everstille. And certainly not at Aunt Gladys' house.

Olivia and Kari became close. They shared secrets and observations about life. They studied together and tested each other on their spelling words every Thursday before the Friday test. When they had to write an essay about their best friend, they wrote about each other. They got in trouble at school when Mr. Taylor caught them passing notes, so they devised a secret written code that just the two of them knew. They ate lunch together and shared sandwiches and treats. Olivia thought she was luckier than Kari because all she had to offer were fig newtons and sometimes, when the Girl Scout cookies Uncle Dean brought home were available, the chocolate mints or the shortbread cookies. Olivia liked these, but she would always trade or share anything she had for her favorites, *kolaczki.*

Living in Chicago, enduring Rose's continual teasing, listening to Aunt Gladys' lectures about behavior, eating her dull cooking, going to Aunt Ernestine's, being bored by the adult talk, living in the strangeness of this city, all were evened out by the fact of Karolina's friendship. She lacked her real family, her father, Uncle Terry, Anne, and missed them endlessly, but the Pinkus family's welcoming warmth, their acceptance and understanding made her Chicago life tolerable.

May 9, Karolina's Name Day

Sixth grade was coming to a close. Spring Break was over. Summer loomed. As they walked home from school, Olivia and Kari talked about the things they would do together during the summer and the possibility, and hope, they would be in the same class during seventh grade.

"Anyway, we can still walk together and study for stuff together. I heard that Michelle from Mrs. Ford's class had a birthday party and all the girls in her class were invited. They went to the Skate-A-Round Skating Rink and Michelle fell and broke her wrist. Did you know that?" Olivia had become expert at listening to the talk on the playground as she and Kari walked around before school and during lunchtime. She seemed to know all the news.

"No, I didn't hear that. One of these days I would like to have a party for my nameday."

"When is your birthday? Wait, did you say *birthday* or something else?"

Kari smiled. "I said *nameday*. My birthday is in March but my nameday is May 9. That's in about a week, and I hope you will come for dinner at my house then."

Olivia stopped in the middle of the sidewalk and looked quizzically at Keri. "I don't understand. Is a *nameday* the same as a *birthday*? And I didn't know you already had a birthday. That means you are twelve; older than me now."

Kari reached back and pulled her forward. "My family still sticks to the Polish ways because Babcia thinks it's important we follow those customs. Birthdays are celebrated, but namedays are really more important. I was named after Karolina, who was a Catholic teacher or something, I think. Her feast day is May 9, so that's when we celebrate. But Babcia's older sister was named Karolina too, so there's that. Anyway, see if you can come," and Kari, sure that Olivia understood all this, stopped at the corner of her street. "Are you going to walk me home and go through the alley?"

Olivia turned the corner with her and asked, "What's a *feast day*?"

"It's like when saints are remembered. I think it's the day they died, but I'm not sure. Babcia says I am being ruined by this public school, but there isn't enough money to send me to a Catholic one. Check with your aunt and make sure you can come over May 9."

Olivia nodded and tucked this strange information into her head. If she could talk to Dad, or Uncle Terry, or Anne, one of them could explain it all to her. Since coming to Chicago, she had only been to church with Aunt Gladys and the rest of the family a few times. And she sure didn't remember all this talk about feast days and celebrations of saints at Everstille Methodist Episcopal Church. There were the beads called a *rosary* Kari's Babcia had, and a cross was hanging in their dining room with dried ferns behind it, but these were never mentioned at Vacation Bible School. However, there was something more important on her mind.

"So, when would my feast day be? When is the name *Olivia* celebrated?"

"Not sure. I'll ask Babcia. She has a calendar with all that stuff. Here we are. Can you come in, or do you have to go home right now?"

"I have to go. Aunt Gladys is mad because I accidentally broke a glass when I dried it last night, so she told me to come right home. I'll see you tomorrow. Don't forget to ask Babcia about my feast day," and Olivia waved as she walked through the side of the apartment, down the cracked skinny sidewalk, out the cinder alley, and over to Aunt Gladys' house where she would have to apologize for the broken glass. Again.

The next morning, Olivia was waiting outside Kari's apartment, anxious to find out her feast day/nameday. She wasn't sure what she would do with the information, but she was excited to learn about this strange custom.

"Hi," she greeted Kari, "Did you ask Babcia about my name day?"

"She said that her book of Polish namedays gives March 5 as *Olivia*'s celebrattion. I even asked her about your middle name, and *Anne* is celebrated on July 26. Are you Polish? Then it counts, but I don't know what country you are from."

"Here. The United States. I don't have another country. And, I don't know about my parents, so I'll just stick with what Babcia said. But one is past and the other is weeks away. I guess I'll just stick with my birthday, May 22. I looked it up, and it's on a Sunday this year, so at least I won't have to go to school. I'll probably have to go to my Aunt Ernestine's and have that dry old sponge cake she thinks is so great."

"Did you check on coming over on May 9? It's Monday, and we're having a special dinner that night."

"No, but I will," and disappointment in her plain United States birthday overtook Olivia as the two walked to school and waited by the red numbers to begin another day.

* * *

Monday came. Olivia had cleared the date with Aunt Gladys, and unsure what she should bring to give to Kari as a gift, and having no money anyway, she made her a card, decorated it, and wrote inside:

> To Kari,
> Happy May 9 Nameday.
> You are the perfect friend!

On the front, she had drawn a picture of the two of them standing outside Kari's apartment building. Kari's blonde hair and her own red hair identified them. Before she left, Aunt Gladys told her to *behave and be polite and be home by eight o'clock,* and as she walked out the back door and through the yard and across the alley at just before five o'clock, she grew excited. This was the first party she had been invited to since moving to Chicago. Unless you counted the dull family parties she was forced to attend.

Olivia entered the apartment building and went up to the second floor where she could hear laughing and talking in a foreign language. She knocked on the door, and Steve answered, "Hey, Olivia, come on in. Kari is over there by Babcia," and he pointed to the back of the dining room which was filled with people holding glasses and talking. She walked to Kari and stood there waiting while an older woman finished talking to them .

"*Wszystkiego najilepszego,*" said the woman to Kari and gave her another bouquet of flowers. Kari was holding two bouquets, and a third lay on the dining table, and she smiled at the woman and said, "*Bardzo dziekuje!*"

When she saw Olivia, Kari said, "So glad you are here! Let's go and put all these in some water. Then we can go to my room, and I can show you what I got."

Olivia helped Kari take the flowers into the kitchen where her mother was talking to another woman and checking things on the stove. They found two vases and a couple tall glasses, filled them with water, and placed the flowers into the containers. As they worked, another couple came into the kitchen with a handful of chocolate bars proclaiming *E. Wedel* on them, tied with red and white ribbons, and repeated the greetings Olivia heard. Once the couple left and the flowers were arranged around the rooms, the girls went to the room Kari shared with her grandmother.

Olivia took the card she had made for her friend and handed it to her saying, "I didn't know your nameday was going to be such a big deal. I wish I had a gift for you."

Kari took the card and smiled. "Thank you, Olivia. This is great. You really made the apartment building look exactly like it is. Don't worry about a gift. I have lots of flowers and candy, and we can share some. I'll bring one of the chocolate bars in my lunch this week. Look. This is what I wanted to show you. Mama and Tata gave it to me. It's *bursztyn*," and she pulled out a necklace that had slipped inside her blouse.

Olivia examined it. It was a piece of amber shaped like a small cross, hanging from a gold chain. "Wow, it's really pretty. What did you call it?"

"*Bursztyn* means *amber*. It comes from Poland. Isn't it pretty? Look how it shines in the light," and she stretched the chain out and held it to the lamp.

Olivia admired it again and touched the smoothness. She remembered the indigo necklace given to her by Uncle Terry and swallowed a sudden lump in her throat.

"It's a great gift. I usually just get underwear or some dull clothes. Will you wear it to school?"

"No, I'm supposed to save it for church and special occasions, but tonight I get to show it off." Kari placed the card from Olivia on the dresser. "There. I can see it from my bed. Thanks so much, or *dziekuje*!"

"That's *thank you* in Polish?"

"Yes. Say it: *dziekuje.*"

"Dziekuje."

"That's good. Let's go out. Mama should have the dinner ready. I don't have to help because it's my nameday. That's why so many people are here."

The group had quieted down, and when Kari came out, there was clapping and cheers, and she was urged to go first in line and fill her plate with the food that was waiting along the counter and on the stove. She pulled Olivia next to her, handed her a plate, and the two of them took their food, found a place in the corner to sit, and began to eat.

"Wow, this looks so good," claimed Olivia. "I know this is Polish sausage and pierogi, and these are potato pancakes. What is this?" and she pointed to a piece of fried food on her plate,

"That's Babcia's *kotlet schabowy*. It's pork breaded and fried, like *schnitzel*. I asked especially for that because it's my favorite. Do you like it?"

"Mmm," muttered Olivia with a mouthful. "This might be my favorite too. Your mother and grandma sure know how to cook. This is Monday, and dinner at home is yesterday's left-overs. This is SO much better!"

They completed their dinner and took the plates into the kitchen where a friend of Mama's was busy washing them. They returned to the corner and discussed the amber necklace, the happenings at school, and as everyong finished eating, Alex came over and took Kari's hand.

"Come on, *siostra*, time to sing to you." He pulled her to the front of the group and amid laughter and clapping, the group began to sing "Stol lat", wishing Kari *good wishes, good health, may you live one hundred years*. This is what the song meant, as Kari explained later to Olivia. And while Olivia didn't know the words, she clapped along when the song was finished. Kari then spoke to the group and her family, but Olivia didn't understand what she was saying because it was in Polish. She heard the work *dziekuje* spoken a few times, so she knew thanks were offered. She wasn't prepared for Kari to wave to her and ask her to join her, and was surprised when she said, in English,

"This is my best friend, Olivia. She was the first person in the entire school to welcome me when I was new, and I am so happy she is here tonight!"

Happiness spread throughout Olivia. This was one of the few times she really felt welcomed in the strange place, Chicago. She turned to Kari and hugged her, and Kari hugged her back. Then it was time for cake.

"This is *szarlotka*, apple cake, and Babcia makes the best one I have ever tasted. She made it especially for me. Come on, here's a piece for you and one for me," and Kari filled the plates again.

As people said their good-byes and began to leave, Olivia looked at the clock in the kitchen and saw that she needed to leave. She didn't want to get in trouble with Aunt Gladys. She waited until Kari said good-night to another woman, and then she spoke up. "This was great, Kari, but I better get home. Aunt Gladys said I had to be there by eight and it's almost that time. Thank you for inviting me. I should say good-night to your parents and grandma. Come with me?"

They found the women in the kitchen, and Olivia spoke to them. "This was a great party. Thank you." And then she smiled and said, "Dziekuje!"

The women laughed, and Kari's mother said, " You are such a good friend to my little Karolina. You are welcome here anytime! Keep coming, and soon you will be speaking with us in Polish!"

Good-byes were said; plans were made for meeting the next morning. Kari walked Olivia out the front door, around the side of the apartment building, back on the skinny, cracked sidewalk, and waved to her as she crossed the cinder alley to enter Aunt Gladys' house.

Olivia walked to the front room where Aunt Gladys and Uncle Dean were watching television. "I'm home," she said.

Without turning around, Uncle Dean asked, "Did you have a good time?"

"Yes, it was a great party."

"That's nice," said Gladys. "Don't forget to make your lunch for tomorrow. Baloney is in the refrigerator," and she laughed at the television program.

"I will. Good night."

There was no answer because the two of them continued laughing at what was happening on the television screen. Rose came down the stairs and pushed Olivia to the side and began to complain about Ivy hogging the telephone when she wanted to make a call. Olivia left the three of them and went to the kitchen to make her lunch. She took the peanut butter out of the cabinet, ignoring the disgusting pinkish baloney on the second shelf of the refrigerator, and quickly make her lunch which she then placed into the folded paper bag. She went up the stairs, still listening to Rose complain about the telephone call she needed to make, washed up, got ready for bed, and went to her bedroom.

The door closed, Olivia opened the small closet, reached in the back and pulled out her suitcase. She opened it and felt in the back for the jewelry box hidden in the zippered part. She opened it and took out the indigo teardrop pendant on the long silver chain and watched, as in the light from the desk lamp, the colors of dark blue, some purple, and a bit of green sparkled and shone, bringing bittersweet sensations to her almost twelve-year-old heart.

May 21, Almost Name Day

"Don't forget to be at my house at five o'clock," and Kari waved Olivia through the side of her apartment building, down the skinny sidewalk and out to the alley.

"I'll be there. I wish you would tell me why."

"It's a surprise. See you tomorrow." And Kari went in through her front door and up to her apartment.

Olivia walked through the back door of Aunt Gladys' house and went into the kitchen for a glass of water. She peeked into the front room where Aunt Gladys was standing, watching the television, and periodically wiping some dust from the furniture with the cloth in her hand. Because Gladys was no longer working, she spent much of her time in the front room with the television on.

"Hi, I'm home. Aunt Gladys, did you remember I am going to dinner at Kari's house tomorrow night?"

Gladys looked over her shoulder at Olivia and nodded her head. "Sure, that's fine. Take the garbage out, and then sweep the front and back porch. I just didn't get to it today," and then she turned back to the set.

Olivia completed the tasks and then went to the kitchen. Since Friday was left-over night, and Ivy worked, and Rose was out with friends, dinner was on her own. She checked the refrigerator and decided that a bit of leftover spaghetti and some of the Italian sausage that had been served with it would do. She got out a pan to heat up her dinner, and was careful to clean up everything afterwards. She didn't want to get in trouble and not be able to go to Kari's house the following night.

Saturday brought the usual chores: changing the linen and re-making the bed, and then washing, drying, and putting away the breakfast and lunch dishes. Ivy's work schedule and Rose's whining meant the job had permanently been turned over to Olivia. She then had a bit of homework to complete and because the day was so springy, she walked around the block. She was hoping to see Kari the three times she passed her apartment, but apparently, she was busy inside. Kari had clearly said that she would not be able to see Olivia until Saturday when she came over at five o'clock, but there was always a chance.

At four-thirty, Olivia went to her room and changed her clothes. She looked through her closet and saw the clothes she had brought with her to Chicago. None of them fit now, and she was stuck with the dull clothes bought for her or handed down to her from Rose and Ivy. She found a pair of dark green slacks and a white blouse and put them on. At least she would put something colorful in her hair. She combed it back into a neat ponytail and found a colorful cloth belt from one of her old dresses. She would use it as a ribbon around her ponytail. However, she would wait until she left the house to tie it on. She had tried that a couple of times, and Aunt Gladys made her take it off. "You look tacky with that," said Gladys. Olivia folded it and placed it in her pocket.

She went downstairs and found Uncle Dean in the kitchen. He was removing the hot dogs he was going to grill for dinner from the package. He glanced at her and said, "Going to miss my world-famous dogs tonight, I hear. Well, have a good time," and then he called out, "Gladys! Olivia is leaving."

From the back bedroom, Aunt Gladys yelled, "Be home by nine o'clock. And behave."

Olivia walked out the back door, out into the cinder alley and up to the side of Kari's apartment building before she pulled the belt/ribbon out of her packet and tied a bow on her ponytail. Now, she was ready. She opened the front door, walked up to the second floor, and knocked on the Pinkus' apartment. Kari opened the door.

"Hi. Here I am on time. I missed being with you today."

Kari didn't completely open the door for Olivia but kept it closed and stood between her and the apartment. She smiled and said to Olivia, "Close your eyes before you come in. Promise you won't peek? It's a surprise."

"What is it?"

"Just do what I say," and when Olivia closed her eyes, Kari took her by the hand and led her into the apartment. "OK. Open your eyes!"

There was a colorful sign that had been taped together and decorated with flowers and butterflies, Kari's signature doodles, which read: Happy NameDay, Olivia! Delicious smells were floating out from the kitchen, and the dining table had been set for dinner. Fresh flowers decorated the table, and Kari thrust another bunch into Olivia's arms. Babcia, Mama, Tata, and Steve stood around her and clapped as Olivia opened her eyes.

She looked at the sign. "What is this? I don't have a nameday."

"Yes, you do," and Kari pulled her over to sit at the head of the table, the place of honor. "We decided that because tomorrow is your birthday, we would make this day, the day before, your nameday. Babcia made your favorite foods, and Alex will be in from work soon.

We wanted you to have a special day. *Wszystkiego najilepszego!* All the best to you, Olivia!"

Olivia grinned and sat down in her place. Just then, Steve came in the door, walked over to her, and placed half a dozen *E Wedel* chocolate bars tied with red and white ribbons into her hand. He greeted her with the traditional greeting, then went to wash his hands as Babcia and Mama began to bring in dinner. When everything was on the table, and everybody was seated, Kari's father stood and raised his glass and spoke.

"We are happy you are here and thankful you are such a good friend to our Karolina. We all wish you *Sto lat*, and here is to your continued long life and health. *Na zdrowie!*"

Everyone picked up a glass and wished Olivia, *Na zdrowie!* and then dinner started.

It was a wonderful night. Olivia and Kari and the family laughed and talked, and Alex and Steve entertained with stories, and Olivia thought she had never been so happy. At least not since Everstille.

When the plate filled with kolacski and the apple cake were brought out, Olivia didn't think she could eat any more, but she found she could. And when it was time for her to go home, after she had thanked everyone by saying *dziekuje,* she left with her flowers and candy and a large bag filled with wrapped cake and cookies. Kari walked her to the alley and waved and watched as she went home.

She walked into the house and saw Aunt Gladys and Uncle Dean watching television. Rose and Ivy were out.

"I'm home."

Uncle Dean looked over and asked, "Have a good time?"

"Yes. I did. Here are some cookies and cake I brought home if you would like some."

"That's nice." said Aunt Gladys, "Put them on the counter. Don't forget, tomorrow we are going to Aunt Ernestine's for your birthday. Get ready for bed."

Olivia placed the wrapped sweets on the counter and looked for a tall glass. She took it upstairs for her flowers which she put on her desk. The candy bars were examined, and she found a secure place for them. *Rose won't be getting her hands on these,* she thought. She was ready for bed and lay on top of the sheets thinking about the evening: the surprise, the dinner, the gifts, the family. It had been a good night. She felt happy. She fell asleep whispering *dziekuje, dziekuje, dziekuje.*

May 22, Olivia's Twelfth Birthday

On Sunday, they went to Aunt Ernestine and Uncle Amos' house. Neither Ivy or Rose came because they had plans with friends. The dinner was roast beef which was dry, mashed potatoes which lacked salt, and a variety of canned vegetables with extra salt. Olivia didn't get a choice of cake, but Aunt Ernestine served the dry sponge cake she made for all the family birthdays. There was no frosting, but the vanilla ice cream helped.

There was a combined birthday gift from the aunts. Olivia knew better than to hope it would be a colorful summer outfit or the cute orange and yellow striped sweater she had mentioned to Aunt Gladys. Aunt Ernestine handed it to her and said, "Happy birthday, dear. With age comes wisdom, we hope."

Olivia opened the box. There was a navy-blue sweater under the tissue paper. It would be useful for the fall weather. There were also new socks. White.

"Thank you," said Olivia.

Grade 7

"…and aren't you mad at her for that?" Kari was listening to Olivia's complaints about Rose again. They continued walking together to and from school even though they were not in the same seventh-grade class.

"Yes, but I am used to her name-calling, and most of the time, I ignore it. She just calls me *Clown* now although never in front of Aunt Gladys or Uncle Dean. It's better, lately, since she has a part-time job at the drugstore. Sometimes I'm the only one home, and that's good. I wonder about the next few years because this year, Ivy graduates from high school, and next year Rose does."

"What will happen then?"

"Not sure, but I think Ivy wants to marry Jeff, and Rose keeps talking about going away to college. That makes me think about my future and how long I have to stay at that house."

Kari glanced at her friend. "Do you want to go away to college? That would be one way of getting away."

"I don't know. I want to go back to Everstille. That's my real home, and I miss it. I miss Uncle Terry and Anne, and don't know what they are doing. There are still times I hear the phone ring, and I wonder if one of them is calling me. I wrote some letters and asked Aunt Gladys for stamps, and she said she would mail them, but I never heard back." Olivia kicked the stone in front of her as they turned down Kari's street.

They were quiet until they arrived in front of Kari's apartment.

"Can you come in? You can test me on my spelling words, and I can test you on yours."

"Maybe later. Aunt Gladys said to come home after school. She's going out with some friends this afternoon and said I needed to get dinner started tonight. I'll call later if I can come. Otherwise, see you in the morning."

Down the side of the apartment and over the skinny cracked walkway and out the cinder alley to the door, which was locked. Aunt Gladys must not yet be home, so Olivia took out her key and opened it. No problem with it now. She perfected the keyhole jiggle over the years. She read the note on the counter listing her required chores. She put her books down, washed her hands, got out the potatoes, filled a pan with cold water and placed the cut potatoes into it. Thursday night. Meatloaf night.

She turned the oven on and got the meatloaf out of the refrigerator. Then she examined the cans of vegetables in the cabinet. She took the can of peas and carrots to the sink, opened it, and poured it into another small pan. The table needed to be set, and she set it for five although she wasn't sure if either Ivy or Rose would be around for dinner. There were a few dishes to be washed, and she began that task when she heard someone come in. It was Rose.

"Hey, Clown. Glad to see you're doing your chores. Meatloaf night. Great. You would think Mom could change the menu sometimes."

Olivia didn't turn around, but continued to wash the dishes.

"Did you see my white cardigan, Clown? I thought I left it in the laundry room, but it's not there."

Olivia didn't turn around, and she didn't answer.

Rose looked at her. "Clown, did you see my sweater?"

Without turning, Olivia said, "My name is Olivia."

Rose stopped looking for the sweater and stared at her cousin's back. "Whatever, Clown. You didn't answer me. I asked, did you see my sweater, CLOWN?"

Olivia turned and faced Rose. Over the past year, Olivia had grown, and they were the same height. Her eyes met Rose's, and there was something in them that Rose had not seen before. Without raising her voice, but taking one step towards Rose, Olivia spoke again, "I am tired of you calling me names. My name is *Olivia*. If you want to speak to me, do it correctly. You don't call me *Clown* in front of your parents, so you know you're wrong. MY NAME IS OLIVIA," and her voice became strident.

Rose stood still. She hadn't realized until just now that she and Olivia were the same height. She hadn't seen those shards of green in her cousin's eyes until today, and Olivia had never replied to her in this manner. Something had changed in the last year, and she wasn't prepared for it. But she recognized it. Then she spoke, "Well, Olivia speaks. Fine. Your name is Olivia. Olivia from Everstille. Did you see my sweater?"

Olivia looked at Rose. She had won although she wasn't quite sure what or how. She continued looking at her cousin, green shards moderating, said, "No," and turned back to the sink to complete the dish washing.

Rose turned away from the kitchen and stomped up the stairs. Olivia washed and rinsed the last glass which she then placed on the dish drainer. She reached over to the side of the counter, lifted the dish towel, and wiped her hands on Rose's white sweater.

Christmas, 1966

Silence fell around the house, and outside Olivia's bedroom window, she watched intermittent flakes enter her vision and sink downward. Detached wetness did not form white piles on the ground. Not yet. Snow was not predicted yet. But soon. In the new year snow would lurch and plummet and plunge to the earth covering the city with a massive snowfall, stopping all traffic, ending work, and school, and travel, forcing winter to be unkind. But that was in the future.

She curled under the extra blankets, thinking through the evening. The five of them had gone to Christmas Eve church service, bundling up against the stony iciness to enter the sanctuary steeped in frigidity because it was night and dark and raw. They sat together, crammed in the pew with another family, singing carols with the congregation. Afterwards, Uncle Dean drove around the neighborhood as they looked at the lighted houses, decorated to greet the season, to welcome the solstice, to bring a sparkle to the wintriness. That was earlier in the evening. Before the silence fell.

She knew now what to expect in the morning. Pancakes and bacon and juice and coffee would fill the table as they gathered to break their fasts, still wearing the warmth of winter nightclothes, and welcoming the amiability of the kitchen, everyone awash in seasonal pleasantness. Then a clean-up of the dishes and themselves, and a gathering in the front room for the gifts. And she knew by now there would be three for her. Two of them sensible, colorless clothes, practical and utilitarian. And the one gift she wanted, that she hoped would be there. A new book inscribed with a promise and a task and signed with the initials: A.O.R. That would happen when the night became light and the moon gave way to the brightness.

The schedule for the remainder of tomorrow was also known. A car ride to Aunt Ernestine's and Uncle Amos' large red-bricked house where family she had not seen for months would gather. Her older male cousins, Enoch and Otis, and their wives, and the toddler which Enoch and his wife had produced, would assemble. There would be noise and laughter, talking, and questions to answer, and she would find a place to hide and begin to read the inscribed book she brought with her. There would be a dry turkey surrounded by its companions: mashed potatoes and dressing and Jell-O molds and vegetables of all sorts. And later, Aunt Gladys' cookies and Aunt Ernestine's dry sponge cake would appear. And she would be encouraged to eat up, eat more, because she didn't eat enough. But the food would present a problem when she tried to swallow it. And it wasn't just the dryness of the meal or the saltiness or lack of salt that caused it. It was memory. It was the thought of Uncle Terry's cooking that made it difficult to chew and swallow and enjoy. But that would be later tomorrow.

And then tomorrow at night, after returning, after the leftovers were put away, after the family gathered in the front room, after Ivy's boyfriend, Jeff showed up, after a Christmas program was turned on and the volume turned up, she would be required to sit with them. There would be laughter and talking, a rehashing of the day, a discussion of the family issues, and everyone would have an opinion or a say-so or a comment, and she would sit quietly in the corner, waiting until it was late enough and dark enough to leave. She would thank them all, and be a *good guest,* and disappear upstairs to ready herself for bed, not caring anymore if they quietly and furtively deliberated about her and her moodiness and sullenness and mentioned her churlishness. After all, they took her in, gave her a home after her father, poor Tobias, died. That would happen tomorrow night. Not right now.

Right now, she was alone and not yet asleep. Her bed was warming up with her body's heat, and her eyes were shutting and opening and then shutting for longer periods of time. This was her time. It was not in the recent past or the near future or the far future time yet to come. It was memory time for her. She was thinking to the long-ago past. To the time when she was with her family. Sitting, with her father and Uncle Terry and Anne, playing a new board game she had received, or listening to Anne read the story from the new Golden Book, or resting and becoming warm when drinking hot cocoa that soothed them all because they had been outside, making snow angels and snowmen or simply walking in the afternoon light, working off some of the delicious, perfectly seasoned, not dry dinner Uncle Terry had cooked. She allowed these memories because it was Christmas Eve, and this was her gift to herself. And tomorrow would be here too soon. And she would be too sad. And for now, just for tonight, she would close her eyes and dream of an indigo room in an old Victorian house in a small town where she longed to return.

Grade 8

To their delight, after a few weeks of school when there was some combining and reorganization of classes, Olivia and Kari ended up in the same eighth-grade classroom. And became seat-mates. Mr. Larson, their eighth-grade teacher, allowed the class to choose whomever they wanted to sit next to because the desks were movable, and he didn't care where they sat. He was young, having taught for only three years, and was considered, by the students, the premier teacher in the upper grades. Not the best. That would be Mrs. Sadowski, a veteran of many years who ruled with a stern look and a soft voice, but Mr. Larson was the favorite. The girls were happy to be together, to walk together to and from school, to study together most nights, and to spend weekends together. They took advantage of every minute together because when high school days arrived, they would be separated. Permanently. They just did not know it yet.

Eighth Graders ruled the school, and although Olivia and Kari were on the bottom rung of the eighth-grade student ladder, they felt the power that came with position. In the years the two of them had cemented their friendship, they had enlarged their bond to include a few of the other such minor girls and sometimes walked home with Kate or Marion or Pam. While they accepted expanded acquaintances, those attachments were never serious. Not like the closeness felt with each other.

Eighth-grade brought privilege. There were fieldtrips and graduation plans, and dresses to be bought. Olivia felt lucky to be allowed a new dress for the luncheon the PTA would be hosting for the graduating class. She had her eye on a blue dress. She wanted the scarlet one, but knew that Aunt Gladys would refuse that request. All graduating girls were to wear white dresses for the actual graduation, and Aunts Gladys and Ernestine were busy remaking Rose's white dress from her graduation four years previously. "Waste not, want not," Aunt Ernestine repeated.

"I can't go shopping to Kresge's on Saturday," explained Kari as they sauntered home in the early spring weather, taking their time because it was…early spring weather, "My family is taking a ride to look at more houses."

Kari's parents were considering a move to a house of their own, and this was making Olivia nervous. "You are? Where are these? I didn't know your family was serious about moving. I thought they had stopped looking at houses. When did this happen?" Olivia felt suddenly panicked. What would she do if Kari moved? Who would she have as a friend?

"I'm not sure where the houses are. My parents have been saving money, and dad is working two jobs, and they have been talking about moving for a while. But I'm not sure that will happen. We are just going to look. Anyway, maybe we can go after school one day next week. Do you think your aunt will let you?"

"I'll see. I just wanted to look and see what they have. Ivy works there, and she said if I find something, she can use her employee discount to get it for me." Olivia had been given a small weekly allowance at the start of eighth-grade, and she was careful in her spending of it. It was meant to teach her to budget, and one dollar did not go far.

"I wanted to look for a blue headband to match my luncheon dress and maybe a new hairbrush. But it can wait until you can go with me. Will your whole family move?" Olivia was less interested in the shopping trip now that she had heard the disturbing news.

"Yes, I am sure they will. Alex is working full time and said he could help pay for the house while he lives there, and when Steve graduates from high school this year, he can get a job where Alex works. But don't worry about it. I think we are just looking."

"I forgot, Rose and Steve are in the same class. Wow, all of us will graduate this year. I'm nervous about high school, are you?"

They discussed the coming high school year and graduation activities and Alex's new girlfriend, and parted when Olivia came to the skinny cracked sidewalk and the cinder alley which led to Aunt Gladys' house. She was worried about losing her best friend, her only real friend, but there was nothing she could do about it. Perhaps Kari's parents were just looking, like Kari said.

One month later, just a few weeks before graduation, Kari's parents found a house. It was in Chicago, but quite a distance from Olivia. The house was close to the southwestern edge of the city where one large street separated the sprawling city from small suburban villages. Although the house was not brand-new, it included enough bedrooms for Kari to have her own. The move had Kari both excited and upset. She would be attending a brand-new high school by herself. She wouldn't know anyone and would have to learn how to take an unfamiliar bus route to the school. And she would miss Olivia who was despondent. This news put a damper on the graduation excitement. And then there was the announcement of the date and times for graduation. Olivia and Rose were graduating on the same night. At two different places.

"I know you understand, Olivia, that we are excited for both you and Rose, but Rose is our daughter." Gladys explained the situation to Olivia. "Uncle Dean and I will be going to her graduation, as will Ivy and Jeff, but it will all work out. Aunt Ernestine and Uncle Amos said they would attend yours. They'll pick you up that night and take you, so you'll have family there. Afterwards, we'll all meet back here to celebrate both graduations. I am getting Italian beef for sandwiches, and Ernestine is picking up a special decorated cake from that good bakery close to her. Now, go and change into the white dress so I can check the length."

Scattered thoughts filled Olivia's head as she walked up the stairs to put the dress on. It was fine. A used dress, but now she didn't care. She didn't care who went to her graduation. And she did understand. She understood that she was a distant third in the line of girls. Ivy had recently become engaged to Jeff, and the wedding was planned for next summer. Rose had been accepted to a small college and would be living there. She was the first one to attend college, and the only happy thought Olivia had was that she would be gone in August. But then so would Kari. August fifth was the last day she would see Kari and her eyes filled with tears whenever she thought of it. Only a little over two months with her best friend. Why was she always losing everyone?

"Come on down and let me take a look at it," called Aunt Gladys, and Olivia walked down the stairs. "Yes, that will do. It looks fine. Perhaps Ernestine can take it in a bit more here, and here, and you seem to be taller than Rose was when she wore it, so let me see the hem," and Gladys pulled and pinned and stood back to examine things. "Hmm, that will work. Now go take it off and bring it back down. And then, better get those dishes done."

On graduation day, Olivia's feelings were mixed. She was both eager and indifferent about her graduation ceremony. She had been quiet all afternoon, listening while Rose chattered on the telephone with one friend and then another and bounced from mirror to mirror examining her hair and deciding upon which hair style was best to wear with the black mortarboard she put on and took off a dozen times.

"Of course, eighth-grade graduation doesn't have a cap and gown like high school does. I suppose in four years you'll wear one. But then, I guess I'll wear another because I'll be graduating from college. What do you think? Does this look better?" Rose in her excitement, forgot that Olivia was her enemy, and when Olivia shrugged her shoulder in answer, Rose said, "Oh, what do you know, Olivia from Everstille? Just an eighth-grade graduate," and went back to her bedroom to restyle her hair.

The family was finally ready, and because Rose needed to be at her high school earlier than Olivia needed to be at the close-by elementary school, they left, leaving Olivia alone in the house.

"Ernestine called, and she is on her way, so you won't be here too long by yourself. We'll see you later," and Aunt Gladys ushered the family through the front door and into the car. "Remember to lock the door and bring your key," she cautioned Olivia who stood there in Rose's hand-me-down white dress.

Ivy turned to her young cousin and smiled as she left. "You look nice, Olivia. Enjoy your ceremony and congratulations!" Ivy was older and kind.

Olivia watched as they drove off and then sat down at the kitchen table. She felt underneath the neckline of Rose's dress for the indigo teardrop necklace she had hooked around her throat just before coming down the stairs. She could not wear it outside the dress where it would show. It was her secret, and she didn't want to explain it to anyone, especially Aunt Gladys whose sharp eyes would see it and question her. It was Olivia's talisman. It was her reminder that someone had loved her; that she had once had a different life, a colorful life, a favorable life. It was her private joy.

Within fifteen minutes, Uncle Amos and Aunt Ernestine drove up in their car. Olivia watched as they got out of the car. Ernestine, carrying in a large bakery box, stepped back as Amos opened the door for her. She yelled out, "Hello, we are here," and as she saw Olivia, said, "Let me get this into the refrigerator and make sure it's safe."

She moved the white bakery box into the refrigerator on the rack under the Italian beef and macaroni salad and then turned to Olivia. She looked her over and nodded her head. "You'll do," she said, and then looked at Amos and instructed, "Now, let's get this show on the road!"

They left the house, and Oliva locked the door. She climbed into the back seat of the car and sat carefully on Rose's white dress so it would not wrinkle. She fingered her indigo necklace, hidden under the neckline of the dress and stared straight ahead as Uncle Dean began the short drive to the elementary school, to Olivia's eighth-grade graduation ceremony.

Days: Name, Birth, Moving

Nameday

As Olivia speared the piece of cheese-filled pierogi and dipped
it into the sour cream piled on her plate, she tried not to think that this
could be the last time she would eat this. It was Sunday evening, May 21,
and her nameday was being celebrated with the Pinkus family. Everyone
was seated at the dining room table enjoying the meal created by Kari's
mother and grandmother, and talking about graduation and summer,
and, of course, the move to the new house. Alex's girlfriend, Julia, was
present, and Alex was being teased about when the two of them would
be married. Julia blushed, and Alex glanced at her, and the entire family
laughed. Olivia was happy. And she was sad.

"This is so delicious," she remarked after she ate all she was able
to, "Thank you for doing this for me again. I love this tradition and really
appreciate it. *Dziekuje!*"

Babcia reached over and patted her cheek and replied, "*Prosze.*
You are very welcome!"

Kari's father lifted his glass and motioned for the others to do so
as he said, "*Na Zdrowie*, Olivia. *Sto lat!*"

"*Sto lat!*" repeated the rest, and they sipped and clapped.

Kari and Olivia went to Kari's room while the older women
cleared the table and readied the dessert. Olivia knew she would be returning to Aunt Gladys' house with a large dish filled with extra kolaczki,
and she was glad because tomorrow night, for her birthday, Aunt Ernestine and Uncle Amos would be over after dinner, bringing the traditional
dry sponge cake. As they waited for the dessert summons, the girls talked
about the upcoming graduation luncheon, and Kari showed Olivia her
new dresses: pink for the luncheon and white for graduation.

"Since both you and Steve are graduating the same night, how is
your family doing that? What will happen?

"Girls with girls and boys with boys is what my dad said. Babcia
and Mama are coming to mine, and Dad and Alex are going to Steve's.
That's how we're working it out. What's happening with you?"

"I don't know yet," said Olivia, "and whatever happens is fine. I
just wish Anne and Uncle Terry could be here, but since that's not possible, I don't care. The good thing is that Rose will be leaving for college
in late August, so I won't have to put up with her too much longer. Ivy is

planning her wedding next summer, and Aunt Gladys is busy with both those things, so I'm left alone most of the time. That's fine with me."

"Well, once we move, you can visit. Maybe on weekends and then during the summer and vacations, you could stay overnight. Don't you think that's possible?"

"I hope so," Olivia replied, sniffing back tears, "I sure hope so."

Birthday

"…Happy Birthday to you!", and everyone ended off-key and clapped apathetically as Olivia blew out the candles. There were only eight of them because that was all Aunt Ernestine could find to bring with her, and Aunt Gladys said she didn't have any.

"Well, I just don't know where the rest of them are. You know what they say: *Things are never lost to you; you are lost to them.* Guess that means I'm lost!" and she laughed although no one else did.

Olivia had no choice of cake. Aunt Ernestine served the dry sponge cake without frosting. Vanilla ice cream was offered. There was a combined birthday gift from the aunts. When Olivia opened the box, she lifted the tissue paper and found a beige cardigan. There was also a beige pleated skirt. And a new half-slip. White.

"Useful for high school," said Aunt Gladys.

Aunt Ernestine nodded and said, "I understand many high school girls are wearing these outfits, and when in Rome…"

"Thank you," said Olivia.

Moving Day

Saturday, August 5, was designated as moving day. But that changed for Kari, her mother, and her grandmother who were moving Thursday, August 3, in order to begin the cleaning and organizing. Babcia's bed would be moved there, and Kari and her mother were going to sleep on piles of blankets until the rest of the furniture was delivered and set up. Kari would be gone two days earlier than Olivia thought. While she did not want to take away Kari's excitement about a new house and her own bedroom, Olivia could barely stop crying while in her own small room each night.

On Wednesday before the move, the girls spent the day together. Olivia had saved as much of her allowance as she could to treat Kari to lunch and give her a gift. Ivy's store discount allowed her to do both. She spent many hours after school at Kresge's jewelry counter examining the various necklaces and bracelets and rings that were there. Many were too expensive; some were too large; others were too ordinary. She finally decided on a bracelet. It was delicate and graceful. It was made of small, dainty white plastic daisies sprouting a bright yellow plastic middle. The clasp looked sturdy, and Olivia was sure it would look lovely on Kari's wrist. She knew it would fit because she had tried it on her own, admiring it often. If she had more money, she would have acquired another for herself. The daisies decided her. She had searched for meaning, and the daisy flower symbolized *friendship and love*. This was the perfect gift.

The Kozy Koffee Kafe, just a couple of blocks from their houses was the perfect place for Olivia and Kari to have their meal. It was warm outside, but fans were stationed throughout the inside of the restaurant. They were lucky enough to get the booth back in the corner where one of the fans gently shifted side to side, bringing a soft tepid breeze, to their table. They had discussed what they would order, and decided that the cheeseburgers were the best thing on the menu. They came with fries which were piled high on the plate, covering the stack of dill pickles and the thin tomato slice and the wilted lettuce, none of which would make it onto the burger. The waitress brought over a a fresh bottle of ketchup for them, and when the chocolate milkshakes arrived, each had two neon red cherries resting on top of the piled, fluffy whipped cream. Straws and almost clean glasses were set down with the check which Olivia picked up and moved to the side. She knew what to do, having eaten many times at Mazie's in Everstille, watching what Dad or Uncle Terry or Anne had done. She was prepared.

For some time, there was no speaking except to ask for the salt or ketchup or another napkin from the silver holder at the end of the table. It was four o'clock in the afternoon, and the girls had decided this time would be perfect, being after the lunch rush and before the dinner hour. Afterwards, they would spend their time walking the neighborhood, traveling to the elementary school, and reminiscing about those days. They took their time, eating slowly, attempting to consume as much of the meal as they could. They had decided if they could not finish everything, they would stop the eating and concentrate on finishing the milkshakes.

Plates pushed to the side, they slurped away at the shakes and sat back in the red leatherette booths and smiled at each other.

"That was great. Thanks, Olivia. Best meal I've had all day!"

They giggled and drank some more and then discussed what the next day would bring. Kari explained that Steve would drive them to the new house early in the morning so the cleaning and organizing could begin. He would pack as many things as he could get into the small truck he and Alex shared, and then later, he would return with Babcia's bed and additional items. Right now, the women were cooking and packing food for the next few days so they would not have to stop and make meals. As soon as they had a telephone installed, she would call Olivia with the new number, but that would not be for some weeks. They could write letters though, and when Kari found a phone booth, she would be sure to keep change in her pocket so she could telephone. They discussed and planned, and, as the diner began to get busy and the waitress was no longer smiling at them, Olivia paid the bill, leaving a tip at the table, hoping it was enough, and they left.

They crossed the busy street at the corner light and walked slowly around the neighborhood, weaving through the small park that had three swings, although one was broken, and a slide. They ambled through the school yard, looking for the red paint, pointing out their old room numbers. As they peeked into the lower windows, they giggled and ran when a custodian moving a large floor polisher looked up at them, and then they strode back to the path they had taken home every day for the past three years. As they got to Kari's corner, Olivia suggested, "Let's not go to your house just yet. Walk to the bench at the park and let's sit there for a while."

At the park, ignoring the young boys who were chasing each other up the slide and then sliding down on their stomachs, they moved to the bench. Kari kicked a browning banana peel under the slats. They sat down, and Olivia reached into her purse and pulled out the package she had wrapped carefully in aluminum foil and tied with the red ribbons she used to place in her hair before being told by Aunt Gladys that they were *tasteless*. She held it out to Kari. "I hope you like this. They symbolize friendship and love, and I thought it would be a perfect gift."

Kari took the package, carefully opened it, and held the daisy bracelet up. She smiled and handed it to Olivia while holding out her wrist. Olivia took it and fastened it to her arm, and Kari grinned as she moved her wrist around allowing the gold in the bracelet to catch the late afternoon sun, glistening and shimmering.

"Oh, Olivia, this is perfect. I love it. Thank you so much. I wish I had thought of something for you," and Kari bent over to hug her friend around her neck.

"Kari, you and your family have already given me so much. You have no idea how happy I was when you got to the school. Fifth grade was awful. I felt so alone. I'm glad you and your family were able to get such a great house, but I'm sad you are leaving. Please promise we'll stay in touch."

"I promise. I was so scared when we moved here, and then I found you. We both got a good deal." She looked again at her bracelet and then picking up the wrapping and the box. "We better get back. I know I have to get up early in the morning and still have packing to do."

Olivia and Kari got up, walking down the familiar street, and said another good-bye. They went through the side of the apartment building, on the skinny cracked sidewalk, out to the cinder alley, and Kari watched as her best friend pushed open the gate and entered the back yard. Olivia stopped and turned around. The girls looked at each other one last time and waved. Olivia darted into the back door and directly up the stairs to her small bedroom as quickly as she could. Rose was standing at the entrance to the kitchen speaking to Aunt Gladys who was in the front room, and she did not want either of them to see or stop or question her. She went into her bedroom, opened the window over her desk, and turned her fan on, allowing a breeze to fill the area. Olivia lay on her bed thinking about the day, permitting tears to flow down her face and, without changing her clothes, turned her head on her pillow and fell asleep.

Early the next morning, before the household was up, Olivia awoke and moved to her desk. She peered out her window into the gray morning light and looked over to the apartment building across the cinder alley. She could not see out to the front of the building, but she strained to hear voices, and thought she could just make out the voice of Kari's grandmother speaking in Polish. She stayed there until any discernible sound had faded, and the gray light had become clear and steady.

Grade 9

One letter and two phone calls later, high school began for both Kari and Olivia, except they were in different parts of the city, attending separate schools. Olivia walked to the bus stop, and while there, she would sometimes talk to Marion or Pam. But while these girls were friendly enough to her, they were not her friends. She had lost Maggie and now Kari, and was hesitant to embark upon another attachment. Despite her loneliness, Olivia thought her life somewhat improved. Rose was gone.

College claimed Rose the last week of August. Uncle Dean and Aunt Gladys packed Rose's many suitcases, bags, and necessary supplies, garnered from a list sent to incoming freshmen, and set off one Saturday morning to deposit Rose in the care of higher education. As a parting commentary to her cousin who was watching from the front porch, Rose looked back and said, "Bye, CLOWN," and smirked at Olivia.

The sight of Rose leaving for months delighted Olivia, so she ignored the remark. A thorn removed from her side. For a while. Ivy, who was older and kind, was working at Kresge's, now as a department manager, and saving money and making plans for her wedding which would take place next summer. Because Ivy was so busy, and Aunt Gladys had found neighborhood friends with whom to spend most of her days, Olivia was often left alone in the house, and she savored her privacy. She completed her chores and her homework, went for long walks in the neighborhood, always passing Kari's apartment building, read, and planned her future. She wasn't exactly sure what she would do when the time came, but the time would come. And she would know.

High school turned out to be easier than she had been warned it would be. If she kept up with her studying, completed homework, and turned in all her assignments, the classes were not difficult. *All this talk about how hard and complex it would be was stupid*, she thought. But then keeping up with her studying, completing homework, and turning in all assignments was the key. Olivia settled into her new educational circumstance with a minimal amount of distress. And she began to save money for what she thought of as her *escape*.

One day, the week before she began high school, after Uncle Dean had come home from work, Aunt Gladys called him into the kitchen, and they sat down at the table with Olivia. She counted out four dollars for Olivia. This was her school allowance. It was to be used for bus fare and lunches, and if she were careful, there would be some left for spending. After all, that was what the dollar allowance during eighth grade had been for: to teach her to budget.

"Now," explained Aunt Gladys, always the expert. "This is what we told our daughters: if you spend wisely and are careful, there will be money for you to buy odds and ends you may want. Or you can save for something more expensive. This will take care of your bus fare back and forth, and pay for a school lunch daily. If you want to make your own lunch and save the money, that is your choice. We think this will help make you a responsible person. Do you understand?" Aunt Gladys pushed her hair back as she spoke. She recently began a weekly regimen at a local beauty shop to get her hair and nails done, but she was not used to the new hairstyle her stylist had talked her into. *I'm going to go back to my old hairdo next week*, she mused to herself.

Olivia thought back to all the whining Rose had done and the new items both girls always seemed to have, but said nothing about those recollections. "Yes, Aunt Gladys, I understand," said Olivia.

"Of course, now that you are older, and we are giving you this allowance, there will be additional chores we want you to complete."

Olivia cocked her head and said nothing. She waited for her assignments.

"With Rose at school and Ivy working full time and planning a wedding, you need to continue with the dishes and garbage duty and occasional tasks I leave you to do in the afternoons when I am not here." Gladys and her friends had decided to form a bi-weekly afternoon card club and sometimes, the afternoons ran into early evenings. "Uncle Dean leaves very early in the morning, and he has been starting the coffee for us, but you are old enough to do that, so in the morning, get up a few minutes earlier and put the coffee pot on. I just love to wake up to the smell of coffee brewing."

"OK."

"And on Saturdays, you are going to take over laundry duties when Ivy has to work the weekend. These tasks are not very difficult, and you will learn from them. Dean, wasn't there something else Olivia was to do? Do you remember what it was?"

Uncle Dean who had the newspaper spread out in front of him wasn't paying attention, and when he heard his name, turned to Gladys and said, "Hmm? What was that, Glad?"

"I said, what else was Olivia going to do?"

"I think you named it all," and he went back to his paper.

"Well, I'll think about it. Any questions, Olivia?"

"No."

"Fine, and this begins tomorrow. So, no lazing in bed on your last week of summer. Get up in the morning and get the coffee started. Now, help me with dinner. Get that pot out for spaghetti. And then make the salad."

Olivia did as she was told. Four dollars! She would have to sit down and figure out exactly what the costs for a week of school would be, and once she got to high school and learned about the lunchroom process, she suspected that making her lunch and bringing it would be what she would do. After all, she had been doing that for almost four years now.

Olivia did make her own lunches. During the weeks Aunt Gladys bought ham instead of baloney, she would make two or even three sandwiches and hide a couple of them in the refrigerator for later in the week. Otherwise, cheese and crackers or peanut-butter would do. Except for Thursdays when the school lunchroom offered pizza. She bought her lunch that day. A few times during the year when the sun was bright and the weather pleasant, she would walk home from school and save that twenty-cents. The walk took thirty-minutes, but she didn't mind it. It gave her a chance to see the neighborhood and to travel past the Kozy Korner Kafe where Kari and she ate their farewell meal. Once a month, she would stop in and treat herself to a chocolate milkshake. The waitress got to know her, and when Olivia came in, the milkshake making was begun. And Olivia always left a small tip.

Thanksgiving came, and Rose was home for the week. But she was so busy seeing friends and telling her family about her brilliant start at college, that she had little time to tease or even speak to Olivia who was grateful for the ignoring. On Saturday afternoon, Rose went to the Skate-A-Round with friends, and Ivy was out with her fiancé, Jeff, and the weekend passed quickly. Sunday afternoon Rose was piled into the car and returned to school. Then the Christmas holiday came and went with the usual traditions being observed. Winter. Then spring. And in the late part of spring, Olivia's art class went on a fieldtrip to the Chicago Art Institute where part of her past showed up.

There were three school buses traveling from the high school to the downtown museum, and on her assigned bus, Olivia shared a seat with Sarah from her homeroom. She and Sarah had three classes together, and this was as close to a friend as Olivia had. After their last period class, they walked to the bus stop, except Sarah crossed the street and took the bus traveling in the opposite direction of Olivia's ride home. But on the fieldtrip day, they sat together holding their lunch bags and the assignment the teacher had given the classes.

"Great," complained Sarah, "an assignment. Meant to ensure we don't have a good time, I bet. Miss Hanson is a real peach. Anyway, we can figure this out together. I'm sure this is just busy work for us. Think so?"

"Probably," answered Olivia, and they continued to talk about inconsequential subjects until the bus dropped them off at the museum's entrance where additional directives were given.

Olivia and Sarah completed their assignment and spent the remainder of time walking, talking, and examining artifacts from the *Arts of Africa* exhibition. Then, lunch in the lunch area at the specified time, and then a line-up with the school group, as they waited for their buses. It was a tranquil day outside, and the girls stood at the front of the group, talking, and glancing up and down Michigan Avenue when Olivia suddenly heard her name.

"Livie! Livie, it's me!"

She turned around and saw a student she didn't know push through the crowd to get to her. His face was familiar, but she couldn't place it immediately. And then he spoke and memories flooded her.

"Livie, hi! It's me, Mike. Mike Jasper. I saw you and tried to get your attention before, but you weren't looking my way. How are you?"

"Mike! That's right, you live in Chicago. I'm fine. It's been a long time."

"My class is here too. This place is so big, I'm surprised I could see you. How…"

"JASPER, GET BACK HERE!"

Mike turned and saw a teacher motioning to him. He glanced over his shoulder and waved his hand so that the teacher knew he heard, then turned back to Olivia.

"I have to go. It's great to see you. Maggie will be thrilled when I tell her. She's a freshman at Everstille High School."

"How is Maggie? I miss her. I miss the great times we had."

"She's fine. I don't spend summers there like I used to, but we get to see my grandpa and the family a few times a year. Where…"

"JASPER. WE ARE LEAVING. GET BACK HERE NOW!"

Mike waved again to the teacher, and turned to go. "Wow, think about us running into each other. Have to go. You look great, Livie. Take care. Maybe I'll see you again," and he ran towards his bus but then stopped and shouted back, "I KNEW it was you because of your HAIR," and he waved again.

Olivia waved and shouted, "Bye, Mike!" and watched as he got on the bus while the teacher who called to him continued to yell.

Sarah looked at Olivia. "Who was he? He's cute. And what did he call you?"

"He is a friend from Everstille, a place I used to live. My family there called me *Livie*, but no one here does. He would spend part of the summer with his grandpa in Everstille and is a cousin to my best friend from there, Maggie."

"What school does he go to? Where does he live?"

Olivia shrugged her shoulders. "I don't know. I knew he lived here, but I'm not sure where, and I don't know what school he goes to. We didn't have time to talk."

As the buses pulled up and the students got on and took seats, Sarah and Olivia sat down and arranged themselves for the ride back to school. Sarah began to talk about something, but Olivia wasn't paying much attention. Periodically she looked at her seatmate and smiled and nodded, but her mind was not in Chicago. It was in Everstille in a tent made of blankets, where the indigo sky was illuminated with sparkles, where laughter was shared, where contentment filtered through her being, and fireflies flickered nearby.

Summer Wedding

It was almost two A.M. as Olivia took off the beguiling teal-colored semi-formal dress with cap sleeves and a full skirt. After shaking it out, she arranged it on a hanger and placed it on her bedroom door hook. Tomorrow when she got up, she would bring it downstairs so Aunt Gladys could take it to the Clooney Cleaners Monday morning. She had been careful with it all day, and it looked new. What a night this had been. What a week! A couple days ago she had no idea that she would end up being a bridesmaid in Ivy's wedding, and now that the wedding was over, and she had been a part of it, she was exhausted and was going to bed. She had never been up this late, and Aunt Gladys said she should sleep in tomorrow. She and Uncle Dean would also, and they would relax until the afternoon. That was when they would go to Saint Camillus Hospital to visit Rose.

Rose was meant to be one of the two bridesmaids at Ivy's wedding. The other one was Sharon, Ivy's best friend. Sharon completed her duty as bridesmaid, but Rose was unable to. She had broken her ankle while skating with friends at the Skate-A-Round Roller Rink on Thursday, and since the wedding was Saturday, there was nothing to be done except make Olivia the substitute bridesmaid. This only added to Rose's agony.

"But why?" cried Rose to Aunt Gladys on Friday morning as she lay in the hospital bed using all the tissue in the box on top of the hospital bedtable. "I can just use a crutch or even a wheelchair. Please! Please!" and she dissolved into sobs again.

"Rose, I am sorry that this is what has to happen. You can't put any weight on your ankle, and the rehearsal is tonight with the wedding tomorrow at one. There is nothing to be done at this point. I'm sorry, but this is Ivy's wedding and we must consider what is best for her. Daddy and I will see you after tonight's rehearsal dinner and call you tomorrow. We'll be here Sunday afternoon and bring you a big piece of wedding cake."

"I want to get the cake myself, and I don't want Olivia wearing my dress!" Gladys looked around the room to find another box of tissue which she opened and placed on the bedtable.

"Honey, I am just as sad as you are, but this can't be helped. Olivia is about your size, and Aunt Ernestine is coming over in an hour to help fit the dress on her. I promise it will be cleaned and fixed and ready for you to take back to college this fall. Now I need to get back. Here, give me a hug." She reached over to hug Rose who didn't want to let her go. Gladys had to remove Rose's arms from her neck as she kissed her cheek again and left saying a final, "We'll see you later," as Rose loudly blew her very red, almost clown-like, nose.

She walked to the elevator and pressed the button while glancing at her watch. Ernestine should be on her way. What a mess this was! While she felt bad for both Rose and Ivy, she couldn't help feeling just a bit angry at Rose for what had happened. No, it wasn't on purpose, but she had asked Rose to NOT go skating with her friends and stay home to help with the final wedding preparations. Rose had been working at the drugstore as a summer job, and she had the week off for the wedding. She told her mother that she deserved some fun, and would be back later, and then fell and ended up in the hospital. The doctor explained that while the break was a stable fracture requiring a short leg cast, she would not be getting the cast on immediately and couldn't put weight on it anyway. She would be fine to return to school in August, but the summer would be spent healing and doing some therapy. And complaining. Gladys was sure of that.

Olivia had been astounded at all the preparations needed for a wedding. She watched and listened to the myriad of calls and meetings and arguments which had comprised the wedding planning for months. She doubted that Miss Kendal's small wedding had been this complicated. Ivy's wedding guest list included one hundred people who would be invited to the evening reception and a full sit-down dinner at a local hall after the afternoon church service. A fancy wedding shower had been given by Sharon, Rose's friend, gifts were delivered to the house, and wedding favors needed to be fashioned and produced. Olivia helped whenever she was asked, and the amount of work that was needed to pull off this social event was startling.

On the day Rose and Sharon brought their bridesmaids' dresses home and showed them off in an impromptu fashion show, Olivia caught her breath and felt faint. The dresses were teal. The color was just a shade lighter than the teal suit her mother, Ruth, wore at her wedding, and almost the exact shade her bedroom walls in Everstille had been. Olivia quickly wiped away the tears that had sprung, unexpectedly, to her eyes, and let her breath go in a silent exhalation. The dresses were charming, and when the sweet hat-like veils, exactly matching the color of the dresses, were adjusted on the bridesmaids' heads, she felt a burn of lust in her heart she hadn't felt since seeing her orange monkey hanging from the tented bottle toss game at the carnival years ago. If only she could wear that dress. That color. That memory. And now, she had.

She didn't wish Rose harm. Rose had been doing her a favor and ignoring her since coming home from her first year in college. The girls had come to a tacit agreement that ignoring each other would be in both their best interests. An agreement that had worked. Olivia was shocked when Aunt Gladys told her that because of Rose's accident, Olivia would not be wearing her newly bought beige dress. The dress matched the beige dresses of Jeff's young sisters, and the three of them were going to hand out wedding programs at the back of the church to wedding attendees. But after Rose's accident, Jeff's sisters would complete the task themselves, and Olivia would walk down the aisle wearing the teal gown. Aunt Ernestine would be coming over to help fit the dress on her. Olivia was a bit thinner and an inch taller than Rose, but the dress would do. Some careful loopy stiches would be placed in appropriate seams, and Olivia would just have to wear her new beige shoes because Rose's dyed-to-match pumps were too large for Olivia's feet. There was nothing else to do.

After Ernestine completed the simple sewing tasks and Olivia tried the teal wonder on once more, the aunts stood back and examined their work.

"Hmm, yes she does look fine, Gladys. And those stiches can easily be removed before the dress is cleaned. They won't even be noticed, and Rose can wear the dress for her college dances. What do you think?"

"It looks fine, Ern. Come here, Olivia, and let's see what we can do with your hair. Obviously, a ponytail won't do. We need to get the veil settled on your head."

Between the two of them, Olivia's long hair was twisted into a knot at the nape of her neck. A few curls were brushed out to her face, and the veil was centered on her head. Olivia went to the bathroom mirror to see what she looked like and gasped. Her mother stared out at her. She had never worn her hair in this way, and as she looked into her eyes and slowly turned her head, she realized this was the way her mother had worn her hair. The teal color was perfect, and she felt grown-up and lovely, both new feelings for her.

She came out of the bathroom. She wasn't glad her cousin had been injured, but she was ecstatic to be in the teal gown. And her beaming face showed it.

"You do look good in that color," said Aunt Ernestine, "but, pretty is as pretty does, so you will need to behave and be careful with this dress at the wedding."

"I will," said Olivia. And through the ceremony and the photography and the greetings and the feasting and the dancing and the smiling…the breezy, blithe, buoyant smiling…she was.

Grade 10

With Rose at school and Ivy living with Jeff in a rented apartment on the north side of the city, Olivia realized an independence not known before. True, she had additional chores to complete, but she didn't mind the dishes and laundry because there were only three people in the house now. Uncle Dean left early each morning and returned late each evening when he relaxed with his paper and television. Aunt Gladys continued her afternoon card games and weekly hair appointments, and recently, had become involved with a neighborhood volunteer group whose purpose was to support and help raise civic awareness, although most of their work involved sharing recipes and gossip. However, those activities kept Gladys busy and gave Olivia treasured freedom.

She missed Kari, but had found no replacement. While some phone calls and a few visits helped retain a friendship, Olivia knew that distance changed relationships. And recently, Kari had acquired a boyfriend which created another shift in their bond. But every May 21, Olivia received a call, some of Babcia's kolaczki, and a wish for *Sto lot* for her faux nameday.

High school was boring. But because Olivia kept up with her studying and homework, her grades, while not spectacular, were respectable, and she stayed out of trouble. Aunt Gladys never had to visit the assistant principal as she had done in the past, due to Rose's antics. While Olivia never discovered friends to match the caliber of Kari, there were some girls and a few boys she walked alongside of and spoke with as she traveled from class to class or to the the bus stop after school. Olivia was not one to join in the school activities or football games or dances. She lived a solitary existence by choice.

She read or went for long walks, or sometimes watched television when Uncle Dean or Aunt Gladys were not at home; she did her chores and kept her room clean, and sat on the back porch watching the squirrels jump from tree to tree; she swept the sidewalks even though she hadn't been asked to, and neatly folded the towels and dish cloths; but mostly, every morning when she got up a few minutes earlier to put on the coffee so Aunt Gladys could awaken to the smell of it, she noted another day had passed. She waited and marked the time, and was grateful for each new day because she became a day older, and slowly, sometimes too slowly, was becoming an adult.

Kozy Koffee Kafe

"....and a side of fries, please, Gail,"

Gail, the head waitress at the Kozy Koffee Kafe, looked at Olivia and nodded as she placed a glass of water in front of her, grabbed the silver milkshake cup and yelled "Ordering frog legs" to Billy the cook. "Special occasion?" she asked Olivia.

"Not really. Last week of school and there's not much going on there. My cousin is getting married next weekend, and my other cousin is home from college, and I just don't want to be around her today. Just feel like some fries. Or *frog legs*."

Gail laughed. She had come to like this girl who stopped in for a milkshake every few weeks. Sometimes she would just get a Coke, and a few times she had ordered a hamburger. Olivia was always pleasant and not snotty like some of the high schoolers who came in, and she always left a small tip. She sat at the counter by herself, and over the last couple of years, Gail found herself smiling when she saw Olivia push open the door. She finished the shake and placed it on the counter with the hot fries. It was a quiet Tuesday afternoon, and there wasn't much to do, so she talked to Olivia as she consumed her food.

"So, are you in the wedding?"

Olivia swallowed her sip of shake and shrugged. "I guess so. Ivy's fiancé has two younger sisters, both in grade school, and the three of us are going to hand out the programs at the back of the church when the guests come in. I did get a new dress and shoes, so that's something. But it's a plain color, just beige. It looks nice on me though."

Gail nodded. "I'll bet beige with your coloring would be great. I remember my wedding. My sister stood up and wore a navy suit. Of course, that was a while ago. Be back; let me wait on these people."

Olivia turned and watched as an older couple came in and sat down at the far booth. The one she and Kari sat in for their luncheon the day before Kari moved. Olivia sighed. She still missed Kari. Since Kari got a summer job babysitting, she didn't suppose she would see her too many times this summer. Gail placed the bread basket down in front of the couple, refilled their coffee cups, and came back to Olivia. She began wiping down the counter and checking the salt shakers while they talked.

"I'm sure you will have a good time at the wedding, Olivia. They can be fun. Any other plans for this summer?"

Olivia finished the French fries and shook her head. "Nothing fun. I'm not sure what I will do this summer. My best friend will be busy with a babysitting job, and I don't suppose I'll see her much. Maybe I should look for a job. I'm just not sure how to even begin, and I'll probably have to wait until after the wedding when all the jobs will be gone. Aunt Gladys is keeping us all busy doing stuff for it. In fact, I should get home now, I guess."

Gail looked thoughtful. "How old are you?"

"I just turned sixteen a few weeks ago."

"Sixteen? Well, that's old enough to get a job. How would you like to work here? We're busier in the summer months, and Billy back there has been talking about getting someone part time to help with the dishes and cleaning. If you don't mind a not-so-glamourous job, it's a start. I have an *in* with Billy because he's my cousin, and this is a family business. What do you think?"

Olivia looked at Gail and smiled. A job! And that meant more money. It would be helpful because Aunt Gladys said that during the summer she didn't really need as much weekly allowance as she got during school, and two dollars was sufficient. Cleaning stuff and doing dishes were things she was prepared to do. She did them all the time at home.

"Really? That would be great. I can do dishes and clean. That's what I do anyway. But I couldn't start until after the wedding. Would that be a problem?"

"That will work out. We will probably only need you for the weekends and maybe one day a week at first, and then we will see how things go. Let me get you some papers to fill out, and why don't you plan on coming in on the Tuesday after the wedding? That's a slow day, and I can train you and show you the ropes," and Gail held up her finger as Billy yelled, "Order up!" and Gail went to pick up and deliver the meals to the couple who were sitting at the booth. Then she went to the back to speak to Billy who looked over at Olivia and gave her a wave. Olivia waved back.

"Here you go, Kiddo. Fill these out and follow the directions and bring them back with you on…June 30? Right?"

"Wow, thank you, Gail. That's great. I promise I will work hard. Now I better get home," and Olivia reached into her purse and brought out her wallet to pay.

Gail held out her hand in a stop signal. "It's on the house today, Kiddo. Think of it as a late birthday present. Here, write down your full name, address, and phone number so I have that information. Tell your aunt if she wants to call and talk to me about you working here, she can."

Olivia took the pencil and paper and wrote the information down for Gail. She passed it back to her and smiled. "Thanks again, Gail. And thanks for the birthday treat. It sure was better than the dry cake my Aunt Ernestine always makes. I'll see you in about two weeks. Really, you won't be sorry; I'll work hard."

"I'm sure you will. Hey, don't you want to know what the job pays?"

"Sure. How much?'

"Not much. It will start out at $1.10 an hour. How does that sound?"

Olivia grinned. "Sounds great," and she waved as she left.

Gail grinned back at her and waved. Then she went to the man who had just come in with the twins and took their order.

Grade 11

"And how did Driver's Ed class go?"

Gail was talking to Olivia while there was a brief lull in the Saturday springtime crowd at the Kozy Koffee Kafe, Olivia's job for almost a year. She had proven she was a hard worker during last summer, and when given the chance, became adept at waitressing. She was so capable that Gail was able to take a few wanted days of vacation and not worry about the diner falling apart. Olivia worked during the weekends, at least one night during the week, and filled in on holidays. Her salary had increased, and the tips were good. So good that Aunt Gladys, after discussing it with Aunt Ernestine, stopped giving her any allowance. "Well, a penny saved is a penny earned," and with Ernestine's sage counsel, the decision was solidified.

"Got an *A*, but still can't drive. Uncle Dean has the car for work although Aunt Gladys keeps bothering him to get another for her. Anyway, there isn't anyone to take me out to practice driving, but that's fine. Between school, chores at home, and working here, I'm busy."

"Well, glad you are keeping up with school. Told my two boys they needed to work hard when they get to high school in a couple years. Giving any thought to your future? College? You don't want to work here forever. It's my family business, but it's not yours."

Olivia was wiping the table and checking the ketchup bottles. She stopped and turned to Gail. "No, I don't know about college. Right now, I just want to work and save some money."

Gail nodded. "I guess you have some time. Saving for a car?"

Olivia shrugged. "Something like that."

Gail laughed. "I remember those days."

Olivia smiled. She wiped the table and the seats, and pocketed the quarter tip.

Grade 12

The late August summer day was warm, but there was a decent breeze drifting through the open windows. Aunt Gladys was in the dining room searching through family photographs and organizing them into several large albums she had stacked beside her. The television was turned to an afternoon program and offered faint chatter although no one paid much attention to it. Olivia had the day off from work and was finishing up the breakfast and lunch dishes and enjoying the semi-silence. Rose was back at college, and there was peace in the house. In a week, her senior year of high school would begin, and as she completed her chore, Olivia deliberated about it. It was Friday, left-over night, and no dinner preparation needed to be completed, so Olivia was thinking about taking a book and going out to the back porch to read when Aunt Gladys called to her.

"Olivia, I ran out of scotch-tape. Would you check on the desk in the laundry room for more? I thought I saw some there the other day. Thanks."

Olivia put the last plate away and wiped her hand on the dish towel before she walked into the laundry room. At the back corner of the room, next to the side door which led out to the backyard, was an old desk used for storage. No one ever sat at it because there was no chair and the top was crowded with an assortment of objects. Olivia had never paid any attention to it, but she went to the desk and moved a few things around looking for the tape which she did not see.

Perhaps there was some in the drawer, so she pulled open the middle drawer. Only a couple broken pencils and some old receipts were there, so Olivia closed it and pulled open the top side drawer. Nothing except a few rubber bands and a stack of index cards yellowed with age. There was a deeper drawer under the top side one, and she attempted to open it, but it would not budge. She pulled it again and nothing happened. She was ready to give up when she remembered that sometimes these old desks had a trick lock, and if you pulled open the middle drawer, the locking devise would allow the stuck drawer to open, so she tried that. Once she yanked on the deep side drawer, it flew open, and there was the tape.

She picked up the tape which was on top of a stack of envelopes bound together by rubber bands and was surprised to see her name written on the top one. She put the tape on top of the desk and reached into the drawer, pulling up a stack of envelopes bound together. As she pulled them up, some postcards fell out. They were addressed to her. She glanced at the message side and caught her breath when she saw the signature. They were from Uncle Terry. Olivia gathered and counted the postcards. There were nine of them. All addressed to her. All signed by Uncle Terry. She looked at the envelopes which were also addressed to her. One was opened; the remainder were sealed. She counted them. Fifteen. The return address was listed with the initials: A.O.R. Anne. There were a few more letters which were familiar because they had been written by her to be sent to Anne and Uncle Terry. These were the letters she had given Aunt Gladys. The ones she asked her to stamp and mail. The ones Aunt Gladys had told her she would send. They hadn't been sent. They were here with the envelopes and postcards. Stacked together. Bound with rubber bands. Next to the letters from Anne and postcards from Uncle Terry. Proof that she had not been forgotten.

Olivia felt her hands grow cold as she clutched the letters and postcards. She pressed then to her chest which was beating faster than she ever remembered it beating. Thoughts spun through her mind and she wasn't sure what she should do. Could do. Would do. And then Aunt Gladys yelled.

"Olivia! Did you find that tape? You've been gone forever! Where is it?"

Olivia walked into the dining room with the stack of mail. She stood in front of Aunt Gladys, blocking her view of the television, and waited until her aunt looked up at her.

"Did you find…" Gladys stopped in mid-sentence when she saw what Olivia was clutching. She sat back on the dining room chair, dropping the photograph she was holding on top of the album page which shut itself. A quick breeze blew a couple loose photos of Rose when she was a baby to the floor where they were ignored. There was an uneasy silence as Olivia accusingly held out the packet of mail.

"These are mine. You didn't give them to me. Why not?"

Gladys let out a deep sigh. She looked down at her lap and then up at Olivia. "Olivia, we tried to protect you. I'm sorry you found those. I should have thrown them out because they will only cause you sorrow. You don't know how difficult it's been to raise you correctly all these years. When my poor brother died…"

"You had NO right to hide these and certainly no right to destroy them. These were sent to ME. All these years I wondered about why the only thing I heard from my family was a book at Christmas, and…"

"Olivia, they are NOT your family. We are. They had no right to you, to interfere, to poke their noses in our business, to show up here unwanted, to call and call and demand to speak to you. We protected you. You don't know what a terrible person that Douglas man is, how he changed poor Toby, how he took advantage of him, how he…"

"STOP IT! You kept this from me. Maybe I wouldn't have spent all these years wondering about Anne and Terry if you had been honest. Thinking I had been forgotten. These are MINE. And if any other letters or postcards ever come here to me, you HAD BETTER GIVE THEM TO ME!" Olivia took a deep breath. She was determined not to cry. She stood up straighter and took a breath. "I can't talk to you anymore. I can't even look at you," and she went to the stairs, walked quickly to her room and shut the door.

She went to her bed and spread out the mail. She placed then in order according to the postmarks. She started with the postcards from Uncle Terry. She discovered he had sent three the year she was ten, three the year she was eleven, and two the year she was twelve. They were postmarked from different states. The last one was sent when she was thirteen and was postmarked from Montana. Uncle Terry had not stayed in Everstille. She had no idea if he was still in Montana. Four years and no additional postcards. Not that any of them were very informative. He loved and missed her. He was fine, and someday, someday…

She turned to the letters next. Some had obviously not been sent in the mail, but her name and the year of the letter was in the corner. She figured out that Anne had included a letter with each of the books for Christmas, and another had been sent around the time of her birthday, May 22. Two letters each year filled with news from Everstille about the people and her friends and Maggie and the library and the festivals. Advice and jokes. Thoughtful ideas. Stories about her mother, Ruth Evans Pinkerton. And always, always assurance that Olivia was loved and missed, and they would be together again sometime. Fifteen letters. The latest one being sent just three months ago for her seventeenth birthday. On that birthday when the dry sponge cake was served, and her gift was a black sweater. To wear in the fall. Olivia read through the postcards and letters twice, and then placed them in the order they had been received.

She looked at the letters she had written; the ones never sent. She didn't open those. She knew what they said. It had begun to be dusk, and she heard voices downstairs. Uncle Dean was home and murmured conversation was heard. She wondered if he knew about the letters. Perhaps he was as guilty as Gladys. She turned on the small reading light next to her bed and sat still just looking at the mail. Now that she had read them, she felt better. Still angry, but better. She had to think.

Footsteps sounded on the stairs. They stopped at her door. There was a gentle knock, and Uncle Dean said, 'Olivia, why don't you come downstairs? You should eat something, and Aunt Gladys and I want to talk to you. I'm sure this can be worked out."

Olivia liked Uncle Dean. He and Ivy were kind in their disregard of her, but she would not be swayed. He knocked again, and asked, "Olivia? Are you alright?"

She spoke to him then. "I'm fine, and I'm not hungry. Really, I just want to sleep. I have the breakfast shift at work tomorrow and need to be there early. I'm fine."

There was a silence at the door and Uncle Dean said, "OK. But come on down if you want something to eat. Or if you want to talk. Good night." The footsteps marched down the stairs, and Olivia heard additional quiet discussion, and soon the muffled sound of the television drifted upstairs.

Olivia noiselessly left her room, went to the upstairs bathroom, and got ready for bed. When she returned to her bedroom, she took the packet of letters, and pulling out her suitcase, placed them inside. Then she put the luggage as far back in her closet as she could, covering it with the extra blanket she used in winter. She set her alarm, turned off her light, and lay down. She thought about her life. Her future. Soon she would be eighteen. Less than a year now. As she drifted off to sleep, she formed a plan. Only a partly thought-out one, but she had time. Most of a year.

Early the next morning Olivia, after dressing and pulling her hair back into a knot at the nape of her neck, went downstairs. It was a cool morning, and the ten-minute walk to the Kozy Koffee Kafe would be comfortable. She turned on the water, filling and drinking a glass, then held the coffee pot under the faucet. She measured out the ground coffee into the basket receptacle, pushed the lid down and plugged it in. She pressed the *on* button, and as the pot began to heat up, producing the wonderful coffee smell Aunt Gladys wanted to wake up to, Olivia gently opened, then shut the side door.

She started to the diner where, smiling and pretending to be someone she was not, she would wait on the customers, pour their coffee, deliver their eggs or pancakes, and thank them for coming. Then she would clean and ready the table for the next customers, placing the coins left as a tip safely into her apron's deep pockets.

Birthday: Age 18

On Sunday morning, May 21, 1972, Olivia spoke for a long time to Kari who had called once again to wish her *Sto lot*. Kari had wanted to meet her, but Olivia told her that was not possible because she was working the afternoon shift. They spoke about the plans Kari had for the job she would be starting at the cleaning company where her mother worked and about the wedding her brother, Alex and his fiancée, Julia were planning.

"It's going to be great, and you'll be invited. It's in October, so make sure you can come. And plan on staying at my house overnight. Babcia is looking forward to seeing you."

Olivia was silent. She knew she would not be going to the wedding or staying overnight or seeing Babcia, but she didn't say these things. She simply listened to Kari talk and agreed with her about the plans. But before they ended the conversation because Olivia needed to get to work, she once more repeated her thanks to Kari for the years of friendship.

"Kari, your friendship has really helped me through these years. And make sure you thank Babcia for the kolaczki she sent. They are delicious. Tell her I said *Dziekuje.*"

They said good-bye and hung up. Olivia stood for a minute, her hand on the telephone receiver, thinking she didn't tell Kari everything she wanted to. Words secreted. Plans veiled.

On Monday, May 22, 1972, Olivia worked the afternoon/evening shift at the Kozy Koffee Kafe. She hadn't planned to, but Gail asked if she could take her shift because her oldest son was in a special school performance that evening. Gail's son was graduating from eighth grade and the class always put on a show for the parents. Olivia was glad to take the shift. She worked as often as she could. She told Gail to have a good time and came to the diner right after her last class. She never said anything to Gail about it being her birthday, and she had told Aunt Gladys she couldn't get out of work.

"Well, that's too bad, being your birthday and all. Ernestine said she would drop off the birthday cake. You can have a piece when you get home. We'll probably be in bed. I know that evening shift gets you home late."

While the relationship between Gladys and Olivia had never been warm, it had become decidedly frosty the past year after Olivia discovered the hidden letters. A few times Gladys attempted to discuss the situation with her, but Olivia shut down any conversation. She continued to complete her chores, do well in school, cause no problems, and Gladys thought everything was fine. It wasn't, but Olivia had become expert in pretending to be someone else. During holidays when Rose was home, Olivia worked as often as she could, and spent most of the time at home in her room. A truce held. And last Christmas, when Olivia found the book under the tree, Anne's most recent letter was inside the cover. Some things had changed.

Olivia and Billy closed the diner together. It was dark, and Billy offered her a ride home. "I know you don't live far, but it's late, and I can drop you off."

Olivia accepted the ride. She said good-night to Billy and used her key to enter the house. A light was on in the kitchen, and on the table was a wrapped gift. A piece of Aunt Ernestine's cake was on a covered plate with a fork next to it, and the unopened birthday letter from Anne was next to it. Olivia took the cake, threw it into the garbage and placed the fork and plate into the sink. She turned the kitchen light off, taking the package and letter upstairs with her.

In her bedroom, after getting ready for bed, she examined the gift, playing a guessing game. *Hmmm, probably another cardigan. Thinking beige.* She opened the box and looked inside. It was a cardigan. Grey. She left it on her desk, not even removing it from the box, and took the letter from Anne to bed with her. This was her real gift. She settled back to read it. It began: *Dearest Livie, I can hardly believe it, but you are eighteen today!*

Olivia read through the letter twice, then set her alarm and turned off the small lamp. She knew she would read it once again in the morning before putting it with the others. Olivia smiled in the dark. Eighteen. She was old enough. She would graduate high school in a week. She was ready. She had a plan. She knew what she was going to do. And, closing her eyes, Olivia laid her head on the pillow and went to sleep.

High School Graduation

Aunt Gladys was ecstatic. Ivy and Jeff were expecting a baby, the first grandchild, around Thanksgiving, and Rose, dear, smart, lovely Rose, was graduating from college. She and Dean were preparing to travel downstate to Rose's college for her graduation, and then stay a few days to help her move into the apartment she would share with three other girls. She was aware that Olivia was due to graduate from high school around the same time, but Ernestine could fill in just as she did for eighth-grade graduation.

"I know you understand, Olivia. Rose is our daughter and right now she needs our help. She's the first person from the family to graduate from college, and we are excited about this."

"Except for Dad. He was a college graduate too."

"Of course. Poor dear Toby. Could you get that empty box from the laundry room, please? Rose needs some kitchen utensils, and I have extra ones."

Olivia delivered the box to the kitchen and turned to go upstairs when Gladys spoke again.

"Olivia, make sure you call your Aunt Ernestine and let her know about the graduation date and time. I'm sure she and Uncle Amos will pick you up and go with you that night."

Olivia nodded and went upstairs. Graduation was next Wednesday night, May 31. She did not call Aunt Ernestine.

On that Wednesday afternoon, Olivia prepared for her graduation. She put on the new dress she had bought for herself and took her indigo necklace out of its hiding place. She arranged her hair in a knot at the nape of her neck, ensuring her mortarboard would fit and placed the necklace around her throat. For this graduation she positioned the silver chained teardrop jewel so that it lay directly against the whiteness of her dress. This time the dress was hers and not a hand-me-down. She gathered her purse and the black graduation robe and cap and walked to the bus stop to wait. The graduates were told to be at the school that evening by five to practice once more, and she didn't want to be late.

When the bus came, she got on, paid her fare, and sat down at a window seat. She looked out at the Kozy Koffee Kafe and saw it was busy tonight. There would be good tips for the new waitress who was taking her place. She had informed Billy and Gail that Friday would be her last day. They assumed she was going to college and would start early. She did not correct their assumption. She needed time to complete her plans, and because Aunt Gladys and Uncle Dean were due back Saturday, she needed to get things done before they returned.

Olivia watched the cars go by and examined the familiar buildings as the bus passed them, wondering if or when she would ever see them again. The bus stopped at her destination, and she stepped down the three steps onto the ground. She crossed the street and walked towards the big sprawling building where she entered the side door and walked down the corridor to join the other graduates. They began to line up, and smiling and pretending to be someone she was not, she took her place.

Monday, June 5, 1972

Olivia had been up for hours, but she remained in bed until she heard Uncle Dean leave for work. Once his car started and she knew he was gone, she began to cautiously move about. She had sorted and organized the things she would take with her, carefully choosing the items because she could not manage it all. Her suitcase was packed with needed essentials. Bulky pieces like the winter coat and boots would not go with her. They were old anyway, and she had restitched the coat pocket and resewn the buttons so often that it was not worth salvaging. The boots barely fit her. She had saved money, and when the time came, she would simply buy needed items.

A double paper bag with sturdy handles held the books. She could not take all of them, but the eight Christmas books from Anne were stored in the bag along with the packet of postcards and letters. Tucked into the side of the bag were two pieces of paper in a large envelope: her eighth-grade diploma and her high school diploma. Nothing else was required. She examined her purse once more to ensure that her money and other important articles and objects were safe. They were. At the bottom of her purse, nestled on top of the wad of bills organized by denomination in an envelope held secure by a rubber band, sat a velvety soft jewelry box. Everything was there. She had checked and rechecked and arranged and rearranged it all over the past few days. She was ready.

Olivia, as soundless as possible, prepared herself. Although it promised to be a warm day, she put on her new sweater. The one she bought herself. It was a lovely shade of blue. Almost teal in color. She left her hair down but pulled it away from her face with a white headband. Not wanting to make noise, she went down the stairs twice without her shoes to carry her belongings to the side door. Before her last trip down, she checked her bedroom, making sure she had left what she meant to and had taken what she required. She moved to the side door, lifted out her bag and suitcase, checked once again that she had it all, and without regret, engaged the lock on the inside of the door and shut it. She stood for a few seconds, took a deep breath, picked up her belongings, and walked directly to the bus stop which would take her Downtown.

During the past couple of days, while she was alone in the house, she planned her trip. She had not been to the Randolph Street Station before, but had the directions written down and trusted that she could follow them. It was there she would purchase the train ticket to South Bend. She knew the train schedule, and the cost, and had Anne's phone number written down on a piece of paper secured in the side zippered pocket of her purse. She lugged her belongings onto the bus, paid her fare, and asked the driver if she were headed in the right direction. She was. She just wanted to confirm it.

At the station, she waited in a short line and when the ticket agent asked if she wanted to purchase a round-trip ticket, she said, "No. Just one way, please," and handed over the $3.20 for the fare. Carrying her suitcase and sturdy paper bag, she walked over to track eight and waited for the signal to board. She would have liked to get a cup of coffee and a donut at the food stand, but didn't think her stomach could contain it because it was filled with fluttering butterflies. And when, at 9:00 A.M., the announcement came that her train, her 9:30 A.M. ride to South Bend was boarding, she picked up her suitcase and sturdy bag and upon entering the train car, found a single seat at the back where she organized her baggage and herself.

Olivia took deep breaths and tried to quiet her mind. She went over what she would do when she arrived at the South Bend station, how she would find a telephone, what she would say to Anne. She didn't allow herself to think beyond that because she could not. The phone conversation was as far as she had planned. She dared not go further.

The train began to fill with other passengers. She was glad she had been able to find a single seat. There was no way she would have been able to converse with a stranger; no polite small talk would be possible. As the train began its slow movement towards her destination, she sighed, and her heartbeat slowed. She watched out of her window, seeing the buildings and cars and then the wide spaces filled with trees zoom past. After fifteen minutes, when she was used to the movement and clang of the tracks, she began to relax. She opened her purse and from the bottom pulled out the velvety jewelry box. Opening it, she cradled the indigo teardrop necklace in her hand. She held it tightly for a minute or two, then unhooked it and moving her hair out of the way, placed it around her neck, against her throat, allowing it to rest on the white dress she had worn for her high school graduation. Looking at her image mirrored in the train window, she noted that the teardrop jewel reflected the blueness of her almost teal sweater, and as she watched the spark of sun against the window, she smiled.

***

Gladys opened her eyes and looked at the alarm clock next to her. It was nine o'clock! She had overslept, but then she had been tired. Dean's side of the bed was empty because he had left for work, and she sat up on her side and sniffed the air. Where was the coffee aroma? She sniffed again. She really needed a cup of coffee. The past week she had been so busy with traveling, and Rose's graduation, and helping to move her into that apartment, that she deserved the extra sleep. And now, she wanted a good cup of coffee. She slipped on her bathrobe, tying it as she slid her feet into into her slippers and walked to the kitchen. The coffee pot was exactly where it had been last night. There was no hot coffee waiting for her. No aroma. Nothing. And where was Olivia? Did she leave for work? Was she working today? Now that she was home, and no longer in school, they needed to sit down and have a talk. A serious one. She would ask Ernestine to join them.

Gladys walked to the bottom of the stairs and called, "Olivia! Are you awake? Are you there?"

No answer. Gladys called louder, "OLIVIA!"

No sound was heard. What's going on? Gladys pulled herself up the stairs and stood at the top. The bathroom light was off, and it was empty as were the two bedrooms in which her daughters used to sleep. The door to Olivia's room was partially opened, and she walked closer and peered in. It was empty. She pushed the door open and walked inside. There was something wrong. The bed sheets were removed and placed at the end of the bed. The blankets and pillows were folded on top of each other. One of the drawers in the chest was partly opened, and Gladys could see it was emptied. The closet appeared to be vacant except for a coat and a few winter things hanging towards the back. The room was unoccupied. Gladys looked around and tried to understand what had happened. Then she looked at the desk Olivia had used to do her home-work, the desk underneath the one window in the room. The window which looked out over the back yard, the garage, the fence, across the cinder alley to the apartments on the next block. There were some things on the desk.

A pile of Golden Books was neatly stacked at one side. On top was a note with the instructions: *These are for Ivy and Jeff's baby.* On the other side was the gift she and Ernestine had given Olivia for her recent birthday. Her eighteenth birthday. The gray cardigan was left in the open box, tags still on: rejected offering. And in the middle of the desk was an envelope. It was not addressed to anyone, but Gladys knew it was meant for her. She picked it up. It was unsealed, and there was a thin piece of paper folded in it. She removed the sheet and heard a *clink*. On the desk, released from the paper into which it had been placed was Olivia's key to the house. The same key she had been given years ago. The one she cried over because, until Ivy showed her how to jingle it, she had difficulty using it. Gladys picked up the key and stored it in her bathrobe pocket. Then she opened the folded paper. There were two lines of writing. The first line was a declaration. The second was a signature. It said:

I am going home.

Olivia from Everstille

III.
Everstille Again

All human wisdom is summed up in these two words: wait and hope.

Emily Dickinson

I pushed the hair back...

I pushed the hair from my face using the small brush I had in my purse, then pulled it back securing it into a pony tail. The June day had turned warm, and the nearly two-hour train ride had too. Leaving my hair down was uncomfortable. Once I lugged my purse and suitcase and bag from the train track, I entered the station and found the bathroom where I took care of my needs, washed my hands, fixed my hair, and took a deep breath. I was here. Almost home. Now I needed to find the telephones and make the call to Anne. I looked once more into the wavy mirror on the wall above the sink. I pulled the white headband out of my purse and placed it back on my head where the curly hairs were already starting to come loose in the heat of the day.

I walked out into the waiting room and looked around. Pay telephones were attached to the far wall, and I made my way there. Placing the bag and suitcase under one of them, I reached into my purse, took out some change, unzipped the side pocket in the purse and removed the slip of paper with Anne's number. I knew this was the correct one because she had ended each of her letters to me with these digits. Placing the required amount into the coin slots, I dialed the number. It rang. And rang again. And again. No answer. I hung up and received the coins back. I tried again, being more careful this time, thinking I might have misdialed. I heard the phone ring repeatedly. I allowed it to ring ten times and hung up. I panicked, and thought through my plan. This had not been an issue when I considered what to do.

I looked around. People were moving, going from one area to another. I only knew I was at the South Bend train station. I had no idea how I would get to Everstille. I glanced at the large clock hanging in the station and stared at it. It told me it was almost one o'clock. Then I realized my mistake. Indiana was an hour ahead of Illinois. And this was Monday. Anne was at the library working. Of course she wouldn't be home!

I took a deep breath and thought. If the library hadn't changed their telephone number in the past eight years, I remembered it. I placed the coins into the slots once more and dialed the library number. It rang twice, and a voice answered.

"Hello. This is the Greenwood Library. Anne Rivens speaking. How may I help you?"

I could not talk. Anne's voice hadn't changed, and I was lost in the past. I waited to hear her again.

"Hello. Are you there? You have reached the Greenwood Library."

"Anne?" I spoke up now, "Anne, it's me. It's Livie."

There was a silence. Then she asked, "Livie? Livie? Is this really you? Where are you? What has happened?"

"Anne, yes, it's me. I want to come home. I'm at the South Bend train station. The one on Washington Street. I need you to pick me up. Can you? Oh, Anne, it's been so long," and I swallowed a wail.

"Livie, why are you here now? What has happened? Are you safe? Are you well?"

I took a breath. This was not the time to explain eight years. "I'm fine. I'm eighteen and wanted to come home. To Everstille. Can you come and get me? We can talk later."

"All right. Let me think. I can't leave for about half an hour, and it will take me some time to get there. Why don't you relax and, let's see, it's about one…come out to the front of the station, at the Washington Street entrance about two-fifteen? I should be there between that time and two-thirty. Will that work?"

"Oh Anne, I am so glad to hear your voice. I'm wearing a white dress and a teal-blue sweater. I'll be waiting."

Anne laughed. "I assume you still have red hair, so I should know you!"

"Still red, Anne. I'll be waiting."

"Be there as soon as I can, Livie."

"I'm waiting. See you soon."

We hung up, and I felt happier than I had in years. Anne was coming to get me. I wasn't sure what I would do later or tomorrow or next week, but right now, I was waiting for Anne, and somehow, I knew, I just knew that it would all get figured out. I was going home.

We carried my suitcase...

We carried my suitcase and bag into the house which used to belong to Anne's parents but was now hers. They were set down at the foot
of the stairs which led to the upstairs bedrooms, and she turned to look at
me. I know I had changed, but except for a few gray hairs and a new pair
of glasses, Anne looked the same.

"Livie, I see your mother in you. I asked Gladys to please send
me a yearly school picture, but after you turned eleven, I never received
any more. There's so much to discuss, and we'll have time to do it, but
I need to get back to the library for a couple of hours. Let's bring this
upstairs, and I can show you your bedroom."

We went up the stairs and I followed Anne into the bedroom to
the left. There were three bedrooms and a bathroom upstairs, and Anne's
bedroom was the one at the top of the stairs. The bathroom separated our
rooms, and the third room was set up as an office with a desk and sitting
area.

"This is great. Thanks Anne. There are so many things I want to
talk to you about and to ask you. But first... about Uncle Terry. Where is
he? Do you know?"

Anne shook her head. "The last postcard I got from him was
almost two years ago. I kept all his cards, and I'll dig them out and let
you read them. We have so much to talk about, and I'm so glad you are
here. There are some leftovers and iced tea in the kitchen. Help yourself
and examine the house. Take a shower and a nap. I'll stop at Mazie's for
some dinner, and we'll spend the night talking. Do you need anything
else right now?"

I did not. She showed me where I could find the towels and
brought the extra fan out of the office and put it in my bedroom. She
suggested I open the windows to let some air circulate in my room,
gave me a tentative hug, and left for the library. It was three-thirty, and I
decided to clean up, change my clothes, and empty the bag and suitcase.
There was an empty space on top of the familiar dresser, so I lined up my
books, according to the year I received them, and placed Raggedy Ann
on top of them. I walked down to the kitchen to get a drink.

I poured a glass of iced tea from the refrigerator and began to
examine the house. I had been here a few times, with Anne, when her
parents lived here, but that was years ago. I know Anne's parents had
bought this house after selling their farm, and Anne's father spent his
time repairing what needed to be, making the old Victorian sturdy and
sound.

There was a side door to the outside in the kitchen, so I started there. I walked down the side drive, around the side yard, and into the backyard where there was a small flower garden next to a shed. Because the house was on the corner lot, it was larger than some of the others on the street, and as I wandered around the back, I saw Uncle Terry's charcoal grill next to the shed. It had obviously not been used in a while, but I saw it and remembered the meals made on it. A back door led into the house, but it was locked, so I went into the house through the side door and walked through the kitchen into the back area. There were two rooms, a sitting room, and another bedroom, and boxes were piled up in the corners of them. The rooms were separated from the rest of the house by a large spacious bathroom and a hallway which led to a library. There were books lined up in the two large bookshelves, and some chairs which also looked familiar placed next to the window. The doorway led to the front room and a dining room which connected to the kitchen. The house was spacious, and as I walked back into the front room to examine the fireplace, I glanced at the window and saw it.

Next to the window in the front room where a large fern swallowed up the sunshine, was the rocker from my childhood bedroom. The rocker upon which my mother's ghost sat. I walked over to it and ran my hands along the back and down the slats. There was a cushion on the seat, and I pulled the rocker out so I could see outside the window without the fern's interference. I sat down and began to rock back and forth, and as I did so, I felt the strain and anxiety from the day disappear. I sat and rocked and finished drinking my tea. I must have been there for quite a while when I heard a car pull into the side drive. I eased out of the rocker, stilled its movement, went to the window, and saw Anne getting out of the car, reaching into the back seat, and bringing out two large brown bags. She was entering the kitchen side door, so I walked over and held it open for her.

"Hi, are there more bags?"

"Hello, Livie. No, these contain our dinner and a few things I stopped at Clampet's to pick up," and she handed me one of the bags. "Why don't you get plates out from that cabinet and set the kitchen table? Let me wash my hands and put these things away, and we can sit and eat and talk. Hungry?"

"Yes, I am. I haven't eaten today except for some coffee and candy from the train station's vending machines. This has been an exhausting day, and I'm starved. Smells great. What is it?"

"Mazie had a special of a ham and scalloped potato casserole. I think she put some green beans and a salad in there too. She makes the greatest corn muffins, and her rice pudding is in this container. How about some iced tea," and Anne got the remainder of the tea out, and we sat down to eat and talk.

There wasn't much talking for a while, and then I started by saying, "I don't even know where to begin, Anne. Eight years. I am an adult, or close to one. I can't tell you how I missed you and thought I was forgotten."

Anne stopped eating and laid her fork filled with ham and potatoes on her plate. "You were never forgotten. I sent books and letters and sometimes toys to you. I know Terry sent things for at least a few years. Didn't you figure out we were thinking about you?"

Now it was my turn to put my fork down. "I never received any toys, and as for the letters and postcards, they were hidden from me until I found them about a year ago. I got the books each Christmas, and they are the ones I brought with me. Why wouldn't I get the toys? Why would Gladys not give them to me?" I was stunned. And angry all over again. Not for the toys, but for the deceit. I sat back against the chair; my appetite lost. Anne reached for my hand and held it.

"Let's finish up here. Don't let those thoughts spoil a good meal. We have plenty of time to talk about it. Come on now, try one of these muffins."

I allowed Anne to talk to me and fill me in on the happenings at the library and the town. We finished eating, cleaned up, and then took our dishes of rice pudding out to the front porch to eat. We sat in the porch swing and finished dessert, and then I took the dishes in, placing them into the sink. I went back outside where we sat, and Anne explained who was living where, who was new to the town, what changes had happened over the past years. I listened and grew tired. There were so many things to ask and to answer, but she was right about there being time to do all the talking we needed to.

Anne grew quiet. The fireflies began to show up and we watched them. Anne spoke. "I think that you need to relax and get used to things here, Livie. You are home, and this is a large house, and you are welcome to stay. I know we have things to sort out, but I think you should take some time to figure out what you want to do and get used to living here again. Rest and sleep in. Go for some walks to town. There are new stores and businesses to see. Come to the library. There are many additions and changes. Maggie works at one of the new shops, and you can reconnect with her and maybe see some of your old friends. And we can talk about anything you want to. How does that sound?"

"Sounds sensible and adult. I'll do that. I might sleep in tomorrow and then look around the neighborhood. Anne, you have Mother's rocking chair here, and I noticed some chairs and the kitchen set from our house. And isn't the dresser in my bedroom from my old room? What happened with Uncle Terry?"

"I can't start to tell you how unhappy he was, how he missed you. He went back to the lawyer and tried to get things reversed, but nothing worked out. I know he visited Chicago at least three times, but was not allowed to see you, and obviously, you never got the toys."

"I remember he came to the door the first Christmas I was there but was gone before I could get to see or talk to him."

"He became more depressed and talked about leaving. He asked me to go with him, but there was no plan. He said he just felt he needed to get away because you and Toby and Ruth were gone. I couldn't go. My parents were still alive then, and my family lives here, and I'm completely tied to the library. Mostly because of Ruth. Anyway, the house was his, and that following spring he sold it to a young family with a small child. They're still living there, but now there are three children. Terry held an estate sale and sold most of the household furniture and effects, but told me to come over and take anything I wanted. You'll see some of your furniture and dishes here. I couldn't allow anyone to buy the rocking chair, so it's here. I took his grill too."

"I saw that in the back. Doesn't look used much."

Anne chuckled. "No, I did try it a couple times, but could never get the hang of it. It really needs to get cleaned. Been in the shed for a few years, and I pulled it out last week thinking to try again. Now maybe I will."

"And you don't know where he is?"

"We kept in touch for a long time, but Terry was never a writer. Every now and then I would get a call from him. He seemed to be working his way around the country, and never seemed to remain long in a place. The postcards show his whereabouts. We'll get yours and mine together and see if we can figure out his travels. He told me he would be back one day. I hope he keeps his word."

"I do too. Anne, while I'm here, I want to help you out. I can clean and do laundry and a bit of cooking. I did learn some things while in Chicago. Just let me know what you want done for tomorrow."

"Nothing I can think of right now, but we'll figure it out. I want to make a suggestion, and I'm not sure how you'll take it."

"And that is?"

"Call your Aunt Gladys. Tell her you are safe. No matter what, she'll be worried."

I didn't answer. I was glad to be at home and not in Chicago, and I didn't even want to think about the Murphys or the Denisons. However, I knew Anne was right.

"OK, Anne, but I'm not sure I'll call tomorrow. I need some time. Can I have that?"

"Sure, Livie. But, call, and don't put it off. Just let them know you are here and are safe. That's all."

I nodded and put my head back and we were silent. There were many things to say to each other, but I knew there was time. We pushed the swing and watched the night approach, and in a while, we decided to go to bed. We went in, and Anne locked the front door. We took turns in the bathroom and spoke briefly once again before Anne and I hugged good-night, and this hug was not tentative.

I went into my room and looked around. I was here, in a different house, in a strange bedroom, surrounded by unfamiliar things, in a town I hadn't seen for eight years, and I felt more comfortable and safer than I had in any of the almost three thousand nights I had spent in Chicago.

The town of Everstille...

The town of Everstille had expanded and changed. The businesses and shops I had grown up with were still there, but the town had additional stores: a specialty candy and popcorn shop (*Sweets to You*), a women's clothing store (*Madeline's*), a toy store (*Play Time*), and a fabric and sewing notions store (*Sew What?*), which appeared to be very popular, and these were just some of the new businesses. However, I did not wander the downtown area immediately. At first, I took Anne's advice and slept in. At least for two days. The third morning, I woke up early and felt like doing something. I started with making coffee and breakfast for Anne.

I woke up when Anne was in the bathroom getting ready for work, so I put on the bathrobe she had loaned me and went downstairs where I started the coffee, a familiar chore. I took out the pot, measured water and coffee, got the oatmeal from the cabinet, and while the water began to boil, set the kitchen table, and began to clean and slice strawberries. When Anne came down the stairs, she saw that everything was ready and she smiled.

"Breakfast made! Thanks, Livie. I wasn't expecting this."

I put the bowl of strawberries on the table and divided the oatmeal into two bowls. "I've been lazy. I haven't done much around here, except sleep and eat, and I need to get moving. Think I will walk downtown today and look it over. I need some things because I didn't bring many clothes and personal items with me, so I may do a bit of shopping. And you have provided dinner the last few nights, so let me do that today. I'll stop at Clampet's and get some groceries. My cooking ability is limited, so don't expect the kind of meal Uncle Terry would make, but I'll have something for us tonight."

We talked and ate, and then I cleaned up as she finished getting ready for work. Before she left, she turned and said, "I don't want to nag you, Livie, but have you called Gladys yet?"

I sighed. "No. But I will today or tomorrow. Promise."

Anne nodded and waved and set off for work. Because it was early and the stores weren't opened yet, I did dishes, emptied the garbage, and completed a few straightening tasks upstairs where I made my bed and finished hanging up the clothes from my suitcase. I hadn't brought many with me. I didn't have many, and any winter items, I left in the closet in Chicago. I readied myself and decided that since Clampet's grocery store was opened early, I would walk there and return with the needed foods for dinner. My repertoire was limited, but I could pull together a hamburger and rice casserole that was tasty. I made a list and set off on the two-block walk with my new house key in my purse. This one I was easily able to use.

Clampet's grocery store was changed, and I spent time walking the aisles and filling the basket I held. I didn't see anyone I knew but after all, it had been eight years, and I was now grown. The checkout clerk was friendly, and I walked back to the house carrying my groceries and thinking through the recipe I would make.

It was still early when I got back, and I decided to prepare the casserole and place it in the refrigerator for later, so I busied myself with that. I washed the lettuce for the salad, wrapped it in a clean towel, and peeled carrots which I put in a covered pot on the stove. I realized I learned a few things in Chicago, and that made me wonder if I should call Aunt Gladys before I left for downtown Everstille. I washed the dishes and glanced at the telephone, but decided: not yet. It was just after ten o'clock and the stores were opened, so I re-readied myself and, locking the door behind me, walked out the side door to town.

There were people walking along Main Street, and while I didn't recognize any of them, I nodded and smiled and said "Good Morning". They smiled and returned the greeting. I got to the corner where Banter's Drugstore stood, turned, and walked past it, stopping in front of Peterson's Bakery. The smells ordered me in, and I had trouble choosing a dessert, but decided on a banana cake with a creamy frosting sprinkled with walnuts which I thought I might taste when I got home. I left the bakery and walked down the street.

The library was across Main Street, two blocks away, but I decided not to visit yet. I wanted to examine the shops I remembered and note the new ones. When I passed Banter's again, I went in and purchased a few items. I didn't recognize anyone there although I saw the owner, Jim Banter at the back of the pharmacy office working on some prescriptions. Perhaps my next trip to town I would call to him. I wondered if he would remember me. Across the street and down the walk were offices I remembered. The Indiana Telephone Company office, where Uncle Terry had worked, was there, and the Everstille Sheriff's Department remained next door to it. There were some new shops, but I passed them up. Across the street the *Sew What?* shop and *Madeline's* were next to each other. I needed to get to the women's clothing store, but it would wait until my next trip. I wanted to see Mazie's Restaurant.

It was there, on the corner. There was a new sign above the door, and I could see that the window on the side of the building was now even larger. I glanced at my watch. It was almost eleven o'clock. Was it too early for one of those chocolate milkshakes? Should I have one? The obvious answers were *no* and *yes*, so I pushed open the door and went in.

Inside, the restaurant was changed. There was still a long counter, but it now wound around the side and seated twice as many customers. New tables and chairs were arranged and decorated with small vases containing what appeared to be fresh flowers, and a half dozen seated customers were quietly eating. As I walked in, at a station where a cash register and a pile of what I assumed were menus were stacked, on a tall black stool, sat Mazie herself. She was older, and her always short hair was salt and pepper. She wore a short-sleeved black Polo shirt with the phrase *Mazie's Best Food* embroidered on it, and when I walked in and stood before her, she looked up with a smile meant for a stranger.

She looked and me and said, "Would you like to be seated?" and then squinted her eyes and cocked her head to one side. "Livie?"

I smiled. "Hello, Mrs. Mazie. Yes, it's me. I'm surprised you remember!"

She came around to the front of the counter and hugged me. "I heard you were back. Spoke briefly to Anne, and she is so pleased. Of course, I remember you. So glad to see you. You are grown! Let me look at you. Brings back old times. Are you here just to say *hello* or can I treat you to one of those chocolate shakes you liked?"

"I think I can manage a milkshake."

"Janie, take over here for a while," and a woman came over to the front station and sat down while Mazie moved me to the counter. "Sit here and talk to me, and I'll make it myself. What are you doing? How was Chicago? Tell me your news. Heard anything from Terry?"

She went about her task of creating the chocolate shake, and we talked the entire time. I told her I had graduated from high school, was anxious to get back to Everstille and wasn't exactly sure what I would do. I was just thinking it through. I sipped the chocolate and listened as Mazie explained the changes in the town and in her life. She was semi-retired, her daughter and son-in-law had taken over the running of the business, and she was just "sitting in the front looking pretty and taking the cash", as she put it.

"However, it's difficult to keep people working here. It's hard work, and I'm always needing someone in the kitchen. Periodically I go back and cook, but those kitchen days wear me out. The business is good, and I don't want to retire completely yet. Still show up most days, at least for a time."

I listened to Mazie talk and glanced around at the restaurant which was filling up with a lunch crowd. I thought I should seize an opportunity and spoke up.

"Mazie, I worked at a diner in Chicago for the past two years. If you need another waitress, I could work here. I don't have a job right now and know the kind of work this takes. Just a thought."

Mazie looked at me and nodded. "I'll keep that in mind, Livie. And, no charge for that shake. Think of it as a *welcome home* present, and come back to visit. I need to get back to work. Lunch time now."

I thanked her and finished up my drink, leaving a tip for the waitress who would clean up after me. As I left, I thanked Mazie once again, and chocolate sloshing in me, walked out and down the street which was busier now. I noted the time and decided I would call Gladys when I got back. Time to get that done.

As I walked back to Anne's house, I glanced at the few gray clouds in the sky and wondered if it was going to rain. I opened the door, put the cake on the kitchen counter, and walked the other purchases upstairs where I combed back my hair and washed my hands. My hair was too long, and I decided that later in the week, I needed to visit the new shop I saw (*Scissors 'N Combs*) to have some of the length cut off. As I walked downstairs and into the kitchen, I passed the telephone and stopped. I reached for it and then grabbed my hand back as if it were burned. I stood there. I needed to get this done. The time was almost three in the afternoon which meant it was almost two in Chicago. Aunt Gladys would probably be at the neighbor's or maybe playing cards, or this might be her beauty shop appointment day, and when Anne asked tonight if I had called, I could honestly say *yes*.

I took a deep breath, picked up the receiver and dialed the number. It rang once, then again. I thought four rings would be sufficient and was waiting for two additional chimes before I could hang up, when I heard Aunt Gladys answer with her usual, "Hello."

"Hello, Aunt Gladys. It's me, Olivia."

There was a hesitation before she answered. "Well, Olivia. So, you left. You never said anything to any of us. Do you think that was right?"

"Aunt Gladys, I'm not calling to argue. I just want you to know I am safe and well. It was time for me to leave. I'm eighteen."

"Olivia, you still should have told us. You have always been just this side of disobedient and obstinate. I can't think what my poor dead brother would say about your actions."

I thought of so many things to say. So many incidents that seemed unfair. The chores, the undelivered toys, the hand-me-downs, the hidden letters and postcards, the graduations, the coffee-making. And most of all, the life insurance policy that she and Aunt Ernestine had been given to take care of me. I could have brought up all these issues, but I didn't want to prolong this conversation. I took a breath and let it out.

"Aunt Gladys, it was time for me to go. I'm sorry if I didn't tell you, but I thought it would be better that way. I'm safe and well. I'm staying with Anne, and plan on living here. In Everstille. I'm old enough to decide about my life."

She hesitated and then said, "Fine, Olivia. We just always wanted the best for you, you know. I guess you're old enough for this decision."

"Good-bye, Aunt Gladys."

"Good-bye, Olivia."

I hung up. There. Done. It wasn't as bad as it could have been. Perhaps I should have brought up some things, but I didn't want the conversation to last. At least I could honestly tell Anne I had made the call. And I did feel better. And when the telephone rang, I wondered if it was Gladys calling back. I almost didn't answer it.

"Hello?"

"Livie, it's Mazie. I figured you'd be home by now. Listen, one of my waitresses just quit because her husband got a better paying job and she won't need to work. But that's not important. She only worked part-time: Thursday and Friday lunch or dinner shifts and Saturday lunch, but if you do want a job, I'm offering you one."

"Yes! That would be great. I promise, Mazie, I'll do a good job. When do you want me to start?"

"Can you come in tomorrow and we can fill out some forms, get you a uniform and talk about your schedule? I won't need you this week, but next week, I will."

"Sure, I can. What time do you want me there?"

"How about ten o'clock?"

"I'll see you then. Thanks, Mazie. I appreciate this. See you tomorrow."

"Alright, Livie. Bye now."

I hung up. Suddenly I felt lucky. It wasn't a full-time job, but it was something, and it was a start. I had saved money from working at the diner, but it wouldn't last forever, and I was worried about that. Now I would have some income. I would talk to Anne tonight. I didn't plan on living with her for free, and now I could offer to pay a bill or two. I glanced out the kitchen window. It appeared the day was ideal. The sun was brighter than it had been, and I saw no gray clouds. What a great day, I thought. A perfect day.

Mazie and I met and talked ...

Mazie and I met and talked the following day about the job I would start in a week. I was delighted. And relieved. And when we finished, I walked across and down the street and entered the Greenwood Library. It was time for me to visit. I also wanted to talk to Anne. I opened the door and stepped through and stood for a minute looking around, remembering the last summer I was here. When I was ten. Before I went to Chicago.

I knew my way around and went towards the Circulation Desk behind which a familiar person stood shifting and organizing some papers. She looked up at me, and then asked, "Livie? Is that you?"

It was Cathy Wesselmann. "Hi, Cathy. I didn't know you worked here. How are you?"

"I'm fine. Miss Rivens said you were back. Good to see you. Can I help you find something?"

I shook my head. "Thanks, but I just want to see Anne, and I know where her office is," and I began to walk back towards it. Cathy's strident voice stopped me.

"Oh, well, let me call her and see if she is available. It will just take a second," and she reached for the telephone to her right.

I remembered why I didn't like her. She was not going to lord it over me that she was working here, and as I walked by the desk, I waved her off and said, "Thanks, but I know my way," and continued my stroll through the stacks into the area where Anne's office was located.

I ignored Cathy's "Wait!" and strode quickly back to Anne where I knocked on her door, and she waved me in.

She laughed when she saw me. "Yes, Cathy just called to inform me you walked past her and ignored her. Sit down. Tell me about your new job."

I did. It was only part-time, but I told Mazie that I could fill in when she needed me, and held up my new black uniform embroidered with the inscription: *Mazie's Best Food* above the left side breast pocket. Anne nodded and asked about hours, and I brought up something concerning to me.

"Anne, I don't intend to live with you and not help with the expenses. We need to discuss it."

"We will. I want you to get started with the job and feel you are secure. I know you need clothes and other items, so for now, get the things you need. Take the summer to do that, and in September, we'll talk about house expenses. How does that sound?"

"Sounds generous, Anne, and thank you. I think I'll walk around and look at the library. I want to go to the Ruth Room and spend some time there."

"Let me walk with you. I need to get up and move, and if I don't spend time out of my office, Miss Wesselmann begins to think she owns the library." I grinned as we left her office.

We walked to the Ruth Evans Pinkerton Room and went in. I looked around at the books and new items, and smiled at my mother's photograph next to the door. Then Anne showed me the updated Children's Section and talked about the new acquisitions. She took me past the fully stocked Research Room and the magazine and newspaper racks, talking about additional ideas she had for the Greenwood Library. As we passed the New Book section, she stopped and reached out to pull out a book which she handed to me. I looked at the title: *The Bluest Eye*.

"I think you'll like this book. Toni Morrison is a new author presenting some important ideas. You can pick something else, but I think that as long as you are living with the head librarian, you should have a library card and use it," and Anne smiled at me.

I looked at the book and nodded. "Sound like a deal. Should I ask Cathy to process a card for me?"

Anne grinned and said, "Oh, I think I can handle that. Come on."

We went to the Circulation Desk where I filled out a brief informational card and received my official library card which I placed in my purse. I thanked Anne and told her I would see her at home, and as I left, I waved to Cathy and said, "Bye, Cathy. Good to see you." She gave me an annoyed side-ways smile.

I felt comfortable that summer. I went to *Madeline's* and found some excellent buys on the sale rack, so my wardrobe brightened with blues and greens and yellows. I also reconnected with Maggie. She was working at *Sew What?* right across and down the street from the restaurant. Some days, we left our jobs at the same time and walked part-way home together. She had worked at the store since she was a high school junior, and was currently managing one of the sections. Her money was being stashed away for a wedding in a couple years to Robert Stevens, the boy who would kick me in elementary school. I spent some of my free time cleaning up Uncle Terry's grill, and Anne and I hooted at my first attempt making hamburgers. The hot dogs were easier to grill, and eventually, I managed to succeed with the ground beef.

One summer Sunday, I slept in, having worked both the lunch and dinner shifts for the last three days, and woke to a delicious aroma. I put on my newly purchased blue-flowered bathrobe and came downstairs where Anne was taking out a cake from the oven.

"What's the special occasion?" I asked looking over her shoulder.

"This is your mother's cinnamon cake. I thought you might want to take a ride to the cemetery. I know you haven't been able to get there since coming home. Are you up to that this afternoon?"

"Yes, I am. I didn't know you knew how to bake anything but the cookies, Anne. This looks and smells wonderful."

"Terry gave me the recipe and taught me what to do before he left. It took a few tries, but I finally succeeded. I usually get out to the cemetery about this time each summer and am glad you're here to accompany me. This could be our little ceremony today. There's still time to get to Sunday services if you want. Do you?"

I shook my head. "Think I'll skip them today. I'm feeling lazy and want to finish the book. It's almost due, and I don't want to have a late return. I hear the librarian is mean."

Anne snickered, and I went back upstairs to clean up and get ready for the day. When I came back down, the coffee pot was full and sliced fruit was on the table. A note said Anne decided to make the Sunday service and would be directly home afterwards. I poured a cup of coffee thinking how strange it seemed to have it made for me, and took the book and some fruit out to the front porch. As I sat on the swing sipping coffee, I looked around the quiet street feeling comfortable and content. I rocked back and forth, picking at the fruit, and ignoring the book. Anne turned her car into the side driveway. Gathering everything up, I went in to the kitchen to greet her.

We ate a light lunch; then, packed the cake and sweet tea to take with us, placing the basket in the back seat. Anne added gardening tools and gloves, and we got into the car.

"Livie, do you want to drive out there? I know you haven't driven since you got here, and you are welcome to do that if you want."

I screwed my mouth to the side and gave a little snort. "Don't have a driver's license. There wasn't anyone to take me out driving, and I walked or took the bus wherever I went. Not a skill I possess."

Anne looked at me and said, "Well, we'll have to rectify that. You should get a license. One day you'll want a car. Let's go before it gets too warm."

She backed the car out of the driveway, and we headed west on Main Street out to the country road leading to North Cemetery. I noted the changes along the way. Houses, newly built, and others being built dotted the land that used to be farms. As we passed the Wells' place, I asked about Michael Jasper's grandfather, Mr. Wells. Anne said he was still living there, and someone in his large family was usually there with him. He drove into the town periodically and often stopped to spend time at the library. I nodded and Anne turned the car into one of the new paths on the expanding cemetery.

"I want to go to my parents' graves first and clean out the weeds. Then we'll do Ruth's and Toby's. Glad it's sunny but not too hot. I'll be ready for tea soon. How about you?"

"Sounds good to me."

She parked the car, and we emptied the back seat and walked to her parents' graves. We pulled weeds and cut back the sedum which surrounded the tall gravestones. Once we finished, Anne bent and kissed both stones, and we stood quietly for a minute.

"I miss them," she told me, "They left the house to me to insure my future. I am grateful because I don't owe a mortgage, and can save some money. They were good people, Livie. "

"I believe they were," I said, and smiled at her.

We left their area and walked over to where my parents were. I hadn't been there in years, and the sight of the stones side-by-side bearing their names was overwhelming. Unexpected tears filled my eyes, and I stood in solitary sorrow as memories filled me. When I looked at Anne, after wiping my face on the edge of my blouse, she nodded and said, "It's good to let the feelings go, Livie. Let's clean up around the stones and then sit down on the blanket. We'll be ready for the tea."

We did our work and wiped our hands, and while Anne walked the tools back to the car, I spread the blanket in front of my parents' headstones, and opened the basket with the cake and tea. Anne came back, and when she sat down, I handed her a cup with some tea. We sat quietly and sipped the tea and cooled off. Anne leaned over and pulled out a piece of cake for each of us.

She held up her piece and said, "Here's to you, Ruth. You were the best mentor and friend ever. I miss you and Toby and think of you both daily," and she turned to me and smiled. I nodded, and we took a big bite of our cake and chewed. Anne placed hers on a napkin, wiped her hands and then her eyes with a corner of a napkin. I swallowed my cake, and put the rest down. Suddenly there was a sorrowing catch in my throat, and my eyes became wet again. The two of us were still, and then Anne picked up her cup and sipped the tea.

"Always feel sad for a time when I come here. Then I remember the great times Ruth and I had, and the fun with Toby and then Terry, and I begin to feel better. I feel bad for you, Livie. You never got a chance to know your mother, and then Toby was taken from you, and the the Chicago stuff happened. I'm glad you are here now. To be honest, I have felt guilty for years because I was never able to keep the promise I made to your mother. Now that you are back, maybe I can. Of course, I will need your cooperation."

I stared at her, and the inquisitive look on my face made Anne grin. "So, what did you promise that involved me?"

She picked up her piece of cake and took another bite. She chewed and looked at the gravestones before she answered. "Before you were born, Ruth and I talked about what your education would be. Not just your formal schooling, but the things she would teach you, the books she wanted you to read, and the discussions she would have with you. I was always a reader, but Ruth organized and monitored additional reading for me. She assigned me books, and we would discuss the ideas and themes in them. She would ask my opinions and encouraged me to question the texts, to not blindly accept what the author wrote. She was a wonderful teacher. In fact, that was what she had planned to be had she been able to complete college. Your mother got two years in before she had no more money and had to go back to her parents' home. She had wanted to teach literature. She would have been terrific."

I waited until Anne took another bite of her cake and drank some tea. I ate mine, and when we finished, she refilled our cups and leaned back on her elbows.

"Right before you were born, your mother had a premonition that things would not be easy with your birth. She was an older woman having a first baby and insisted on being at home for your birth. Up until the last six weeks or so, she seemed perfectly healthy, but then…" Anne's voice trailed off and she closed her eyes. Then she pushed herself up and turned to me.

"Your mother wanted me to take her place as your teacher should anything happen to her. I promised I would guide you in your reading and talk with you about the books if she couldn't. I was sure she would be here to do it. Anyway, she started with me when I was almost twelve, and while I read to you, and we talked about books, I thought I would start with you at that age. And then you were gone."

We were silent for a while, and then Anne started to clean up our picnic. I helped her. We put away the napkins and cups and together folded the blanket. I picked up the basket, and we walked slowly back to the car.

"Anne, I don't have any objection to book discussions. I'll be happy to read what you think I should. I always liked reading, and it took up plenty of my time in Chicago although I'm sure I don't read as much as you do. I'll help you keep your promise to Mother. We can start with the book you suggested I read. I'm almost done, and maybe this week we can talk about it. Will that work?"

Anne opened the car's back door, and we put the basket and blanket inside next to the gardening tools. She closed the door, walked to the driver's side, and looked at me.

"Let me know when you are finished with the book. Of course, we can discuss it. After all," and she grinned as we sat in our seats, "why do you think I suggested it?"

Because Cathy Wesselmann...

Because Cathy Wesselmann left for college in early September, and quit her part-time job at the Library, Anne offered it to me.

"I thought I would be able to fill in with some of the other part-time staff, but it isn't working out for one reason or another," she explained to me, "so I thought you could take over her hours. I can adjust the schedule so that you are free on the days you work at the restaurant. I would need you at the library during the first part of the week. It's only part-time, but if you don't mind a minimum wage, it will help you with the purchases of new clothes and shoes you need. What do you think?"

"I think I am grateful. I also think there will talk about you offering me the job over anyone else."

Anne laughed. "Well, this won't be the only time the town has discussed my actions. I'm not worried. Plan on coming in next Monday, and I'll show you around and explain your duties."

"I'm sure if Cathy Wesselmann was able to do the job. I can," and I barely regretted the statement.

We were sitting down to the dinner I had made. Another chicken and rice casserole, and this was the third one I had made since taking over cooking duties. We took a few bites, and I said, "I guess I need to look up some more recipes if I am going to continue this chef business. Wish I knew how to make some of the delicious food Kari's grandmother made. Maybe I'll write to her and ask for some recipes."

Anne nodded and swallowed. "Well, we can continue to split the cooking. I can fend for myself on the nights you are at Mazie's, and do the chef duties on weekends. And just so you know, fall is a busy time of year for me. The annual festival is coming up, and I volunteer for some committees. There will be some late nights for me. There is always a need for volunteers, so if you find you have some extra time, you might consider that. It's actually fun."

I said I would think about it. I was looking forward to the festival after all these years. Things had changed in Everstille. There were no longer four parades and festivals, but more effort was put into the two that were kept: the fall festival and the spring festival. Both events still included the parade and an expanded sidewalk sale from the town's stores, but added arts-and-crafts booths from out-of-town artists and craftsmen. This brought additional visitors into the town and was helpful to the town's merchants. Anne said food trucks lined the streets, and there was a carnival atmosphere. I thought back to the carnival Uncle Terry and I went to and looked forward to that weekend.

On Tuesday night, after eating our leftovers from the previous night, Anne said, "I took tomorrow off, Livie. If you want to, we could take a ride to South Bend and do some shopping at Robertson's and JCPenney's and some of the other stores. I know you need some things, and there are some great sales going on now. We could eat lunch there and enjoy the day. Are you free?"

"As a bird," I answered. "Great, now I sound like Aunt Ernestine."

The shopping trip was both productive and pleasant. I was able to expand my small wardrobe and spend time with Anne. We ended up discussing the last book I read and talking about what I saw as a future for myself. Honestly, I didn't know what that would be, and when Anne brought up college, I hesitated.

"Come on, Livie. After all, if Cathy Wesselmann can do it, so can you."

I gave her a side-ways grin and looked out the side car window. I didn't exactly know what to do about the rest of my life, and while I didn't want to hurt Anne's feelings, I was pretty sure working two part-time jobs was not it.

"My time in Chicago was not awful, but it was not wonderful either. I missed you and Uncle Terry, and it took me a long time to get over the fact that I was there and not here. Not sure I ever got over it. I concentrated on getting back here, to Everstille, and now that I'm back, I just want to enjoy it. I never thought I would get to college. Not because I wouldn't be accepted or be able to complete the work, but there's the money factor. How could I afford it? My grades were good but not spectacular, and I never applied for entry or a scholarship or even thought about what I wanted to do in college. I don't know, Anne. I think I just need to be here for a time and consider things. Maybe I should talk to Cathy Wesselmann about it when she is home for the holidays."

Anne snickered, but then said, "Not the worst idea you've ever had, Livie. There is time. You are right. You've only been here for a few months. When you're ready to talk about things, let me know."

I nodded. We went home, took our packages out of the car, and rested with some iced tea. I was grateful for Anne's support and advice. She listened to me. I cherished her concern and interest in my ideas and thoughts. That was something I had missed for eight years.

Winter came, and with it, Christmas...

Winter came, and with it, Christmas, and I was as excited as one of the children I read books to each Wednesday afternoon at the library's Read-Aloud Story Hour. After a couple months of assisting Anne in the task, she asked me to plan the book and an activity to go along with it, and then the responsibility became mine. Wednesdays I started at noon and worked until five, so I had the morning to get things ready. On those days, I came to the library early and spent the time organizing and preparing. I discovered that I enjoyed reading to the three and four-year-olds almost as much as they seemed to enjoy listening. Perhaps I enjoyed it more.

Through the month of November, I read animal stories (*The Poky Little Puppy, Millions of Cats, Corduroy*), favoring the Golden Books that lined the Children's Section. But now, it was December, and while there was cold weather, there was no snow forecast, so I brought the snow to my little listeners with *Frosty the Snowman, The Snowy Day,* and *The Big Snow*. Afterwards, I gathered the five or six children who were there and used up almost three bags of cotton balls creating snow scenes. Then there was the clean-up.

Anne came over to help me, and we talked about Christmas preparations as we gathered the loose cotton balls and wiped up the glue. Anne's family took turns hosting Christmas Day, and this year was Anne's turn. Her house was large, but put eight additional adults and a dozen children in it, and it wouldn't seem so spacious. We needed to move things around to create some space for the Christmas tree. We would start decorating over the weekend and talked about what cooking and baking needed to be done.

"Of course, I will make my world-famous orange Jell-O, bake the cookies, and I make a decent scalloped potato dish. But my sister and sisters-in-law will bring the real food," and we laughed.

"How about the cinnamon cake?"

"Hmm...maybe I could do that, but the recipe is your mother's, so why don't you try it? Maybe you could make a practice cake this weekend and then make one for Christmas dessert."

"O.K. I'll attempt it. And if I make the pierogi recipe again, maybe they'll turn out better this time. Those will take practice."

"Sounds great. Tonight, we'll get a shopping list together after dinner. By the way, what is dinner? We ate the leftovers last night."

I stood up and stretched out. We were finished with the cleaning, and I knew I still had a couple hours of work to complete before going home. Anne would be home about an hour after me, and I wasn't sure I could pull a real meal together before she came home.

"Well, it's Wednesday, and Mazie's has a blue-plate special. Think it's a tomato mac-and-cheese. Sound good? I'll stop after I leave and pick two dinners up."

"Sounds fine. And after dinner, let's also get to the back rooms. Those boxes have Christmas decorations, and we can pull them out. I want to show you some of the things."

Our evening planned, I completed my tasks, went to Mazie's and then home. After Anne arrived, we ate, cleaned up, wrote out a shopping list, and walked to the back rooms where we moved the boxes piled up in the corner.

"Are all these Christmas decorations?"

Anne pulled off the top three boxes. "These contain the decorations. Let's stack them over there," and we moved them against the doorway. "These other three contain memories. I just left them all stacked up in the corner, but should put them somewhere else."

I looked at the boxes which were labeled: *Toby, Terrence* and *Livie.* I looked speculatively at Anne. "What memories do they contain?"

"When Terry was packing up and selling the house and the furniture, I asked if I could keep some of the things and pack them away for you. I was positive that one day I would see you again. The box with Toby's name is yours, and you can look through it. There are some mementos from his teaching, some odds and ends, photographs, and a sweater and hat he wore. Terry didn't have any place to keep them, so I stored them here. Terry's box contains items he couldn't take with him when he left, so I kept those here. There are clothes of his hanging in that closet. He was limited in how much he could pack in the car. I kept his things because I'm just as sure we'll see him again."

"And the box with my name?"

"It's yours. Open it."

I pulled off the tape that kept it shut, and the first things I pulled out were the orange monkey and the yellow banana. I gave a yelp and looked at Anne.

"I was positive I had packed the banana and just forgot the monkey. I can't believe these are here. They'll go next to the Raggedy Ann upstairs on my dresser. What else is there?"

I pulled out various toys and games and the notes Uncle Terry used to leave me on my freshly made bed each week. There were colored hair ribbons I used to wear and a handful of old school papers including the weather and the cloud diaries from Mrs. Smith's third-grade class. I looked at the papers and toys and photographs, all pieces of my childhood which had been saved in this box by Anne.

"Thank you, Anne. I'm taking this upstairs tonight and I can't wait to look through it all. It's like lost pieces of a puzzle have been found. Let's put Dad and Terry's boxes away for now, and I'll drag this to the stairs."

We moved the two boxes to the room's closet, pushing Uncle Terry's clothes to the back, and between us, carried the decorations out to the front room. I placed the box with my childhood things near the bottom step and went to the front room where Anne was moving things around.

"What can I help you do?"

"I think we need to move the fern and rocking chair over there and leave space for the tree we'll pick up Saturday from the corner lot. The youth group at the church sells them. We can do that once you get home from the restaurant, and we'll decorate it Sunday after church. I'm looking forward to the scent of a fresh pine tree in here. Livie, open that box and take out the ornaments."

I pulled the big cardboard box to me and ripped the tape off. When I reached in and took out the top ornament wrapped in newspaper and looked at it, I gasped. "Anne, these are mine! These are the ones Dad and Uncle Terry and I bought each year to decorate the tree. I never thought I'd see them again." I carefully took the ornaments out, unwrapped them, and lined them up on the sofa. Then I stood back and changed a few around. And, then changed two again.

"What are you doing?" laughed Anne.

"Trying to put them in order from the first one to the one I got when I was nine. I'm sure this is right."

Anne looked at them. "Maybe. I don't remember. But there are the photos we took when the tree was decorated, and they are in your box. You can check them and see. Anyway, when we decorate, these will all need to be placed high on the tree and away from the tiny hands that will be here on Christmas. If we open the other boxes, we can see what old decorations might need replacing. Maybe before work tomorrow, you can go to the Emporium and look around."

"Sure, I can do that," and we continued to examine the decorations and reminisce about past holidays.

I took my box up to the bedroom and before I looked through all the toys and games and photos, I lifted the orange monkey and yellow banana out and rearranged them on the top of the dresser next to Raggedy Ann. I stood there looking at the colors. The red of Raggedy Ann's hair, the orange of the stuffed monkey and the bright yellow banana looked like the start of a rainbow. The memory of my rainbow painted bedroom filled my mind. I touched the indigo stone necklace which I always wore around my neck and sighed. But it was a sigh of contentment and satisfaction; a partial release of the frostiness which had held in the center of my chest from the time, winters ago when I heard Uncle Terry's voice, but the front door was locked, and when I finally wretched it open, my past had disappeared into the hostile iciness of a Chicago winter.

It was a new year...

It was a new year, and I felt I had a new life. While I had been back in Everstille for only ten months, I was beginning to feel I had never left. There were remnants of the Chicago life, and reminders of it, but they seemed increasingly faded. Ivy sent me a picture of her new baby, a boy named Evan, and a thank-you for the Golden Books I had left for him. I received a Christmas card from Aunt Ernestine which had been signed by both her and Aunt Gladys. In it, Aunt Ernestine hoped that I was well and happy and ended her brief note with the reminder that *Things are not always what they seem*. I wasn't sure what she meant and didn't spend much time pondering it. No cardigan was included with the card.

Despite the years we were apart, Maggie and I reclaimed our friendship, and we would shop together at the new stores in the town. She introduced me to her friend, Liz, who worked at *Scissors 'N Comb,* and was able to trim off some of my hair so that it became manageable. There were some old friends who welcomed me back, and some new acquaintances who were friendly, and with my two jobs, I was busy and the year passed quickly.

Easter was April 22, and when my nineteenth birthday came one month later, it was a Tuesday, and I was at the library. Anne had asked me to open the library that morning, and when she came in about an hour later, she brough with her a large cake from Peterson's Bakery which was shared with all the patrons who came in that day. She had arranged for the Story Hour group to make me home-made birthday cards, and on Wednesday, another smaller cake was shared with them after they sang "Happy Birthday" to me in their cute high voices. It was a satisfactory birthday, and no sponge cake or gray cardigan was present. Or wanted.

The following weekend was the Everstille Spring Festival. Although I had to work extra hours on Friday and Saturday at Mazie's, we were still able to see the entire parade as it passed in front of the restaurant. But that was a good weekend for working; I made double my usual tips. Saturday night, Anne and I walked over to the end of the street where we had a perfect view of the fireworks, and after Sunday church, grilled hamburgers on Uncle Terry's grill which I had almost mastered.

That afternoon, Anne and I sat on the porch and rocked on the swing and sipped iced tea and watched the clouds move in. The next day was Memorial Day, and the library was closed. We both were looking forward to a day off doing some light cleaning and catching up with laundry. When the rain began to come down in larger drops, we moved into the house and made ourselves comfortable in the front room. Anne sat on the club chair and put her feet up on the footstool while I sat at the corner of the sofa, moving my recent library book off to the side. Anne looked at the book she had suggested and then at me.

"Have you finished it?"

"Yes, I have. Did you want to talk about it now?"

She looked gravely at me and asked, "Was it a good story?"

I glanced at the title: *Giovanni's Room* by James Baldwin. It was a book I had many questions about and was unlike any other book Anne had suggested to me. It centered on a young man living in Paris who had a girlfriend but was also involved with a man. I wasn't sure what to make of the book.

"The story itself was thought-provoking. I guess I don't understand things, but I'm sure you can help me figure it out. So, yes, it was a good story."

Anne sat still for a few seconds. Then she finished her glass of tea and stood up. "Do you want more?" she asked.

I shook my head, and she went into the kitchen and returned with a full glass. She sat again on the chair and looked solemnly at me. She sipped at the tea, then the put the glass down.

"What do you know of Toby and Terry's relationship?"

I considered the question. "I know they called themselves *cousins,* but they weren't. Uncle Terry explained that to me when Dad died and before I left for Chicago. He said they were friends in Chicago, and when he came here to live with Dad and my mother, it was just simpler to explain they were cousins. They had decided that when I was born, I would be taught to call Terry *uncle*. That's about all I know. Why? What else is there? Anne, I'm old enough to know these things."

Anne nodded. "I know you are. I wanted you to get settled here and feel comfortable before I gave you something. Wait here, I'll be right back," and she got up and went upstairs.

She came back down in a few minutes holding a large brown envelope. She sat down again and was quiet for a while, staring down at the envelope in her hand. Then she looked up.

"After your mother died, around your first birthday, I spoke to Toby and Terry. I told them that one day you needed to know the truth about them, your mother, and your history, and that they should write it down. Toby was willing to do it, but Terry said he was not a writer and couldn't. Eventually he did. They gave me their letters, and I told them I would keep them until you were grown enough to understand. Then the whole Chicago thing happened. I put these away and have never looked at them. What they wrote to you is for you to read, and I think it's time. Today seems like a good day to do this. The night is cool and rainy, and tomorrow neither one of us needs to go to work, so you'll have time to digest this. The letters in this envelope have been in my bottom desk drawer for almost two decades now. Here, they're yours."

Anne handed me the large brown envelope which I placed in my lap. I wasn't sure what would be in it, and was uncertain I even wanted to know. I had a thousand questions, but seemed to be struck dumb. I just looked at her.

"I'm going upstairs. Think I'll read for a while after I take a bath and then try to sleep." Anne came over and bent down and kissed my cheek. "Truth is important, Livie. And you are mature enough to process it. Good-night."

I waited until I heard Anne place her glass in the kitchen sink and walk up the stairs. I could hear her in the bathroom running the water, but I felt like a statue. I looked at the envelope in my lap and saw that on the front was my name: Olivia Pinkerton. Turning it over, I saw that the years had yellowed and curled the tape which held it shut, and it was easy to open. Inside were two smaller envelopes. On one was the name of the man I knew as Dad: *Tobias Pinkerton*. On the other was written *Terrence Douglas*. They were both sealed with the same yellowed, aged tape.

I got up from the sofa and shut the front door because the rain, while not harsh, was steady, and had brought with it a cool late spring breeze. I walked over to shut the side window and went into the kitchen where I made a cup of hot tea. I was starting to feel chilled but suspected the weather had little to do with it. When I returned to the front room, I switched on the floor lamp next to the sofa, took the light coverlet from the back, and sat down, spreading the warmth over me. I took a sip of my hot tea and put the cup on the table next to me where it would remain until the next morning.

I took a deep breath and let it go with a loud sigh. The library book we hadn't discussed was on the opposite end of the sofa, and looking at it, I had a realization. Anne had never intended to discuss *Giovanni's Room* with me. The book was not meant for discussion. It was meant as preparation.

I reached beside me and picked up the larger envelope, the one with *Tobias Pinkerton* written on the front. I tore off the yellowed tape and took out the sheets which had been folded into thirds. With the rain dripping onto the planks of the front porch, I settled under the coverlet and began to read.

The morning sunlight...

The morning sunlight streaming in from the side window warmed my face and woke me up. I had not gotten upstairs to bed. The night was spent reading and rereading the letters Anne had given me, and then I laid down on the sofa to think and consider. I fell asleep there. It was early, and I did not hear Anne moving around, so I assumed she was still in bed. I replaced the smaller envelopes into the large one and left it on the sofa. The coverlet was folded and put back, and I took the full cup of cold tea into the kitchen. I went upstairs to take a shower and dress. I moved quietly because I saw that Anne's door was still closed, and no sounds emanated from the other side.

I readied myself for the day, pulling my still wet hair into a ponytail, and went downstairs to make coffee. As I filled the pot and measured the grounds, I wondered who was making Aunt Gladys' coffee. I hadn't heard from the Chicago family in a few months and wondered what was happening with Ivy's baby, but I was not interested enough to contact them. I put bread in the toaster and set the table for a light breakfast. Anne came downstairs, still in her bathrobe.

"Seven o'clock. I am up early even on my day off. Coffee smells good. Morning, Livie. How are you?"

I placed some toast on a plate and put in down in front of her. Then I placed additional bread in the slots and moved over to the table with my coffee.

"I'm fine, Anne. But I have questions. You knew I would."

Anne poured milk into her coffee, began to butter a piece of toast, and looked over the table at me. "I'll answer what I can, but it will be from my perspective. I haven't read the letters, but I suspect I know what's in them."

"Anne, you can read the letters. I don't have a problem with that. I'll get them," and I started to get up. Anne stopped me.

"No, Livie. I don't need to read the letters. I remember."

We took small sips of our coffee and I began to butter the toast I didn't really want. I took a small bite and put it on the plate. I had thousands of questions in my head, so I just pulled one out.

"Anne, did you know about the relationship between Toby and Terry?" I wasn't sure what to call the man I had known as *Dad* anymore.

"That was one of the first things Terry told me. As you found out, I was part of their group. There were rumors in the town which was smaller then, and, like small towns, had little to do except gossip. But Terry didn't tell me anything I wasn't aware of, at least sort of. But, yes, eventually I was aware of their…closeness. That had been ongoing since their days in Chicago."

"And, my mother knew about it too, right?"

Anne nodded. "I'm sure you read about why Ruth and Toby married. To call their marriage *convenient* is to demean it. They loved each other, Livie, just not in the way a man and woman would. They were the best of friends, and I say that while claiming Ruth as my best friend too. It was all complicated. Terry was so likable and friendly that he fit right in with the town. After a few years, the fact that the three of them lived together was simply accepted. And of course, Toby and Terry had been introduced as *cousins* and continued that story. It's still what the town believes. Or pretends to. Now that Terry has been gone for years and this place has expanded with more businesses and people and houses, it's old news and no longer discussed."

"Mazie asked me if we had heard from Terry. That was one of the first conversations we had."

"Mazie is a friend, and while I have never divulged any of their secrets, she is smart and worldly. While she has never asked me anything about them, she had said enough to me to let me know she at least suspects the truth. Livie, I need to say… you don't seem upset. At least we are discussing this calmly, and I didn't know how you would take it all."

I reached down and pulled off a piece of the now cold toast and chewed it. I took a final swallow of the coffee and then got up to refill my cup, raising the pot to ask Anne if she wanted more. She did, and I poured her another cup too. We sat in silence for a while as I thought about how to answer her.

"That's why you gave me the James Baldwin book to read."

"I thought it would be a way of approaching the subject, yes. Of course, the situation with your family and the book's characters is not the same and can't be compared. But your mother and Toby were married in name only. And now you know both parts of their secrets."

I sat down and looked at Anne. "When did you know that Uncle Terry is my father?'

"Honestly, not until the first time I held you. You were about a month old, and after your mother's funeral, I was away for a time. When I returned, seeing you was the first thing I wanted to do, so I went to your house. When your little bonnet was removed, there was your hair, matching Terry's. And eventually, when your eyes were fully opened, they were his eyes. Of course, there was talk in the town, but Toby and Terry handled it well, and your mother was so honored and admired that no one wanted to think such a thing was likely. After your mother died, that the two men, the two *cousins*, would live together and raise you, was accepted. Toby had a stellar reputation, and Terry was honestly liked by everyone, and he and I continued to show up at places together. I was asked often about when the wedding would be, and had to side-step that question."

"Did you ever think of marrying him?"

"We discussed it. However, I knew I could not be as tolerant or understanding as Ruth, and there was no thought of me moving in with Toby and Terry. I like my solitude and independence too much, and, frankly, the leading objection was the thought of your mother. I could never marry Terry knowing that she truly loved him. At least I assume she did. We never discussed it. Until I saw you as a baby, I thought Toby was your father, the same as the town did."

"My mother never told you about Terry and her?"

"No, Livie, and that was probably the only secret your mother and I didn't share. And that was fine. Ruth had a right to her secret thoughts and feelings."

"I think the most difficult thing to accept is that Toby isn't my father. It's heartbreaking because after Dad died, I belonged with Terry. I should have been able to stay here and should have never been sent to Chicago. If Tobias Pinkerton isn't my father, then the Chicago family isn't my family at all. I am angry about that, and I don't even know who to be angry at. You knew. Terry knew. Are you telling me the Murphys and Denisons had no idea that Terry was my real father?"

Anne took a deep breath. "That was the worst part of it all, Livie. Legally, according to your birth certificate, Toby was your father, and until his death, those families never really knew that Terry was even living here. There were plenty of questions and accusations. But Terry was determined not to tarnish Toby's reputation. And the idea of two men loving each other and living together was not accepted. It still isn't. Then there was the judge's decision. It was a mess, and I am sorry for my part in it, but there it is."

I hadn't expected tears to appear, but they did. Anne got up to get some tissue and put the box next to me. I cried, and then, I stopped. I looked at her and attempted a smile.

"Anne, I'm not angry anymore, but last night, when this realization hit me, if you hadn't been upstairs sleeping, I'm unsure how I would have reacted."

Anne gave a rueful smile and sighed. "Honestly, I was afraid of your reaction, so I made myself scarce. The feelings were and are, yours to work through. If there are more answers you need, I'll try my best. Do you have more questions right now?"

I thought and then shook my head. "I'll probably want to talk this through again, but now I just need to let it all sink it. No, wait, I do have one. The Murphys and Denisons were awarded Dad's life insurance policy by the judge, right?"

"Yes."

"Do you think that is why they took me?"

Anne shrugged. "I think they were convinced that you were Toby's child. After all, the birth certificate said that, and that was certainly proof enough for the judge. I believe they felt a duty to you as Toby's child, and the money was just an extra incentive."

"That's how I felt: a duty. I didn't suffer in Chicago, but there wasn't much affection shown to me. Looking back on it all, I was showered with love by all of you. I was probably spoiled. I don't know. I need to think things through."

We sat at the table finished the coffee, and finally, Anne said, "Here it is, almost nine o'clock in the morning and I'm not even dressed. Let me get ready and then, let's do what we planned. Laundry needs to get done, and those back rooms need to be aired out and cleaned. Been meaning to do that for months now."

I began to clear the table as Anne placed her plates in the sink. I thought for a minute and then said, "If anything positive has come out of this, I'm delighted to realize that I am *not* related to either the Murphys or the Denisons. That's a great thing!"

"You are home, now, Livie, and I hope you know that. *Home is where the heart is*, so they say."

I looked at her and commented, "Wow, now you sound just like Aunt Ernestine!" We grinned.

There were many conversations

There were many conversations over the next days. Anne never put me off or refused to answer questions although she did not know all the answers. I spent more time than I should have staring into the bathroom mirror looking for any sign of Dad, just in case everything was a mistake or a joke, but there he was: Uncle Terry looking back at me. I reread the letters many times, and then finally, put them away in my bottom dresser drawer, underneath brightly colored winter sweaters. Truth hidden under a rainbow.

While I had some difficulty comprehending the relationship between Dad and Uncle Terry, I kept coming back to one of the comments in Dad's letter. He wrote that "… human nature is complicated and there are many kinds of love", and I had to agree with that. Both parts. The complication and the many kinds.

I wasn't even sure what to call Tobias Pinkerton. He was *Dad* and yet, he was not. I asked Anne what she thought and she, in her usual wise way, suggested I just continue to call him that. "After all, that's who he was to you while he was alive. And Terry remains your *uncle*. I suspect Terry would agree."

We talked about Terry. When we compared the postcards he sent to us, we figured out part of his travels. After he left Indiana, Terry spent some time in Illinois. Then the dates and the postcards showed him traveling west to Iowa, South Dakota, Montana, and Washington State. The last postcard I got from him put him in Montana, and Anne's last one was received over two years ago when he was in Washington State. We pulled out a map in the library one time and looked at his travels. I ran my finger along the states, wondering where he had gone and what he was doing. Neither one of us wanted to say out loud that not hearing from him was a bad sign. But I thought it, and am sure Anne did too.

I continued working at the library and at Mazie's, and while they were different jobs and experiences, I enjoyed them both. Anne would periodically ask me if I had decided on any plans for my future, but I had not. She brought up the possibility of going to college, and talked about regretting never being able to, and said there were always ways to afford an education. Once when we drove to South Bend for a shopping trip, she drove around the Indiana University campus to show it to me. I know she wanted the best for me, but money was an issue, and I was unsure about the possibility of scholarships. We continued our book discussions which I enjoyed. And learned from them. It's too bad that Anne never got to college. She would be a wonderful teacher, and I told her that. She replied that my mother was the teacher and had taught her everything she was teaching me.

Late spring brought lovely weather. It was warm, but not uncomfortably so, and the blue sky made me happy. Mondays and Tuesdays were generally slow days at the library, and that allowed Anne and me time to complete weekly tasks which were time-consuming and laborious, but necessary. When it was pleasant, we walked to the library enjoying ourselves and relishing being in nature. The first Monday, June 4, was such a day. As we walked, I reminisced.

"Tomorrow marks one year I have been here, and I want to celebrate. Let's go to one of those new restaurants in Elkhart, and I'll buy dinner. How does that sound, Anne?"

"Sounds like you want to get out of your cooking night, but yes, that would be nice, Livie. Where do you want to go?"

As we completed our walk to work, we discussed the celebration for the following night. We talked about where we would go, what we would eat, and made plans for the dinner which, it turned out, we would not have.

I stood at the Circulation Desk

I stood at the Circulation Desk with a stack of notecards in one hand and a pencil in the other. Anne was in her office working on new book orders. It was about nine-thirty, and the only other person in the library was Mr. Owens who showed up every Monday morning to peruse the weekend newspapers from Elkhart, South Bend, and Indianapolis. The papers waited for us at the front door, and every Monday, I put them on the table towards the back where Mr. Owens liked to sit. He would spend a couple of hours reading, and then replace all the sections, leaving them just as they were found. So far it was a typical Monday.

I heard someone open the library door and from the corner of my eye, I saw him stand there. I did not look over to see who it was because I was concentrating on the numbers I was trying to add up in my head, but there was a sudden peculiar feeling in my stomach, and the hairs on my arms began to stand up. Suddenly, I was afraid to look up. I kept my head turned downwards, and the man moved slowly towards me. When he stopped a few feet in front of the desk, I got up the nerve to move my eyes forward and look at his shoes.

He wore cowboy boots, and above the boots were Demin blue jeans. My eyes traveled up to his mustard-colored leather jacket which had fringe hanging from the shoulders to the cuffs. As I looked up to meet his face, he removed the cowboy hat he was wearing and held it to his side. His hair, which was longer than I had ever seen it, still matched the color of mine, but there were white strips above both ears which traveled back to meet the red at his collar. His face looked the same, although it bore a brownness from the sun and sported new wrinkles at the corners of his eyes. Smile wrinkles. Our eyes met, and I took a breath realizing that I hadn't in what seemed like an hour. He smiled and spoke.

"Hello, Cabbage."

The notecards fell from my left hand, spreading out on the desk, and the pencil I held in my right dropped, rolling away and onto the floor where I would find it later. I turned to the swinging half door separating me from the rest of the library, pushed it open, and flew towards Uncle Terry. I threw my arms around him. He held me, and I pushed my face into his neck and inhaled the soap smell of his freshly washed skin, the leather of his mustard-colored jacket, and a scent I could not identify but which I knew was *family*. We stayed like that until he took his hands, placed them on my shoulders, pushing me back to look at my face.

He positioned his hand under my chin, smiled as he glanced at my indigo pendant necklace, and moved my head to the side. Then he nodded and said, "That's how Ruth wore her hair, pulled back in a knot. You look like your mother."

I took my hand and brushed back the lock of mottled hair above his ears. "I look like my father too."

There was a contorted smile on his face. "You know then. Anne told you, or gave you the letters."

"I think that, somehow, I always knew, but, yes, I read the letters, Uncle Ter…," and then I stopped. "Honestly, I'm not sure what to call you."

"How about *Terry*? Toby was always your *Dad*, and I think he should remain that. We'll talk, Livie. I'm sure you have questions."

"I do, and the first one is how did you know I was here?"

"I didn't know you were *here*, in the library. I traveled back through Chicago and stopped at Gladys' house thinking to find you there. Was told you were in Everstille, so I came here to find you. I planned to see Anne and find out where you were. I should have known you would be here. Library in the blood!"

We laughed, and the past years melted. He was here, in Everstille, with Anne and me. I thought my heart would explode. There were so many sudden questions that my mind teemed, but now wasn't the time, and here wasn't the place for them.

"Where's Anne?"

"She's in her office. I'll take you there. Wait until I do something," and I reached behind the desk to pull out a bell and wrote a note which said *Ring for Service*. Sure that Mr. Owens would be occupied for at least another hour with his newspapers, I was satisfied, and taking Terry's arm, we walked through the stacks and towards the office where Anne was seated at her desk reading and shuffling papers.

I knocked on the partially opened door as I pushed it. "Anne, there's someone here to see you."

She held up one finger to indicate she would need a minute, and finished reading the sheet in her hand. Then she looked up with that professional smile she kept for meeting patrons, and her mouth opened, changing her taut smile to surprise. The papers left her hand just as the notecards had left mine, and she stood, moving like a bolt into Terry's arms. He hugged her, and then, as they stood there, he looked over to me and pulled me in to their circle. I remembered the last time we were like this. I was ten, and leaving them, and wished that we would float up to the sky to stay. We were there.

"Why didn't you call and let us know you were on the way?" Anne wiped her eyes, and I wiped mine.

Terry grinned. "I was always one for surprises. Besides, I knew you were both here in Everstille, and I didn't want to lose travel time making a telephone call. I'm just glad to be here."

Anne sat back at her desk and motioned to Terry to take a seat, and I stood in the doorway. "Terry, there are so many things to ask you, but the first thing is, where are you staying?"

"Nowhere, but I'm hoping there is a hotel close so I can get organized and settled. Haven't thought about much else other than getting to see you two. What can you suggest?"

"I suggest you come and stay with us. There's plenty of room, and for some reason Livie and I cleaned the back bedrooms just recently. I must have had a premonition about you and just ignored it. Terry, we all have too much to talk about for you to be far away. Can your car hold me? Let's go to the house, and I can get you settled."

"Are you sure, Anne? I have a truck, and I believe I can squeeze you into the front seat. No car?"

"We walk on nice days. Livie, will you be OK here for a couple hours?"

"Of course I will. Besides, Mary Lou is coming in at noon. Go on, Terry, and get settled. I'll be home a little after three. There's so much we need to discuss."

Terry looked at Anne and then at me, and stood up to hug me once again. "Won't take much convincing. I'm happy to stay with you. Come on, Anne. My truck is in the front."

Anne reached over to grab her purse, and the three of us walked past the Circulation Desk. I saw Mr. Owens was still reading, and no one else had come in, so I took my place behind the desk and watched as Anne and Terry walked out. I would have preferred to go with them, but supposed the price of being an adult meant I had to stay at work. My heart was still beating rapidly, and I wasn't sure I could concentrate on needed tasks. I stared at the clock, figuring out the hours before I could be home; before I could see Terry and talk to him; before I was able to be with my father. Too many, I thought. I bent down to find the pencil which had rolled off the desk and tried, although not very successfully, to concentrate on completing my job.

As it turned out...

As it turned out, I ended up working not only with Anne at the library, but also with Terry at the restaurant. The days after Terry arrived felt different. I hadn't realized that I was waiting for him, but once he showed up, I knew a missing piece was back. That first night, Anne and Terry and I stayed up talking until well past midnight, and it was only when the three of us were yawning we decided to stop the questions and discussions and go to bed. Anne and I both needed to be up the next morning, and Terry said he was going to sleep in and then take a walk to the town to check out the changes. But, the next morning, I woke up to noises downstairs, and when I went to the kitchen, Anne and Terry were up, drinking coffee and talking, while Terry stayed busy making the buttermilk pancakes I hadn't eaten for years.

Nine years had gone by, and the three of us had plenty to say about our lives during that time. Anne told us of her dealings with the townspeople and the Library Board, the activities and growth of her large family, and her nascent efforts at writing. A short story of hers had been published in a women's magazine, and she was working on a children's book. Although Anne had heard most of my experiences in Chicago with the Murphy and Denison families, I repeated them for Terry. I spoke about my difficulties with Aunt Gladys and Rose, my attachment to the Pinkus family, Kari's friendship, my job at the Kozy Koffee Kafe, and my decision to save money and come home to Everstille. But it was Terry's accounts and narratives of his travels and exploits throughout the country that enthralled Anne and me.

When Terry left Everstille, he was unsure where he would go or what he would do. He spent a few weeks in the Chicago area looking up old friends and determining whether making a life there was even possible.

"I thought I could be close to you; maybe spend time with you, but attempts to see you were denied, and talks with the Murphys became angry shouting matches. Gladys threatened to call the police if I showed up anymore, and I was so depressed at losing most of my family that I just left. I traveled out west and stayed for a while in one town or another, rarely staying more than a few months. The only place I ended up for a longer time was Montana where I worked on a ranch."

"Thus, your cowboy look," teased Anne.

"Yes, Ma'am," said Terry using a western drawl which made us laugh.

We talked about his adventures. Terry said he could always find a job as a cook in a diner or restaurant, but he did other things too. I started to list his other jobs once, and he said I had a great memory, and it was better than his. Besides a cook, he worked at a gas station, as a bartender, a gardener, and a delivery man for some small company. But both Anne and I wanted to hear about his ranch activities.

"I was in South Dakota, working at a bar, west of Rapid City, and a couple of ranchers came in. It was a slow day, and we began to talk. When they got hungry and the kitchen wasn't yet opened, I told them I could cook something for them, and when I did, they asked about my expertise in the kitchen. We spoke for a while and the older man, Hank, gave me a piece of paper with his phone and address on it. He said if I ever wanted to work at a ranch kitchen, they were always looking for staff. I put it in my pocket, and about a month later, when I figured it was time to move on, I went to Montana and eventually found the ranch they owned. I asked to see Hank, we talked, and that's how I began there."

"Did you do the cooking for everyone on the ranch?" I asked.

"The Sunny Day Ranch was big and busy, breeding and raising both cattle and horses, and there were plenty of ranch-hands. I was one of three cooks in two large kitchens. The long-time cook, Mac, was basically in charge of organizing and ordering and maintaining the pantry stores, and the other cook, Jim, and I did most of the work. There used to be more cooks, but it was hard to keep workers there, and Jim and I were always busy. We really needed three cooks, so Mac would pitch in, and after I was there a couple months, another cook was hired."

"Did you ever get out of the kitchen and ride horses or help on the ranch?

Terry nodded. "There were times the kitchen staff was needed to help out. We usually knew ahead of time and prepared double food which would be stored away until we all came back."

Anne leaned forward to ask, "So what did you do?"

Terry shook his head. "It wasn't as exciting as you would think. The cattle were free-roaming, and when it was time to round them up for a market drive, someone was needed to work at the groundskeeping, doing mowing, and raking, and baling the hay. Then barn livestock and horses needed to be fed. Sometimes the out buildings or fences needed maintenance, so we were all kept busy doing that. Not much glamor in it, but we were outside, and it was a change."

"Did you ever get to ride the horses? That's something I'd like to do."

"Well, Cabbage, I did. But it wasn't a success. That's one of the reasons I stayed at that ranch for quite a while. Some of the cowboys there thought that since I wanted to ride, they would play a trick on me, and about my third time on a horse, they saddled up one of the wilder ones. I couldn't handle him and was thrown. Broke my leg and was laid up for a time. They felt bad, especially when the food was not what they expected. I couldn't get out of bed for six weeks, and once I could limp around, I had to sit at a table and cut up vegetables until the doctor gave me a go-ahead to work."

"I suppose," said Anne, "that was the end of your horse riding."

"For a while it was. Once I healed, I did get back on and ride. Cowboys made sure I got an old, slow horse, and I think I did it just so they wouldn't say I was scared. I liked the ranch, and most of the guys there were good ones, but after a time I knew it was time to move on. Went to Oregon and Washington State for a while after that."

We listened, and talked, and asked questions of Terry, and he was happy to tell us about his adventures. I had the feeling that there were more to his adventures than he was sharing with me. He and Anne would spend time talking, and often, when I showed up, the two of them would stop their discussion or quickly change the subject. Once, when Anne and I were alone, I mentioned this to her and asked about it.

"Livie, there are some things Terry isn't comfortable talking about in front of you, so just accept that. He still sees you as his little girl."

I thought about this and said, "Well, if it's about his love life, I've already figured that out. I did read the letters."

Anne just looked and me and smiled. Then she laughed. I never did find out what their conversations were about.

Terry stayed around the house doing chores and fixing things which needed to be repaired. He kept the grass cut and worked at the small garden for which neither Anne nor I had much time, and when he saw his old grill, he was thrilled. We had great meals because he took over the cooking, and during the warm summer days, would grill outside. We ate at the old picnic table Terry had found, repaired, and painted. In the good weather, it was picnic time nightly.

That lasted for a few weeks. One Wednesday, Terry announced to Anne and me, "Well, I'm a working cook again." While in town, he stopped at Mazie's to say hello. She needed a cook and offered the job to Terry. "My ready cash won't last forever," he explained, "and kitchen work is something I know. So, Livie, I guess you'll be working one job with Anne and the other job with me. How does that sound?"

"Sounds great to me. When do you start?"

"Tomorrow at lunchtime. We can walk to work together. So, who's cooking tonight, and what's for dinner?"

That night, I made hamburgers on the grill, under the direction of Terry although I knew what to do. We talked about the Sunny Day Ranch, planned dinners for the weekend, and Terry and I discussed his coming restaurant job. And that was how I ended up working with both Anne and Terry.

Our work schedules were complicated...

Our work schedules were complicated, and the three of us couldn't spend much time with each other except for Sunday afternoons. Anne and I decided that it wasn't fair that Terry worked in a kitchen all week and then made a Sunday dinner, so we took turns. Poor Terry got the bad end of that deal. When we had time, Anne and I would pour through the magazines at the library looking for new dinners to try. Sometimes they were successful. Not always. But Terry was a good sport about our attempts.

One Sunday in late summer after Anne and I cleaned up after Terry's delicious dinner, she reminded me she was going to her sister's house. Liz's son had a book report due and she thought Anne could help him. "Besides," explained Anne, "we haven't seen each other for a while. I should be back by six o'clock or so. I'm sure you and Terry can entertain yourselves."

"I suspect we can. Enjoy being a teacher!"

Anne left, and I went to the backyard where Terry was just finishing up weeding the garden. He turned to me and asked:

"Did Anne leave yet?"

"She did. Is there something you want me to help with? The place looks great, Terry. Much better than when we were working at it."

"Think I'm done for now. Since Anne isn't here, I thought you and I could take a ride to the cemetery. I know the two of you were out there earlier in the summer, but I think I'd like to visit today. How about it?"

"Sure. Let me get the old blanket and pour some iced tea to take with us. If I had known you wanted to go, we could have baked the cinnamon cake. Guess that will have to wait."

Terry nodded. "As long as we are traveling on the country road, I thought you might want to practice driving. Anne told me you don't have a license yet, and she hasn't been able to go out with you often. How about that?'

I sighed. Not that I didn't want to learn or get a license, but driving made me nervous, and Anne and I had only been out twice. Terry saw my hesitation.

"Livie, the only way to learn something is to do it. Go on and get the things ready, and I'll clean up. Meet me by the truck in five."

I went into the kitchen and gathered the tea and grabbed my purse and the old blanket. Terry was waiting by his truck and waved me into the driver's seat.

"No, Terry, I can't back out in this. I haven't even backed out in Anne's car, and this is so different. Please, back it out, and when we get to the country road, we can change seats. Please?"

Terry looked at me and nodded. He got into the driver's seat, and I crawled into the passenger side, placing the tea and blanket on the floor. I was feeling nervous and barely talked as we drove out to the road where Terry pulled over to the side, and we exchanged places. Then Terry began to talk in a foreign language.

"Now Livie, look at those three pedals on the floor. They…"

"Three? Anne's car has two."

"Let me explain. Gears help to move the power of the car from one part to another, and you need to change gears to increase or decrease speed or do things like go up a hill. Anne's car is an automatic. That means the car shifts itself into different gears. This truck is a stick shift. That means you will need to use the clutch, the one on the far left, to start the car and to change gears. Use your left foot for that and your right foot for the other two: the gas and the brake. This is the gear box."

"Terry, this is not what Anne's car is like. If I can drive her car, why is this so different? It's not what I'm used to."

"It's always good to know how to drive different vehicles, Livie, and this is the one I have now. Try it. Let's get the truck started."

Terry continued to talk to me about the shifting (upshift, down-shift), the use of the clutch pedal (Push it all the way down, and leave off the gas pedal to push in the clutch when moving to second gear.), and changing gears when I heard the engine's RPM change (I never heard anything.) After several false starts, I got the truck going and Terry told me when to shift, but I saw him grit his teeth when there was a grinding sound which was apparently not good for the vehicle. It took a long time to travel the mile or so to North Cemetery, and when I tried to turn into the narrow lane, Terry told me to ease off the gas pedal, slowly apply the brake, shift into neutral, and coast. The car lurched forward and stopped with a weird sound. Terry took a deep breath.

"Guess we're here," he said.

"Sorry, Terry. I'm not sure I can do this. I don't want to damage your truck either. Maybe driving is just not for me."

He turned to me and shook his head. "No, Cabbage, you need to know how to drive, and I can teach you. We just have the wrong vehicle here. I doubt that you'll be driving a stick anyway. I'll talk to Anne tonight. I'm sure we can figure things out. We're here. Let's go."

We spent an hour or so at the graves of Ruth and Toby. I cleaned up a few weeds that had grown in the month or so since Anne and I had visited, and we sat on the old blanket sharing the tea I had packed for us. Terry was quiet for a long time.

Finally, he spoke. "The two of them were the most important people in my life before Anne and you came along. I know you read that in my letter, and it might seem strange that Ruth and Toby loved each other too, although not in the normal husband and wife way. The three of us were happy and looking forward to you being in our lives. Life is funny, Livie."

He stayed quiet after that, and I wasn't sure what to say, so I didn't answer him. We stayed for a while longer, and then he said we should probably get going.

"Terry, I don't want to drive back. Is that a problem?"

He laughed. "No, that's fine. I'll get us home, and we'll figure out a way to teach you and get that license. Come on. I have a taste for some of that ice cream in the freezer. How about you?"

We got into the truck, and he drove us home. That night, the three of us discussed using Anne's car, and a plan was devised. Terry usually had Sundays and Tuesdays off and started late on Wednesdays and Thursdays. We drove on those days, and he proved to be a patient teacher. I learned to back in and out, pull forward, turn the corners, and come to a full stop without flinging us both into the windshield. Driving was one thing, but parking was another. Terry had a plan for that too.

One day, I watched as he drove into the side driveway of the house with bales of hay in the back of his truck. During my next driving lesson, I was instructed to park between the bales of hay which had been placed quite a distance from each other. Slowly the bales came closer together, and eventually, I became a better parker. The day I was able to parallel park between the bales without touching either one, Terry picked me up and twirled me around.

"I knew you could do it. Now there is one more thing you need to do before I take you to Elkhart for that license."

"And that is?"

"You need to learn to drive in the bad weather. When the snow and ice come, it's a different ballgame in a car. But, don't worry. We'll practice through this winter and in the spring, the road is yours!"

That's what happened. The following spring, I was ready for the driving test. I wasn't worried about the written exam, but the driving one made me nervous. When I passed and held up my license for him to see, Terry nodded and said, "That's my girl!"

I hugged him. And without thinking about it or expecting the words to come out, I said, "Thanks, Dad."

That year with Terry...

That year with Terry seemed so normal that Chicago almost faded in my memory. While I kept in touch with Kari, her life was evolving. Babcia had died, her two brothers were married, and Kari was engaged. Our phone conversations were short, and the time between letters lengthened, but I would always be grateful for the kindness and friendship of the Pinkus family. Having discovered that I was not related to either the Murphy or Denison family made it easy to have little to do with them. I considered telling them why I had no interest in maintaining a familial friendship, but both Anne and Terry thought it wasn't necessary and would only tarnish Toby's memory in his family.

"Leave it be," said Anne, "Sending a yearly Christmas card and including a short note isn't that much of a duty. And once a year or so when Gladys calls, the conversation is never long. Don't let it bother you."

"I suppose," I answered, "but I would sure like to know where all that life insurance money went. I suppose to Ivy's wedding and Rose's college education. Also, to Gladys' hair and nails."

Anne shrugged. "Livie, I agree, but I told you there would be some way of affording college if you decided to do that."

I said nothing. Anne and I had spent some time discussing the possibility of my attending college. She suggested I send for the application and catalogue for Indiana University, which I did. "Just look through it," she encouraged. Anne had always wanted to go to college, and I accused her once of living through me. She sighed and said, "You're probably right," and I let it go.

The town's fall festival came, and Terry, Anne, and I stood and watched the high school band marching and wearing their red and white uniforms and playing a new march, one I did not recognize. The parade had been expanded, and the floats, which were now all pulled by trucks, had increased to three. The assemblage of arts and crafts vendors lined the side streets, bringing in additional visitors, and the marching organizations now included both the Boy Scouts and the Girl Scouts. I stood and watched and vividly remembered my childhood at the parade with Dad and Terry. Terry and I were pressed into working extra hours that weekend, but neither of us minded, and the extra tips were handy. I was saving up for that car I would one day own.

Thanksgiving was a spectacular family feast held at Josh Rivens' house. Anne's youngest brother and his wife, Beatrice, had a lovely and large home, and Anne's considerable family piled into it making for a crowded, exuberant, and entertaining time. That day turned out to be exceptionally warm, so the men took all the children out for a long walk while an early evening dinner was readied. When they came back, they claimed *starvation*, and we all filled our plates, ate, and talked. Anne made her cookies and the scalloped potato casserole, while Terry and I, following Babcia's recipes, worked together, creating dozens of pierogis and kolaczki, bringing a tasty bit of Poland to the Thanksgiving meal. None of them were left which I took as a testament to their deliciousness.

The warmth and dryness of that November lasted into December, but even without a snowfall, the Christmas celebrations were joyous. I'm unsure if it was the weather which accounted for my cheerfulness during that time or the fact that Terry was back to spend the holiday with us. We did some shuffling of work schedules and all claimed the same free Saturday afternoon. Just as we used to when I was young, we drove to South Bend for a day of lunching, shopping, and deciding on a special ornament for the tree. That night, we decorated the tree in Anne's front room, carefully placing the ornaments and reminiscing about each one. I don't think that even Christmas Day was as festive as that Saturday evening with the three of us laughing and talking and remembering.

I spent New Year's Eve with some friends at Maggie's house. At first, I wasn't going to go, thinking I should spend the evening with Anne and Terry, but they insisted.

"Livie, go be with your friends. Have a great time. We'll spend New Year's Day together and relax," Terry reassured me, "Anne and I are old folks here, and we'll watch some television and talk."

"Not so sure I like being called *old folks*," laughed Anne, and then she added, "Go on. Livie. Welcome in 1974 with Maggie and the others."

I did go and enjoyed myself. But the following day, I was just as happy to spend it with Terry and Anne making a *Hoppin' John* casserole that apparently my mother once insisted would bring luck in the new year. As we ate, I listened wistfully as Anne and Terry recalled the occasions they spent with Toby and my mother, and could only imagine what my life would have been like had they remained in it.

The following months were some of the driest on record. Terry insisted I continue to drive and bemoaned the fact that it looked as though I might need to wait to practice driving in snow for another year. But he said my driving was getting better, and even insisted on a few more lessons driving his stick shift truck. "You just don't know," he explained for the umpteenth time, "when you might need this skill."

When March passed and April appeared, and the thought of snow was eliminated, Terry told me to review the Indiana's Bureau of Motor Vehicles' written test questions because after Easter, he would be taking me for my license. I reviewed and studied but remained nervous.

"You'll be fine," he said as we traveled in Anne's car towards Elkhart's BMV. "Do you need to look over the questions again?"

"Not worried about the written part. I know that. I'm just nervous about the driving portion. What if I fail? Then what?"

"Then you take it again," Terry said, "but I have faith in you. You had a great teacher!"

I did have a great teacher. I passed both parts of the test, and when I held up my new license to Terry, he smiled and nodded. He insisted we stop on the way home to pick up dinner as a celebration, and when Anne got home that evening, we celebrated.

Spring came, and when it got closer to my birthday, Anne and Terry began to talk about having a party for me.

"Twenty years old! That calls for some celebration, don't you think?"

I wasn't excited about the prospect. "No, Anne. Please, I'm too old for a birthday party."

"You had one last year, with the Story Book group."

"Right, and they were three and four years old. Just a dinner here with the two of you is fine. Please."

Terry looked at me. "So, what do you want for that dinner? And choose your cake. At least we can continue that tradition."

I thought. "Make your meatloaf and mashed potatoes, and if there are some early strawberries, shortcake would be perfect."

And that's what we did. I was touched by the lovely bracelet Anne bought me, but Terry's gift was typically generous and practical. He paid for a year of automobile insurance for me.

"Who knows?" he explained after I hugged him in thanks, "Maybe you'll get that car of yours sooner than you think."

I wish I had known then. I wish I had realized the meaning behind his comments. I wish I had understood that this birthday dinner was the last one he would make for me. I wish I knew what he had planned. I wish.

During that spring, I noticed...

During that spring, I noticed a reserve in Terry that hadn't been there before. When we sat on the porch he would suddenly stop talking or not answer a question and stare into space. When Anne or I called his name, sometimes it took three tries to get his attention. He would sometimes tell us he was going for a short walk, and then return two or more hours later. I asked him once if anything was wrong, but he just smiled and shook his head. Sometimes he would reach over to me and push my hair back or hold my cheek for a second and look pensive. I asked Anne if she thought something was the matter, but she just shrugged. Terry was simply not present.

The last Sunday we were all together, Terry got up early in the morning and baked a cinnamon cake. "I thought that when you come home from church, we could visit the cemetery. The day is going to stay cool and it might be a nice outing for us. Think so?"

We did, and when Anne and I returned home after the early service, we changed clothes and prepared to go. I pulled out the old blanket to spread on the ground, and Anne packed the basket with cups, napkins, and a knife to cut the cooled cake. We went to her car, and she handed me the keys. "Go ahead," she said, "you're the chauffeur for today."

As I drove to North Cemetery, Anne and I kept up a running conversation about minor things; the weather, town gossip, our new dinner casserole for the evening. Terry was sitting quietly in the back seat, and as I glanced in the rear-view mirror, he sat with his chin propped up on his hand, looking out the window, not paying attention to the conversation. I pulled into the narrow lane, stopped the car, and said, unnecessarily, "We're here."

Terry carried the basket, I took the blanket, and Anne held the wrapped cake. We walked together to the graves of Ruth and Toby, and I spread the blanket for us. Anne bent down to remove a few weedy growths in from of the stones and then joined us on the blanket. We sat silently until Terry spoke.

"I feel at ease, here with my family, present and past. Anne and Livie, I hope you know how much I appreciate being with you both through this time. Everstille is a special place; a hometown to me. Of all the places I have traveled to and lived in, this town is the one I claim. When asked where I am from, I always answer 'Everstille, Indiana'."

I nodded my head. "I know, Terry. All the time I was in Chicago, I never felt it was my home. Here is where I belong."

Anne looked solemnly at us and mumbled, "Umm," and we were all still again. After a bit, Anne reached into the basket and pulled out napkins and the knife. She unwrapped the cake and cut generous slices and poured glasses of tea. She held up her glass and toasted, "Here's to Ruth and Toby and us, *Family*, as Terry said, past and present."

We sipped the tea and ate the cake, and I listened as Terry and Anne told stories about Ruth and Toby. I had heard them before but never tired of them, and we spent a pleasant time in the June afternoon.

That evening, after dinner was eaten and dishes were done, we went out to the front porch and got comfortable. In a while, Anne went in and brought out three dishes of ice cream which we ate in companionable silence. It was getting dark and fireflies were visible. It was the end to a comfortable day, and I should have been feeling content, but there was a troublesome element in my heart, and I couldn't identify it. I decided I was being ridiculous and ignored it.

"Well," and I stood up and collected the dishes, "think I'm going to get to bed. I want to finish the latest book, Anne. Maybe later in the week we can talk about it."

"Yes, we'll do that," she said.

"I'll put these in the sink. Coming in soon?"

Terry looked up at me. "Soon, but I think Anne and I will talk out here for a while."

"Goodnight, then. See you in the morning," and I turned to go into the house and the kitchen where I rinsed out the dishes and placed them in the sink. I turned to go upstairs, and Terry was standing next to the stairway.

"Oh, I didn't hear you come in. Thirsty?"

He shook his head and then said, "Come here, Livie," and when I moved closer to him, he brought me in for a hug which he held. "I want you to know that I'm proud of you. You're smart, and kind, and clever. I just wanted you to know what I think."

I was surprised at this emotion from him, and I hugged him back and said, "Thanks. I love you; you know."

"I know."

After a few seconds, he looked at me and pushed my hair back. "Livie, I want you to consider going to college. There's always a way, and I think you'll find it. Will you do that?"

"I'll think about it, Terry. You know money is an issue, but really, I'll consider it."

"Good," he said. "Now, I think I will get some water for Anne and me. Go on up, and read that book. Good-night."

"'Night, Terry," and I walked up the stairs as Terry poured two glasses of water and took them outside to the porch where he and Anne sat and talked while the fireflies flickered nearby.

The morning sun was not shining yet...

The morning sun was not shining yet, but I was wide awake. I listened and heard slight noises downstairs and thought Anne was awake and moving around. Putting on my bathrobe, I glanced at the alarm clock which claimed 5:45 A.M., and shut it off. Anne's door was still closed, so I figured Terry was the one making soft noises. We could have coffee together and talk before he left for his breakfast shift in half an hour. I walked quietly down the stairs expecting to see him in the kitchen making coffee, but he wasn't there. The back laundry room light was on, and I looked out the back door to see Terry placing his suitcase and some bags into his truck. His duffel bag was inside, waiting.

Terry turned around to walk back to the house and saw me standing there. He stood outside and looked at me. Then he came in.

I stepped back. There were so many emotions in my core, I didn't think I could talk, and when I did, anger and sorrow was mixed in my voice. "You're leaving. Why? Where are you going? Why are you leaving, Terry?"

He stood inside the back door and leaned against the wall as he looked at me standing in my bare feet, clutching my bathrobe shut, winding my arms abound my middle to keep myself together.

"Livie, as much as I feel at home here, it's time for me to leave. Over the years I've moved from place to place, and gotten used to seeing new sights and meeting different people. Starting a life over was always exciting. Being with Anne and especially with you has been important for me. I needed to see you, to know that you are grown and safe. I wanted to spend time with you, and I have. You are an adult, and I'm proud of you and know you'll do well."

"Stay with us and make sure of that! How can I lose you again?" I could not help the tears.

Terry came over and held me while he talked. "You are not losing me. I promise. I just need to do some traveling before it's too late, and I haven't seen whatever it is I need to see. That sounds strange, but it's how I feel."

"But where are you going? Where will you be?"

"Not sure. Livie. I've been out west, and I think I'll travel east for a bit. Ohio, then Pennsylvania, and New York. I always wanted to see New York City. And then maybe back to Virginia or up to Maine."

"Then take me with you. I can pack and go. I want to see those things too."

"You have a life here, Livie. And you promised to think about college. There's plenty of time for you to see and do things. Anyway, traveling on the road isn't easy. What about Anne? You don't want to leave her."

"But you're leaving. Why didn't you tell me or say something? I knew there was something you were thinking about; that there was something wrong. I could tell. How could you leave and not even say anything to me? To Anne?"

Terry pointed to the countertop along the side of the room. "There. I left a letter for you explaining it all. Anne and I talked last night, and she knows. I wouldn't just leave, but I thought it would be easier this way. I didn't want this to happen. I didn't want to make you cry."

"Please, Terry, at least stay and let's talk about this. What about Mazie? Does she know?"

"I told her last week."

"Then this was planned, and everyone knew except me. Why?" I felt in the bathrobe packet, finding tissue, and pulled it out. I blew my nose and hic-cupped.

Terry had his arm around my shoulders and pulled me to him. "Livie, I don't always do things right, I know that. I'm sorry I've hurt you. That's the last thing I want to do. But I promise you two things. Are you listening?"

I nodded; I placed my arms around him, not wanting to leave his warmth, and looked up at him.

"First, I will be better about keeping in touch this time. I will write and call, and when I land at a new place for a while, I'll let you and Anne know where that is. Alright?"

I nodded again.

"Secondly, I promise I'll be back. I need to travel a bit. I can't tell when, and it may be a year or more, but I'll return. Bad penny showing up again! I told Anne the same things I'm telling you. I'll stay in touch, and I'll be back."

"Why don't you stay just for a while. We can have breakfast and talk. Please?"

Terry pushed my hair back and caressed my cheek. He smiled but it was a sad one, and I knew he wouldn't prolong this particular pain.

"It's better that I go now. I'm packed and ready and staying here will just make it harder when I do leave. I promise: I'll stay in touch; I'll be back," and he pulled me in again, and we held onto each other, and my father said to me, "You are mine, Cabbage. You always have been and always will be." Then he let me go.

I stood quietly crying as he picked up the duffel bag and loaded it into the truck. He got in and started it, pushing down the clutch to the floor as he taught me. He slowly backed out of the side driveway, and I followed his slow movement as I walked from side window to side window, observing him leave.

Just before he backed up onto the street to head out of town, he stopped and regarded me standing in the window, watching him. I placed my hand on the window in the same way I once, long ago, signaled a farewell to him and Anne and my mother's ghost, and I kept it there until he backed up and pulled forward, and I could no longer see him or his truck.

I stayed at the window and then realized I was cold, and it was not due to the early morning chill. I walked over to the sofa and took off the blanket throw which I wrapped around my shoulders. I walked over to the rocking chair my father had bought for my mother so that she could sit in it and rock me when I cried. I sat in it, alone, and cried.

I watched as the sun slowly begin to lighten up the sky and rocked so slowly, I didn't appear to be moving. I wasn't sure what time it was, but I could hear Anne coming down the stairs. She paused at the bottom, then walked around the corner where she stood surveying me. "He left, didn't he? And you saw him off."

I nodded and wiped my eyes with a corner of the blanket throw. Anne turned around and came back with a box of tissue which she put down in my lap. She allowed me my sorrow. After I didn't think I could cry anymore, I stopped. I gathered the dozen tissues I had used and squeezed them together in my hand and looked at Anne.

"He said he would keep in touch and that he would return, but not for a while."

"Yes, I know. And, Livie, I believe him. I hope you do too."

I sighed and took one more tissue. I blew my nose and took a breath which I expelled in another sigh. Anne came over and brushed back my hair in the same way my father had. She smiled at me and kissed my forehead.

"We'll be fine, Livie. All of us. We can talk more if you feel up to it, but right now, I'm going to make coffee and start oatmeal. Go on upstairs and wash up. Hold some cold cloths to your face, and when you're ready, come back down. I'll have breakfast ready. You know, we have a library to run. It's Monday, and Mr. Owens will be waiting for those papers."

I did smile at that. Then I placed the blanket throw back, wadded up the tissues, walked over to the kitchen trash, and threw them away. I walked upstairs to do what Anne had instructed. I needed to get ready for the day. Mr. Owens would be waiting.

It wasn't until the next day...

It wasn't until the next day, after work, that I remembered the letter that had been left. I walked to the countertop, picked it up, and brought it to the kitchen table with me. I poured myself some water and sat down to open it. There was something in it, and when I shook it out, a key fell onto the kitchen table. I hadn't seen a key like this one, so I read the explanation Terry left me.

The letter was short and to the point. It basically repeated everything he had told me the morning before. He needed to travel again. He knew I would be well and safe. He loved Anne. He loved me. He was proud of the person I had become. He would stay in touch. He would return. And the key was for me to take to the Everstille Bank. It was a key to a safety deposit box, and someone at the bank would help me with it. I should ask for Howard Jones, Jr., the bank's manager (and the owner's son), who expected me. There was a letter with additional explanations in the box.

I reread the one page. I looked at the key and thought this was so like Terry...making mundane things interesting. I sipped at the water and looked at the time. The bank would still be open for another hour, but I decided that tomorrow morning would suffice. I wanted to talk to Anne first.

When she came home, I had a simple dinner of hot dogs and beans waiting. I didn't have much of an appetite, and was waiting on the front porch as she walked home. I had the letter in my hand and as she came up the steps, I handed it to her. "Here, read this," I instructed.

She sat down on the swing next to me and looked the letter over. Then she looked at me.

"Pretty straight forward, Livie. I'm surprised you didn't go right to the bank. You're more patient than I would be."

"What's in the safety deposit box? I know he told you. Is it money?"

"Yes, he told me, and yes, it is."

"Where did he get it? Why didn't he just give it to me, or better still, why couldn't he use it and just stay here with us?"

Anne took off her glasses and cleaned them on the bottom on her skirt. She sighed. "Terry has a reason for it all. I am sure the letter in the box will explain it. Tomorrow, go and find out, Livie. It's his surprise for you."

"Tell me, Anne."

She put her glasses back on and stood up. "I will, but let's go inside. I want some water and need to take these shoes off."

We walked inside, and she went up the stairs to change her clothes and shoes. I finished setting the table and placed the dishes and beans and hot dogs out and put large glasses of iced water next to our plates. Anne sat down, and we ate while she spoke.

"When you were taken to Chicago, Terry was beside himself. He went there, and you know that he wasn't welcomed by either Gladys or Ernestine. He was as sad as I had ever seen him, and he told me that he just needed to leave, to travel, to clear his mind. He asked me to go with him, but I couldn't, so he planned to leave in late spring after the house and furnishings were sold. I never asked how much he got, but I knew there was money. Once day he came into the library to see me. He had just been to the bank and talked to Mr. Jones, the old man, and discussed financial things with him. He planned things for you."

"That's where the money came from then. Didn't he keep any? After all, the house was his."

"Terry said the house was yours, and he couldn't keep it. He kept some money to travel, but his plan was always to give it to you when you were grown. I think that's why he returned when he did. He needed to check on you and make sure you got what he thought was rightfully yours. No, I don't know how much money is there. I know that was your next question, Livie, but you'll find out tomorrow."

We sat for a while, and I picked at my meal as Anne finished hers. We cleared the dishes, and I swept the floor as Anne emptied the trash. When she came back in, she asked, "Are you up to discussing the book tonight? We can sit on the porch and do that."

"Porch sitting sounds great, but I don't think I can concentrate on a book discussion tonight. I'd rather we talk about Terry and Toby and my mother. Tonight, I need you to tell me the stories again. Feel up to story-telling?"

She did, and that's what happened. Anne and I sat on the porch swing and I listened to her. She spoke of my mother and how they met. She described the way Ruth taught her with the library books and trained her to work at the library. She explained how Toby came to town to teach, and became the high school principal, and how he and my mother met, becoming fast friends. Anne talked about when Terry first came to town and how he lived with my mother and Toby, and how he charmed the town and became accepted. She revealed that she was part of their group and described the fun the four of them had. Anne repeated the story of my birth and the pain of my mother's death afterwards, and reminded me of the rainbow-filled home both my fathers crafted for me. She communicated to me the stories of my family, although I knew them. As the moon became apparent, and the silence of the evening was interrupted by occasional crickets, I sat, and listened, and remembered; when the fireflies began to spark, there was an ease that surrounded us, and a gladness that engulfed me.

After three weeks...

After three weeks, we heard from Terry who was working and living in Columbus, Ohio. I was glad he was keeping his word, but I continued to be upset and a bit perturbed at the way he left. Still, it was good to hear his voice.

There was a Certificate of Deposit which would mature in a few months, and a generous amount of cash in the safety deposit box. The letter with it instructed that I should get a decent used car and go to college. At first, I was upset with Terry's instructions. Who did he think he was? And then I realized who he was, and that he was giving me the advice a father would. Anyway, that's what Anne said, and after I thought about it, I realized she was right. So, we went to Mackie's Service Station and Used Car Lot, and Mackie himself helped me pick out a car. Not a new one, but a decent running one. I did, however, refuse to get one with a stick shift.

I made an appointment with a college counselor at the Indiana University extension in South Bend, and Anne arranged to go with me. I began to get excited about the possibility of going to college, but I felt strange about starting because I was older than most freshmen. I remained unconvinced this was the right thing for me, but Anne and the counselor suggested I begin as a part-time student, take a few courses in the fall, and make a decision after that. That's the plan. And because I have a car, I'll commute.

I feel bad about the fact that once I start school, I won't be able to keep both of my jobs. One will have to go. Anne said to do what I have to, and both she and Mazie said they would work around my class schedule. I love being at the library with Anne, and I hate to give up the Story Book Hour, but I need to be practical. Working at Mazie's, collecting tips, created more money for me than working at the library, so once I start classes in the fall, I'll continue at the restaurant. But through this summer, I'll work both jobs.

I like driving my new used car. It's a Volkswagen. It's called a *Super-Beetle* because it's three inches longer than a regular VW Beetle. It's sky-blue which reminds me of my bedroom walls when I was five and had Miss Kendal for kindergarten. Anne wasn't thrilled with my choice because she thinks it's too small a car to drive, but I think it's perfect. There is a sunroof, and Mackie fixed it for me when it rained, and I discovered that the right side of me got soaking wet. However, I didn't tell Anne about the leaking sunroof due to her prejudice. I wash the car weekly, and in a a few days, I'm going to take a practice ride to the IU campus to time the trip. I'm planning ahead.

Last Sunday afternoon I was invited to go with Anne to her sister's house, but I wanted to drive my car and stop at the cemetery. After we ate lunch, we both took off, and I opened the sunroof and waved at her. I drove around Everstille looking at the new businesses in town and the new houses out on Country Road 8. I drove past the cemetery a few times and then turned into the narrow lane where I parked the car and walked over to spend some time with my mother and Toby. It was a perfect summer day, not too warm, and the breeze was comfortable. I sat for a time in front of the graves thinking about them and Terry and Anne and the coming fall at college. Suddenly, I felt a cramp in my leg, and I stood up to stretch it out. As I stood there, I heard someone calling to me.

"Livie! Livie, it's me!"

I turned and watched a man come towards me. He seemed familiar, and as he got closer, I realized it was Mike Jasper. He was tall and had a beard, and I was surprised to see him.

"Mike! It's been years. How are you? What are you doing here? I almost didn't recognize you with that beard."

"I just got here Friday. I'm staying with my grandpa and going to IU in the fall. After high school, I found a job and took some classes at a junior college. I couldn't afford full-time college, so I had to save some money. Grandpa's getting older, and needs someone to be with him, so I volunteered. If I'm living in Indiana with him, I can go to IU. I'll also look for a part-time job. How are you? Maggie told me you were back here."

"She didn't say anything to me, but then I haven't seen her for a while. She's been busy; I've been busy. What are you doing here at the cemetery?"

"Taking a walk. My aunts and uncles and cousins are coming over this afternoon to see me, and we're going to have a potluck tonight. I suppose some of them are there now, and I should get back. Maybe now that I'm here, in Everstille, we can get together with Maggie and Bob."

"That would be fun. Did you say you walked here?"

"Yep. My car is at Grandpa Wells'. Thought a short walk before seeing everyone would be good. Besides, Grandpa took a nap. He's probably up now."

I pointed to my VW. "That's my car. I can drive you back to the cabin. I was leaving anyway."

"Sure, that'll be great."

We went to the car and got in. I backed it up and pulled forward and drove slowly so we could talk. I told Mike I was taking some classes in the fall at IU, and I asked him some questions about the classes he had taken.

"There are general classes everyone takes, and eventually you get to concentrate on classes for your degree."

"What do you want to do?" I asked.

"My father teaches history, and that's what I would like to do. That's what I'm planning to do. What about you? Have you thought about it?"

Until then, I hadn't, and I'm unsure where the idea came from, but I said, "Literature. I think I want to do something with that. Not sure I want to teach, but I'm not ruling it out. I need to think about it."

Mike smiled and nodded. Then he pointed to the right. "Here," he said, "this is where you turn."

"I remember," and I turned into the path and saw that there were several cars parked in front of the cabin. "I guess your company is here."

"Some of them are. Listen, Livie, why don't you come in? You probably know most everyone who will be here. And Maggie and Bob are coming later. Come on, stay."

"Well, I need to call Anne and let her know where I am."

"That's not a problem. Come on in and stay for dinner. I should warn you though: there will be plenty of small kids running around. Watch your toes!"

I chuckled, and we left the car and walked up the stairs to the cabin where faint laughing and talking could be heard.

"We can go in, and you can call Anne. Then we'll join everyone in the backyard," Mike stopped. He tilted his head and regarded me. "You know, at the cemetery, I knew it was you because of your hair."

I looked at the cabin's door window where my head was reflected. In the glass, my hair was revealed a darker copper penny hue which contained a bit of orangey gold that was mixed with burgundy. I contemplated my reflection. Then I smiled at Mike.

"My hair. Yes. I take after my father."

He considered my hair, nodded his head, pulled open the door to the cabin, and together, we went in.

Terrence Douglas' Letter
1955

You don't have to have the same blood to be family.
Unknown

Written the week after Christmas, 1955

Dear Little Cabbage,

I have some time off, and it is cold, and Christmas is over. I am starting this in the afternoon as you are napping, and Toby said he will take care of you while I get this completed. I want to continue writing until I am done; otherwise, I am afraid I won't succeed. So, here goes.

I have been forced into writing to you. That's a bad choice of words. Of course, I want you to know about your family and background, but I read what Toby wrote, and it seems like it's all there. I want to do what's best for you, but I guess Toby and Anne are right. They think I might be able to add something to our story. I suppose there are some things I can tell you. Maybe, because you are reading this and are much older, you already know them. Perhaps I have told you things. But in case I haven't, I'll try to do it now. This letter will be short. I can't write as good as Toby can and don't have the patience he does.

I grew up in Chicago with my mother and younger brother, Thomas. In fact, if you had been a boy, we were going to name you after him. Didn't turn out that way. Tommy and me and Mom lived in a small apartment in a neighborhood on Chicago's southside, and things were rough growing up. Tommy was born when I was four, and then my father left. Mom never much spoke about him or about that time, and I have no idea where he went or why he left, or what happened to him. I don't have a picture of him, but I do remember he had red hair like mine. And Tommy's. And yours. That's the saddest part of my life. Until your mother died. When Tommy was about four (and I was eight), there was a bad influenza going around, and Tommy got it and died. Mom was working as a seamstress in a factory and she got sick too, but she lived. At least long enough to bury Tom and find me a place where I could live and be safe, and then she died too.

There was a family who lived on the next street and the woman and Mom were friends. They had worked together, and I guess Mom did a great favor for the woman, Jenny. I never knew what the favor was, but it had to be a big one because once Mom died, Jenny and her husband took me in and raised me with their two older girls, Clara, and Mabel. They were nice enough as sisters, but didn't pay much attention to me. Part of that was because they were in high school, and after that, they went and moved on with their own lives. Later, after I left, Jenny got real sick and died, and the last time I saw them was at her wake. Lost touch with them. Jenny did me a favor because she insisted I go to school. I think that if she had not been so hard on me in that area, I wouldn't have met Toby. Things turn out funny sometimes.

I went on to high school and was mostly an average student. I always had a job of some kind, and that seemed more important to me, but Jenny said Mom made her promise I would get an education. Don't know if that's true or not, but I believed it when I was young, and it made me finish school. I wasn't the best student, but that wasn't the teachers' faults. I caught on quick, did little studying, and it seemed to me that school was easier than some of the jobs I had.

The high school senior class was mostly girls, and so some luck came my way. There was a stipend to take some college classes that was available to a male senior who had at least a "C" average and showed what was called *promise*. A few teachers got together and thought I should get it. I was sure at the time they were nuts, but since then, I realized they were just desperate to give it out and not have it wasted. It wasn't much, but paid for a small room at the "Y" near the Chicago Normal College, with some cash left over for books and supplies and a bit of food. I hadn't planned to or wanted to, but I found myself out on my own, living in a room hardly big enough to stand with my arms outstretched, and going to school as a part-time college student. It was pure luck because Jenny's husband was never much of a fan of mine, and he told me that I had to get out as soon as I turned eighteen.

I took a class or two here and there, just enough to keep to the letter of the stipend, and got a job working for the college. The college was one that trained teachers to work mostly in the Chicago schools, but I wasn't drawn to being a teacher. The institution turned out to be an interesting place for someone like me. And now comes the hard part, Livie, and the part Toby and I hope you are old enough and smart enough to understand. I suspect you are. Toby and I haven't quite figured it all out yet, but we agreed that we would raise you to accept and honor people who are different or at least feel that way. That's important.

Chicago Normal College is where I met Toby. We ended up in a class together, and I noticed him right away. Actually, all the students, especially the women, did. Toby was like a Greek god in his younger days. He was tall and blonde and had great-looking eyes. Still does. He was always polite and friendly to everyone, and he was well liked. I liked him immediately too.

I don't remember what the class was, but I had to do some research and read something for it at the school's library. I went there one day after I completed my janitorial work. I was in the stacks looking for the book and reached for it at the same time Toby did. That's how we met. We shared the book, and then shared a friendship. I never finished college; it really wasn't for me, but am ever glad I went there and spent time in the library. Funny how libraries fit in all our lives.

When Toby moved back to Everstille, and you have read about that, I missed him. I always had some women friends, and I began to see one or two on a regular basis. Yes, Livie, I like women too, and that's hard to explain. I can't figure it out, so I'm not sure you can either. But I was regularly seeing a woman, Betsy, and was thinking that maybe I could have a normal life. Maybe I could marry Betsy, and settle down with her, and get a full-time job, and feel that I was the same as other men. That was the problem I had. I didn't feel normal, didn't feel like other guys felt. I listened to the college guys talk and knew I had to hide my feelings and actions. I was always afraid of being caught doing something I could be arrested for. Toby already explained that we had to be careful when we saw each other on those weekends he came up to Chicago to visit. So, with Betsy, things were just easier in lots of ways. But I missed Toby, and when he came up, and we talked about me moving to Everstille and what life might be like, I realized that was what I wanted. I ended up going back to Everstille with him. And living with him and Ruth.

I knew about Ruth. I knew that Toby thought he needed to get married, and she had agreed to. I also knew that Ruth didn't really like me when I came to live with them. Toby had told me about the arguments they had, and it was understandable. My feelings about Ruth were mixed too, and I didn't know what to expect. I didn't intend to stay with them forever, but that changed. Ruth and I had our troubles at first. Then, we became friends. And then more than friends.

I can write about this because Toby and I have discussed it at length. We fought about what happened, and then the three of us argued about it, and it seemed to go on forever. Ruth and I felt guilty, but then again, strangely, we didn't. The peculiarity about it is that the three of us loved each other. I don't think I have ever used that word before. It is easier to write it than say it. We knew the town was watching and listening. Small towns have big ears and watchful eyes. That was one of the reasons Anne and I started a sham relationship, so the town could see and hear, and hopefully, forget their suspicions.

Anne is part of our lives. She always will be. Perhaps it would surprise you to learn that I have discussed marriage with her. Toby and

Anne and I have had many conversations over the past months about that and about her moving in with all of us. Anne has remained insistent about not marrying. She said she is married to her books and the library. Anyway, as she explained, a marriage to me would be the ultimate betrayal of Ruth, and she is probably right. I read Toby's writing and he left out what really happened between Ruth and me. He said it was my responsibility to tell you and to tell you as much as I thought you should know. And I think you should know.

I watched a bird build a nest once. First some twigs and loose hay were laid around making a base. Then, little by little, more small twigs and hay, some hair like substance, and odd-and-ends were placed into the base, and then one day when I looked, it had changed. There was a nest. It had been built with small pieces and slowly turned into a home for the eggs she would sit on and hatch. That was the way it was with Ruth. We tolerated each other, and I was grateful that she let me and Toby be together. We kept our spaces, and I let her have her way around the house because I was just a guest. At first.

I watched as she did things for Toby. His shirts were cleaned, and ironed, and hung up. Then one day, mine were too, and she never asked, but just did. I saw her make the baked apples just the way Toby liked them, and one day I came home to the shortbread cookies I had told her were delicious. Ruth worked the same as Toby and me, and how she got the time to do these little things, I don't know, but she did. There was the time Toby broke the coffee cup he used every morning for his coffee, and in a week or so, a replacement appeared. Apparently, Ruth went to the Emporium in town, and they were able to find one just like it. Flowers from Ruth's garden were placed on the table, and the back porch where we sat and watched the sunset was always swept. I noticed these things. I watched as Ruth brought in her twigs and hay and created a nest. A comfortable, clean, organized, and, to my surprise, happy nest. I began to like Ruth who gradually accepted me. She was always polite and never pouted when, on those rare occasions, Toby and I came out together in the morning from my back bedroom.

I assume you are old enough now to understand the sleeping arrangements. Ruth had the main bedroom downstairs. I slept in the backroom upstairs that was farthest from the main staircase, and Toby stayed in the large bedroom above Ruth's. At least, most of the time. We just naturally had our own spaces. When I moved to Everstille, I realized that Toby and Ruth had separate rooms, and I tried to be as unobtrusive as I could be. We all attempted to give each other privacy, and for the most part, it worked.

One early summer Saturday morning, I looked out the window of my room and saw Ruth working in her garden. She was clearing, and weeding, and taking care of the flowers and a few vegetables she had planted. I knew she had to work that Saturday, but she weeded and worked with the flowers until she had no more free time. She came into the house, and I heard her get ready to go to the library. Toby was downstairs, and they were talking, and drinking coffee, and asking each other about their day's duties. Toby had to go to the high school for a meeting and then show up at a baseball game in the afternoon. He was often gone during weekends and busy with meetings and such which made for plenty of late nights, but that was what his job required. I waited to come downstairs that morning until they both had left; then, I put on my old work clothes and went out to the backyard to the flower garden.

I saw where Ruth had left off with her weeding. When I had the job at the college in Chicago, part of my duties included keeping the grounds cut and neat, doing weeding and such, so I knew what to do. I started to work and finished the garden. Then I got out the grass mower from the shed, oiled it up. and cut the lawn. I raked and swept the cut grass off the walk. When Ruth and Toby came home, I wanted the outside of the house to look neat and cared for. I wanted them to see the yardwork was done, and they could rest and relax. I knew Toby planned on doing the yardwork when he came home, but there was no reason for me not to do it. I needed to show them both that I appreciated their kindness. I especially wanted Ruth to know that I was thankful for her tolerance.

The yardwork became my job. I didn't mind (still don't) because I don't work on Saturdays, am able to do it, and enjoy the task. Ruth still worked in her flower garden, but when she couldn't get to it, she would tell me what needed to be done, and I was happy to assist her. Things between us became pleasanter after that. Then there was that one incident that changed my feelings towards Ruth; that made me see her in a different light.

One Saturday when she did not have duties at the library, Ruth was out in the garden, Toby was at the high school, and I was cutting the grass. I had stopped to clear some of the clumps away from the blades, and out of the corner of my eye, I saw one of the neighborhood girls come around the side of the house. She looked at Ruth who was standing just outside the flower patch looking at her accomplishment and removing her garden gloves. The little girl, it was Amy Jackson, was holding a book in her hands and looking upset. I watched as she came closer to Ruth and stood next to her until she was noticed.

"Hello, Amy. Did you need something?"

Amy took a deep breath and started to talk, but tears began to come down her face. She wiped them away and held out the book in her hands.

"Miss Ruth, I am so sorry. I was reading this book and my little brother came by on his bike, and he fell off it, and it fell on top of me, and the book fell, and I tried to catch it, and the cover tore off, and I am so sorry," and Amy held out the torn book to Ruth.

Ruth took the cover and the book and reached into the pocket of her smock and took out a handkerchief. She handed it to Amy, turned her around, and the two of them went to the back porch and sat down on the steps. I listened as Ruth spoke.

"Amy, accidents happen, and thank you for coming to me with this. It is repairable. There is a way to fix this book and place the cover back on it, so it will be fine. I have a thought. On Monday, after school, can you come over to the library? You and I can repair it together. I'll show you what needs to be done. Then you can take the book home and finish it. How does that sound?

Amy blew her nose and stopped crying. "Really? I'm glad it's not ruined. Yes, I'll be there after school Monday, but I don't need to take the book back and finish it. I've read it three times. It's my favorite."

Ruth looked at the book: *Little Women* by Louisa May Alcott. She smiled and spoke again.

"Have you read the other books by Miss Alcott? If you liked this one, you might like the others."

"I didn't know there were more. This one was really good. I'd like to read the others."

Ruth nodded, and then she asked. "What makes this book good, Amy?"

Amy thought for a while and then said, "Well, the story is real. The sisters sometimes fought, and I fight with my sister, so I know how that goes. And it's sad too. Every time I read about Beth dying, I cry. I guess it's just a good story."

Ruth nodded once more. She held the book so that the cover fit over the pages and said, "That's the secret, Amy. A good story is the most important thing. You have discovered the trick to writing. I also cried at

Beth's death, and when a book's story makes you feel strong emotions, then you know it's worthy."

They sat on the porch for a few more minutes talking about other books Amy liked, and Ruth suggested additional reading for her. Then Amy, the stress and trouble she arrived with clearly gone, left. When she got to the corner, she turned and waved to Ruth telling her, "See you Monday." At Ruth's wake, I saw Amy come into the funeral home with her parents. She was carrying a book, and placed it on top of another stack that was being started, and I didn't have to walk over to see that a copy of *Little Women* was there.

I remember standing at the lawn mower and looking towards Ruth. She saw me looking at her, and her grass green eyes met mine, and something changed for us both. At least it did for me. Her gentleness and graciousness with Amy touched me, and I saw another side to her. In hindsight, my feelings for Ruth changed at that moment. But it was months before anything happened between us.

The three of us, Terrence, Ruth, and me, became a real unit, a group. Everstille was, and is, a decent place to live, but it was a big change for me. A real change from living in Chicago where there were so many people and so many problems that most people were just concerned about themselves and their families. I had no family. Just some friends and sometimes a girlfriend, and Toby. But when he moved back here, to Everstille, I wasn't sure we would continue our friendship. He wrote to me often, and I wasn't too good at sending letters back to him. Writing is hard for me. I hope you understand this, Livie. This letter is taking a lot out of me.

When I did move here, folks were friendly to me. But I suspect it was because of Toby's position and Ruth's work. They were important to the town, and I came along on their coattails. When I did get a job at the telephone company, I was glad. I was able to help pay the bills and support myself. Things were good for a few years, and then there was some talk in the town.

At first, Toby told me to ignore it. We hadn't done anything to encourage the talk, but I partly blame our neighbor, Mrs. Wilson. She thought she was a bigwig at the church, being in the Rachel Circle and leading the music and playing for the choirs. She was always saying things like, "Oh, Mr. Douglas, I am so glad Ruth's house is a large one so all of you can fit comfortably in it." And "Oh, Mr. Douglas, I saw that you and Tobias were sitting on the back porch, talking, late last night. I hope Ruth is not ill, and that's why she couldn't join you." She was making insinuations about our relationships and it annoyed me. Toby said she is an unimportant busy-body and to ignore her. Ruth said she wanted to be a big fish in this small pond and to ignore her. She was hard to ignore. Partly because she was not totally wrong.

About the time your mother was expecting you, the three of us had a conversation and decided that the only other person we could trust with our secrets was Anne Rivens. I like Anne. She's friendly and helpful and smart and not all full of herself the way so many people are. We got along good enough. When Ruth and Toby suggested that seeing a woman would help to stop some of the talk and rumors, it was Anne who was the logical choice. So, Anne and I began to go to events as friends. And after a time, we became real friends.

On one of the first occasions we went out together, we had a real serious discussion. Ruth and Toby agreed about what I should say if the time was right, and after a short time, I was sure Anne could be trusted. Ruth and Toby both knew what I was going to tell her. We were trusting her with our lives, and we were right to do that. She was then and still is now, the truest friend we have. I told Anne about Toby and me and how we met at the college. I explained, in as careful terms as I could muster, our relationship. I let her know that I was not moving out of their house, and Ruth knew all about Toby and me. And then, I asked for her help. I suggested that we could be friends and just be seen around town together. She listened and asked one or two questions, and then said she would help in any way she could. I was relieved and thankful to her, and so, our friendship was cemented.

Well, Livie, I guess I have wandered all over these papers and wrote all around the subject, and have finally come to the place I need to be. This is the hard part. I promised Toby I would be honest and tell you about your mother and me. I guess I have talked about everything else but that. I watch you in your crib, holding that doll Anne gave you, and you looking like the sweetest thing, and although I know you will not read this until you are grown, these words are difficult to write. There is no other way to write this: Ruth and I became lovers.

We didn't mean to. We went from *circling each other like cats,* that's how Toby put it, to being tolerant of each other, to being friendly, and then to having stronger reactions. Yes, Livie, I loved your mother. There, I wrote that word again. My feelings for her were what I thought a man should feel towards a woman. I have struggled throughout my life trying to understand and explain myself. I cannot. Or maybe I can. The relationship with Ruth permitted me to feel the way I thought other men did. The emotions I experienced with Ruth were different than those I had with Betsy or other women. They were like the feelings I have about Toby. I know I have no excuse for my actions, but the truth is, I don't regret them. I only regret hurting Toby. Even though he got over it. Or said he did.

Toby was traveling. He was doing some work with different principals and schools and would sometimes be away for part of the week on these trips. At times, he would be gone on a Friday and return on Saturday night. Other times he would not come home until Sunday. The times varied, and Ruth and I got used to having dinner together or sitting on the back porch at night watching the sunset, or working in the garden side by side. Over the years we learned to rely on and help each other, and this was comforting. I have always gotten along with women, and I think this was due to my foster mother, Jenny, who was a good sort of person.

Anyway, when Toby was gone on these trips, Ruth and I were together. We went shopping at Clampet's for groceries and sometimes to the Bijou Theater to see a movie on Saturday afternoon when Ruth didn't have to work. During those Saturdays when Toby was gone and Ruth was working at the library, I would try out a new dish for dinner, often including ingredients I knew Toby did not like, just to see how it would taste. Ruth was always willing to try different dishes, and we had fun eating dinners together. We talked about our lives and our beliefs. We grew closer.

One Friday in August, Toby left for a weekend seminar and would be gone until Sunday night. Ruth did not have to work the following Saturday, and we had planned on getting up early and working at the weeding and the flowers and the lawn, and then cleaning up and seeing the new movie at the Bijou. We had asked Anne to go with us, but she called on that Saturday from the library as she was closing, to cancel out. Her parents were both sick with a summer cold, and she was going over to stay with them and nurse them through the rest of the weekend.

Ruth and I decided that we would skip the movie. After the weeding, we cleaned up. I made us a light supper, and we ate. Then we did the dishes, and straightened the kitchen up together, and went out to the back porch to sit and try to catch a breeze. It was a warm August night, but it soon cooled off, and we saw some welcomed rain was rapidly approaching. We went into the house to close the windows and lock up, and then stood there talking about going to church the next day. There was a sudden flash of lightening and some deafening thunder claps, and it surprised both of us, and we jumped. Ruth let out a strange squeal, and we laughed at each other, and then, we kissed. I'm not sure why it happened, but I will spare you the details except to say that we did not get to church the next morning.

I wish I could say there was just that one time, but there was not. Ruth and I finally decided that we needed to end whatever it was we had begun. And by early October, the fall session of school was in full swing, and the three of us were back in our usual arrangement. It seemed as though those times between Ruth and me had never happened. Except, Ruth was expecting a baby. She was expecting you.

Once she was far enough along, she told me, and we had to decide what to do. The truth is always best, Livie. Not easy, but best, and we sat down with Toby and admitted what we had done and waited for whatever pronouncement he would give us. I was even prepared to be thrown out of the house and, if she wanted to, would ask Ruth to go with me. I didn't know what would happen. There were tears and anger and hurt and many, many discussions that night and many nights afterwards. Then things got quiet. For a time, the three of us went around ignoring each other and trying to work out in our minds what to do. And then, somehow, and I am not quite sure how, we came together and talked again and agreed that whatever had happened, whatever Ruth and I had done, something amazing was going to come from it.

We became a unit again. This time we seemed to be even more united because we had a purpose. We would be a family, and the three of us would raise the child Ruth was expecting. To maintain what Toby called *social decorum*, it was agreed that Ruth and Toby would be the legal parents, and I would be "Uncle Terry", and we would continue to live together in the large house where we had all been content for so long. Plans were made for cleaning and organizing and painting the birthing room and the nursery, and Ruth discussed her eventual withdrawal from the library and her possible return in years to come when our child, you, Livie, was in school. That will never happen now.

There was, and is, no doubt about who your father is, Cabbage. For one thing, you only need to look in a mirror to determine that, but before you were born, we did not know what your features would be. The other fact is that Ruth and Toby were married, but it was a marriage in name only. They had never shared any intimacy other than a brief hug and kiss on the cheek. That had been the agreement from the start. I guess it is fair to say that we all knew what our sins and offenses were, and Ruth and I bore most of them.

246

There is not much more to write. The plans Ruth had for you will not be realized, and Toby and I are poor substitutes for her. Anne is here to help us, though. None of us know a thing about raising a baby and caring for a child. I am going to apologize here and now for whatever stupid things we have done. For mistakes I am sure we will make. At least the ones I am sure to make. The one thing you can be absolutely sure of is that we all, Anne, Toby, and me, cherish you. We have planned and talked about how we should care for you and teach you. Our hope, at least mine is, is that we will not do too much damage in raising you.

When you are grown and read this, there may be other things you want to know. Come to me, and ask. I'll answer. I promise you that. I owe you that much. I am here for you. I hope you know this by now, but, Olivia, all my love is yours. That word is easy to write when it comes to you. I will practice saying it to you too.

Uncle Terry

(Terrence Douglas, your father)

While this is the end of the *Everstille* series, there are more stories to be told.

Susan M. Szurek's next book is *Tomas' Children* which will be out soon.

The beginning of the book follows.

Warning: This is a dark journey.

From: *Tomas' Children*

Prologue

As Tomas watched his third child come into the world accompanied by screams and blood and puke, he wondered whether he should drown it in the same manner his father used to drown the kittens on the farm.

When he was young, the barn cat had crawled into the corner of the kitchen to bring forth a mass of wet, mewing blind creatures. She had been allowed into the house because she was a good mouser, and the cold brought in those creatures. When Tomas' father found the litter, he scooped the lot of them up with an old flattened box he kept for clean-up and shoved them into a sack. He tightened the top and turned to his watching six-year-old son. "Here, go to the stream and hold this under until there's no movement or sound. Then throw them into the heap for burning."

Tomas looked at the bag, retreated one step, and shook his head. The father, not one for wasted words or sentiments, looked at Tomas, hit him on the side of his head, and did the deed himself. It wasn't the last time the task was demanded. When the dog, Molly, had a litter the next summer, the father called Tomas over again to the side of the barn. "Look there," he pointed, "Them three are fine. This one here is the runt, and she won't feed it. If you don't take and get rid of it, it'll die anyway and suffer." He scooped the runt up, grabbed an old sack and thrust the animal in it. "Go on now. Drown it, and be fast about it."

Tomas took the sack and walked towards the stream. Before he got there, he found a soft spot under a tree, pulled some leaves together and made a bed for the runt. He was going to return later and try to feed it, but the father kept him busy doing late summer chores, and he was delayed in getting back to the spot. The next morning, he found the runt partly chewed up by some animal hungry for soft meat. Tomas kicked some leaves over the remains and went back to the barn to complete his given tasks. He figured the father had been right. Save the pain and suffering by providing an early death.

The father was not a waster. He believed in quick action with a minimum of work. When Tomas went to school and learned about Thomas Jefferson and Thomas Paine in his history book, and later when told the *Bible* story about Doubting Thomas and having read the Sunday School tract for himself, he noted the missing letter in his name, and asked the father about it. "Can't hear the letter. Why use it?" was the explanation given. Later, when Tomas left the farm and set off for his own life, he took back the letter of which he had been deprived and spelled his name *Thomas* from then on.

It didn't matter to the father who he left lying in the bed at the farm, moaning with his final breaths as the cancer finished its job, looking at his son, begging for an end without suffering further. Tomas considered him, thinking of the dozens of drowned kittens and runts over the years; remembering the last dog he had, the last Molly. He looked at the man he had lived with for years and felt empty. There was no anger, no gratitude, no spite, no hope. Tomas looked around at the bedroom which was crowded with the deathbed, the casket, the dresser. Being taught not to waste emotion, Tomas reached into the back-dresser drawer where he knew the father kept his hidden money, pulled it out, placed it in his pocket, picked up the worn satchel, and left without a word

He gathered items he thought he would need and packed the satchel. He made a bedroll using blankets and placed his three books and some tools in the middle, tying it with rope, ensuring things would not fall out. An old knapsack held additional tools, a few kitchen items, some leftover cornbread, jerky, apples from the tree in the back. He walked to the porch and placed his belongings on the bottom step so he could free the chickens and horse. He opened gates and cages, allowing them to fend for themselves or to be found by neighbors. He filled the feeders with whatever he could find and wished them luck.

He gathered the packed belongings and proceeded to the wooded area to check that Molly's grave was undisturbed. He walked to the copse of trees underneath which his mother and siblings were buried, looked at the graves, bent over to remove the leaves and weeds grown around the stones. He did the task without feelings; they been expended years before. He stood up, stretched his back, and looked once more at the house where he thought he could hear, faintly, hazily, feebly, his name being called. He ignored it. Arranging the necessary items on his back, making sure his three books were safe, throwing his old jacket over a shoulder, he grabbed the full satchel and stood up.

Tomas walked past the outbuilding, the woodshop, and he paused, but decided he could not manage additional tools. He moved towards the main road which split into two: one leading south to the town past the schoolhouse, church, and small businesses struggling to succeed, and the other north away from the town, to unknown places, new circumstances, strange locales. He turned north and began his journey.

Chapter 1   Late Summer, 1918

I almost went back. I turned north on the road and walked about one hundred feet and stopped. I was far from the bedroom, the porch, and path, but I swear I heard his moans and cries. I thought he yelled my name even though I knew he barely had the strength to whisper. I knew his shotgun was on the dresser because he placed it there a month ago, saying it was loaded and ready, but I ignored it. If he wanted to use it on himself, I wouldn't stop him, but I would not shoot him like he shot Molly, even if he deserved it. He had refused all my help except for the past couple weeks, and then only because he feared he would piss the bed like a baby. Even when I helped, he chided me, told me I should be working harder, doing better, refusing to speak about anything of importance. He was dying, and I wanted him to answer my questions. I wanted to know about my mother, and my twin brother, and the other brothers, things he never told me, questions he had refused to answer, but he just looked at me and sneered. He would die in that bed in a day or two, unless he gathered strength and courage and used the gun. Either way, I would never know. I would be gone. I stood still for a minute, then readjusted my belongings and continued to walk.

I had no idea where I was headed. I knew that I could find the city of Champaign if I turned around and went the opposite way. I considered going there. My Aunt Jennifer and Uncle David had moved there some years ago. For a few years, Christmas days were spent with them at their place, although my father complained about it the entire time he drove there and back. Uncle David had started a business in the city, but I didn't know what it was. I was confident he would help me get a job. Aunt Jennifer would make him do that. There was also a chance of getting a high school diploma, just like Mr. Jensen told me I could, but I hadn't even gotten the eighth-grade certificate, so I didn't know how that would work. There was something in me, a stubbornness my father said I had, that made me travel a different way, away from what I had known, into a different place where I could meet new people. I continued the northward direction.

Parts of the road I traveled on were familiar. I had left the town of Levett, where I grew up, but some of the farmland was known to me. I knew some of the farmhouses I was passing contained a bedframe or a bookcase or a table that my father and I had produced in the wood-shop. I remembered traveling to this area and delivering some of the items. I wondered how they were holding up, if they needed any repairs or re-staining. I was sure I could do that, and it would be a way to earn money. But I couldn't just go to the door and knock. There would be questions about my father, and why I was alone, and where I was going. It was too risky, so I forgot that idea and just continued to walk.

I kept to the main road but over to the side; not that there were too many travelers down this way, but a couple automobiles and a horse and wagon had driven by. They hadn't seen me. When I heard their noise, I walked into the field and sat low until they passed. I was nervous and anxious. I doubted if anyone who knew me would actually come this way, but I didn't want to have to answer questions or give explanations. I kept walking until the heat beat down around me, warming my head until I took off my cap and pushed my sweaty hair back. I decided to find a tree and rest and eat some of the cornbread I packed, along with some sips from the jar of water in the knapsack.

As I rested, I began to think through my plan. Or rather, lack of one. I wasn't sure where I would spend the night or, after the food I had with me was gone, what I would eat. In my hurry to leave, to get away from the farm, I hadn't planned for all consequences. I was unafraid to sleep in the woods or to be alone, but lack of food and water had me worried. Once I reached a town, I knew I could buy some supplies, but until then, I had to ration what I had. After sitting for a while, I took stock of my supplies and thought I could last a day or two with what I had, if I were careful.

Looking around to make sure no one was spying on me, although I couldn't imagine who would be in this wooded place, I took out the money I had pocketed and brought with me and decided to count it. Some was my own saved cash. That was three dollars and some change. Together, with the cash I took from the dresser, I had twenty-two dollars and eighteen cents. Most of it was single dollars although I had one five-dollar bill, and it sure seemed like a lot. Because buying supplies for the farm and the woodshop had been one of my duties, I knew some of the costs of foodstuffs at the Nelson General Store, but wasn't sure if things would cost the same in other stores and different towns. I looked at my money and thought about what my father had once said: "Don't keep all your money in one place. Spread it around in hiding spots. If a thief comes, he is likely to only get some of it." I divided the money up, putting some in the books in the bedroll, some in the bottom of the knapsack, and secreted more in the satchel, in the pocket of the other pair of pants I packed. I left the change and two dollars in my pocket and thought I was being smart. Then I thought back to the advice and felt stupid. What made me think this was the only money my father had? He was sure to have taken his own advice, and there had to be more cash hidden away in the farmhouse. I never looked. Wasn't going back now, and didn't think the hidden cash would do him much good anyway. I wondered if whoever found my father's body would also find his money.

I decided to continue walking and get as far as possible before I needed to find a spot to sleep for the night, so I got up and readjusted my belongings, and started out again. There was a breeze, and I was grateful for it because although it was the second week of September, it was still summer-warm. I kept changing the satchel from hand to hand and began to wonder why I had packed it. There were some clothes and an old towel and a few things I just threw in, not knowing what I would need, but it was heavy. I wondered how much room I had in the knapsack and the bedroll. Maybe I could fit the items in them and leave the satchel. But, if I carried the satchel into a town, I might be able to sell it and get some money for it. Probably not much, but it was in decent shape and I hated to just leave it. In the morning, I would try to rearrange everything and empty it which would make for easier carrying.

My feet were starting to hurt, and I was getting hungry and tired. I didn't recognize the farmhouses I was passing, so I was sure this was an area where I knew no one. And no one would know me. I thought it was time to look for a place to spend the night. If I could find a stream, I would be able to refill my water jar and splash some cold water on my face. What would it cost to rent a room in a hotel should there be one in the next town? I had never been in one, but the thought of a bed and some warm water sounded inviting. I wasn't sure I could afford that pleasure. Tonight, I would find a soft spot under a tree and make my own hotel. I walked on and noted that the farmhouses seemed closer together and figured that meant I was near to a town. Wasn't sure how far I had traveled, but thought at least fifteen miles. I hadn't stopped for any length of time except for a lunch break, and I had kept a good pace. Time to look for a spot.

Up ahead there were a couple of farmhouses. I considered going to one and asking for a drink from the well and if I could stay in their barn, but I was still travel-shy and worried about strangers. I noted where I was and looked towards the east where I could see a small wooded spot, and I headed towards it. As I crossed over to the trees, I saw some autumn berry bushes, and taking my cap, I filled it with as many as I could and stuffed my mouth with the juiciness. September was the season for them, and I was glad to find something to add to my meager dinner. I took the capful and walked into the trees and looked around for a place to make my bed.

I found a spot and checked it out for poison ivy. I knew the leaves were probably dropped, but the stems could still give a bad itch. I also looked for snake-holes, and once it all seemed clear, I set up my bedroll and secured my belongings behind me. Tomorrow I would need to look for a stream or a friendly farmer's well, but tonight I would need to make do with the food I allotted myself and the remaining water from the jar. I was grateful for the berries and saved half of them for morning breakfast. No coffee and eggs then. That made me think that I should have hard-boiled some eggs to bring with me. I felt stupid again.

I ate slowly, thinking about what I would do tomorrow, hoping I would find a small town to refill supplies, and wondering about my future. I took out the Sherlock Holmes book Mr. Jensen had given me and was able to reread one of the stories before it became too dark to see the words. This was the book into which he had written his address in Champaign, and I wondered if he were married now, if he still taught school, and I supposed I would never know. I could write him, but what would be the use of that? I wasn't sure he would even remember me; after all, it was over two years ago he left.

I gathered the blanket around me and settled back. The tree was sturdy, and the rustling leaves were soothing. I looked upwards where a few stars were starting to show and wondered if my father was dead yet. I guess I should have felt sadder than I did, but I had made up my mind and chosen my path. Tomorrow I would, with luck, find a town, get some supplies, and maybe sell the satchel. Beyond that, I wasn't sure what the future held. As I drifted off, as I fell asleep under the tree and the leaves and the stars, I remembered this day was my birthday. I was sixteen.

***